CONGRATULATE THE DEVIL

PARTHIAN

LIBRARY OF WALES

Howell Davies was born in 1896 on a farm at Felingwm near Carmarthen. He joined the Royal Welch Fusiliers on his 18th birthday in 1914 and served throughout the First World War, being wounded twice and commissioned Captain. Educated at the Sorbonne, Oxford and Aberystwyth University, he became a freelance journalist and editor for a wide variety of publications and organizations. He was editor of *The South American Handbook*, from 1923 until 1972. His best-known works are the three novels published by Gollancz just before the outbreak of the Second World War, most notably *Minimum Man* (1938), which was widely serialized. This was followed in 1939 by *Three Men Make a World* and *Congratulate the Devil*. Howell Davies died in 1985.

CONGRATULATE THE DEVIL

HOWELL DAVIES

LIBRARY OF WALES

Parthian
The Old Surgery
Napier Street
Cardigan
SA43 1ED
www.parthianbooks.co.uk

The Library of Wales is a Welsh Assembly Government initiative
which highlights and celebrates Wales' literary heritage in the
English language.

The publisher acknowledges the financial support of the Welsh
Books Council

The Library of Wales publishing project is based at
Trinity College, Carmarthen, SA31 3EP
www.libraryofwales.org

Series Editor: Dai Smith

First published in 1939
© The Estate of Howell Davies
Library of Wales edition published 2008
Foreword © Adrian Dannatt 2008
All Rights Reserved

ISBN 978-1-905762-47-7

Cover painting *Love* by Keith Bayliss
Cover design by Lucy Llewellyn

Typeset by Lucy Llewellyn
Printed and bound by Gwasg Gomer, Llandysul, Wales

British Library Cataloguing in Publication Data

A cataloguing record for this book is available from the British
Library.

LIBRARY OF WALES

FOREWORD

'No, no, I'm Welsh actually' is always my riposte when accused of being English, partly to avert the cliché of being just one more Englishman living in New York, but mostly as homage to the very Welshness of my grandfather Howell Davies. This notable Welshness was not a question of mere nationality, though he was born on the hills of Felingwm, nor of language, though he indeed spoke and wrote Welsh with pride and accomplishment, but rather of character and attitude, his unique approach to the whole thing of it.

Thus I grew up with the sense, never stated nor defined, that Welshness required verbal wit and linguistic dexterity in whatever tongue it might be expressed, a cunning born of a long history of being the minority, the marginal, maverick even. That to be Welsh was to prefer the amusing or outrageous over the factual and actual, to believe the imagination more vital than any reality and that all liberties taken with the truth were proof of one's ultimate loyalty to those most important things of all, the story, song, poem.

By the time I knew my grandfather he was more or less retired and though I was aware he had been a writer, I thought of him rather as a reader, talker, pipe-smoker, sage and wit, the one adult who would come up with something scandalous, inappropriate or just funny. So much of my childhood seemed to be spent at that small, bright pink cottage, Number Two Pond Square, right at the top of Highgate Hill, a magical place of narrow stair and tiny rooms with the scent of books, newspapers and literary journals, pipe smoke and coffee.

Here Howell would eat his rice-pudding every day, hand-grind his own beans in the kitchen, read his copy of *The Times* at the worn-smooth table in the downstairs living-room, always keeping an eye on the square outside, to spot an old friend or spy a new potential one coming by. For Howell always loved to meet new people, preferably young, ideally writers or those involved in the arts, and sometimes to this end he would sit outside on the low brick wall of his front yard, puffing away in his Parisian beret, accosting suitable strangers.

Though he spoke a good deal, Howell had the supreme elegance of never talking about himself, least of all if he felt unwell, and never referring to the years he had suffered in the trenches of the First World War. There was a shiny bronze shell canister used as an umbrella stand in the hallway and down in the basement there was a captured German helmet, as well as his own Tommy's helmet shockingly pierced with shrapnel from when he had been so seriously wounded, but he said nothing.

He also never spoke of his own life as a writer, nor did he really care about keeping copies of his innumerable articles, short stories, radio scripts, plays and essays; that archival instinct must have seemed pompous or pointless, alien to his inherently anarchic nature. Thus it was only much later that I discovered the few battered books he had bothered to keep on his shelves, as if by chance, and was happily able to appreciate his prolific career as journalist, script-doctor, travel guide editor and science fiction novelist.

Howell, or Hywel as he sometimes spelt it, was born on 3rd September 1896 at Court Farm, Felingwm, near Carmarthen, one of eight children in a respectable if surely far from rich farming family. This rural upbringing was a source of certain nostalgia as well as earthy comedy, and he enjoyed telling tales of farming life, trapping a vicious swan's neck under the tine of a fork, singing at chapel, playing tricks on his brothers. These siblings went on to successful careers in education, science and medicine, suggesting that Howell perhaps slightly exaggerated the rustic simplicity of their origins.

The war obviously changed everything. Howell volunteered for the Royal Welch Fusiliers on the very day of his eighteenth birthday in the summer of 1914. As a foot soldier Howell must have seen the very worst of the war, the brutal reality recorded in two small wartime field diaries, both later transcribed and donated to the Royal Welch Fusiliers' Regimental Museum at Caernarfon Castle. One of these is from his first year of active service and the other presumably from 1917 as it mentions the Russian revolution.

During those very long years Howell was not only promoted to Captain but also wounded twice, the second time sufficiently seriously in the head to recuperate back in Wales. It was here that he met Robert Graves, who was to become a permanent off-and-on friend, a professional colleague if not mentor. As Graves puts it in *Goodbye to All That*: 'Few officers in the battalion had seen any active service. Among the few was Howell Davies (now literary editor of the Star), who had a bullet through his head and was in as nervous a condition as myself. We became friends, and discussed the war and poetry late at night in the hut; we used to argue furiously, shouting each other down.'

Immediately after the armistice Howell took advantage of his veteran status to enrol at the Sorbonne, and though he was not there for long and failed to garner any actual academic qualification, as a handsome young officer he surely fully sampled Parisian café cultural life of the era. Whilst doubtless 'arguing furiously and shouting down' a wide variety of other bohemians Howell did manage to meet certain celebrities from this community of exiles, most notably James Joyce. Indeed Howell even owned a first edition of *Ulysses*, whether signed or not always remained a moot detail, eventually given to one of those ambiguous, ill-defined female 'friends' he seemed to easily accumulate. Likewise his impressive 'Bardic Chair', supposedly won at some unspecified Eisteddfod, was given to a female friend to decorate her fashion boutique. These friends, often of a strong literary or artistic bent themselves, may well have interfered with more formal scholarly obligations. For, right after the Sorbonne, Howell went up to Oxford only to come down again remarkably rapidly amongst rumours of romance, though he always remained a sworn enemy of Cambridge in their annual boat race.

Howell then continued his education at Aberystwyth, where again he refused matriculation, describing himself as leaving the place 'degreeless and inconsolable'. This comes from a surprisingly honest essay by Howell in the 1928 anthology *College by the Sea*, where he admits 'I learnt at Aberystwyth that it is not life that matters. It is the way you get out of it.'

He also described the effect of all those returning ex-servicemen: 'We fought for extended bounds. We got them. We wanted to meet the women in cafes, in cinemas. We wanted to walk with them into the country. It was given us, after a most undignified scuffle. We clamoured for booze, for the right to enter public houses. Some of us were drunk with vain glory.'

Howell did, however, successfully edit the college magazine *Y Ddraig* (*The Dragon*) during 1920–21 and was proud of the important papers they published, including the inaugural address of his only local hero Alfred Zimmern, who had just been appointed first Woodrow Wilson Chair of International Politics.

Howell concluded: 'speaking honestly for myself, I remember with joy... only the wooing of my wife.' For it was at Aberystwyth that he met Enid Margaret Beckett, my mother's mother, and married her, though not without opposition. For 'Becky', as she was known, was from an altogether more solid background, her father Thomas Beckett being Senior Wrangler at Cambridge, with a maths theorem named after him, and longtime head of mathematics at St Paul's School, whilst her mother, Zoe Stevenson, was a direct cousin of Robert Louis from Edinburgh. By contrast, Howell had no degree and no visible means of support, having happily found occasional employment making Lyons Swiss rolls or selling encyclopaedias door-to-door.

However, by 1923 Howell had not only won a *Cassell's Weekly* essay competition on 'Is There A New Wales?' he had also found work with Trade & Travel Publications Ltd, a company affiliated with the White Star Shipping Line, which put out a series of compact, hardback guides crammed with information. The most famous of these, still published today, is *The South American Handbook*, a thoroughly detailed compendium of information on that continent which Howell single-handedly created as its inaugural editor in 1923. Impressively he continued to create this chunky tome every year for the following four decades, being called out of retirement to edit it again in the late sixties, his final volume coming out in 1972, a full fifty years after the first.

Howell naturally had an extensive network of contacts and correspondents throughout those countries and the faintest wisp of clandestine communication if not actual espionage accompanied their activities. Appropriately Graham Greene called it 'the best travel guide in the world', Howell also became something of a media pundit on the whole region. Hearing him pontificate on the radio about revolution in Bolivia or inflation in Argentina, only his immediate family were probably aware he had never been anywhere near South America and in fact regularly refused free shipping-line trips there. For Howell was not a great traveller and apart from walking tours of the Black Forest and an early enthusiasm for skiing, or 'scheeing' as it was then called, preferred London, if not Highgate itself, and the wider domain of imagination.

Howell also edited *The Traveller's Guide to Great Britain & Ireland* (1930) and an accompanying Spanish version, *Anuario de la Gran Bretaña*, where we learn that: 'Gales es un país aparte de Inglaterra, con lengua propria y distinta característica nacional y de rica y variada hermosura. El interior es magnifico e inspirador.'

Howell also worked for a long a time for the BBC, but always as a fiercely independent freelancer refusing any staff contract whilst pounding out the widest possible variety of material, much of it describing particularly British topics, whether Dr Barnardo's or the bowler, for the Overseas Service. He much enjoyed that BBC Broadcasting House social culture of the period, and was an habitué of the neighbouring pubs of Fitzrovia and Soho as well as the Café Royal. With his flair for friendship Howell maintained a generous roster of higher acquaintances, whether poets such as Dylan Thomas, Robin Leanse and Dannie Abse, science fiction writer John Wyndham, Alison Waley or Laurence Gilliam, head of BBC Features. Another poet-friend was Alun Lewis, whose biography by John Pikoulis grants some sense of Howell's lure: 'Alun was equally pleased to meet a conversationalist of the greatest vivacity, purveyor of the higher gossip, literary and political.' Howell, he thought, had 'said many sharp and illuminating things as well as helped me to find a general sense of purpose and direction.'

But Howell wrote as much as he talked; such as 'The Five Eggs' included in *Welsh Short Stories: A Collection of Best Stories by Famous Authors* (Faber 1937) or a full-length play *The Mayor*, staged by The Repertory Players for one-night, 6 May 1951, at Wyndhams Theatre, with its cast including the young Alec McCowen.

And then there are the novels, a trio of science fiction/ fantasy books published by Victor Gollancz between 1938 and 1939, books Howell himself never mentioned and which, due to the strange nom de plume 'Andrew Marvell', forced upon him by his publisher, few realised were his own work. Of these, the first, *Minimum Man,* was the most successful, a veritable bestseller, serialised in the evening paper, republished by the Science Fiction Book Club in 1953, and in August 1947 issued in an unauthorized version by American pulp magazine *Famous Fantastic Mysteries*, with striking cover-art by illustrator Virgil Finlay. Certainly the book is included in most of the reference works and web sites devoted to the fantasy genre and its theme, of the next stage of human evolution being a new race of tiny beings attempting to push us aside, struck some acute public nerve of the era.

The following novel, *Three Men Make a World,* might seem the most topical as it concerns the deliberate sowing of a chemical bacterium that contaminates all petroleum, jams every form of oil-based consumption, and brings contemporary transportation and existence as we know it to an end.

The book is overtly anti-capitalist if not 'green', and is clearly ahead of its time in an almost beatnik attitude, featuring a central character from a wealthy background who rejects it all in the quest for an existential freedom from consumer goods and society's mores. 'He wanted, in a way, to sing, to have flowers in his hair. That was it. You could sum up the general temper of his desires by saying that he wanted flowers in his hair, to trip it through life, gay, happy, unoppressed by material considerations...' Even Seán O'Faoláin gave 'Three asterisks for this yarn, which combines excitement and uplift in a melange not too high- or low-brow for any common reader.'

Congratulate the Devil is the third, last, least known and hardest to find, probably due to the outbreak of war just after it was published in 1939. It is as fantastical as the others and in its casual discussion of mescaline-based hallucinogens also has something of an avant-tang of the later counter-culture. But I do not want to give anything away regarding this book's truly bizarre plot, a narrative that whilst highly improbable does obey its own odd logic.

It is stylistically very much of its time, the late and fevered 1930s, darting forth out of its quick-fire patter and rapid scene-cutting; dated of course, but on the whole more amusingly than annoyingly, with a certain durability to aphorisms such as 'Every Man has a book and a crime in him, and many people commit both, once.' There is also the rather disconcerting effect of having what is now London's revered Serpentine Gallery for contemporary art blown sky high by artillery shells. It is the most Welsh of all Howell's books, beginning and ending in Wales and featuring a most amiable Welsh 'wandering minstrel', naturally an unemployed one, as a central character; and it is packed with Howell's remarks regarding his nation and its apparently curious ways.

'For that was the worst of being Welsh, once you got into the spirit of a thing, and though you began by acting, in a moment, quick as anything, you were serious and inside the skin of the song, mournful as midnight and feeling a black sort of ecstasy.'

My grandfather wrote, too, of 'The Welsh being very Welsh, with memories as long as donkey's ears', and it is true that sometimes my own memory seems improbably long, irreconcilable with the Manhattan of 2008 where I reside. Every year it seems more impossible, illogical, that I should really have known, and known well, someone who fought in the First World War, who was actually born in 1896, born before even the motor car we both despise. And I bless that Welsh memory, as long as donkey's ears, without any trace of English embarrassment, I bless it for ever.

Adrian Dannatt

CONGRATULATE THE DEVIL

In seven days I shall be killed, but I don't know yet how it is going to happen. I cannot make up my mind whether to do it myself or to let those soldiers and policemen who surround this village do it for me. I shall probably toss up in the end and leave it to chance – if there is such a thing as chance. I don't think about it much, but death takes a good deal of not thinking about. I try to forget, but now and then I find that I am pressing the artery at the wrist with my fingers, the way doctors do. The blood goes flip, flip, flip, like minnows rippling along. Then I lift my fingers and there is no flip. You are dead now, my boy, I say. The blood is still. So many flips for seven days and then no more.

That is as near as I can get to realising what death is.

I doubt whether you will ever know how it happened. I shall tell you later whether it is to be by their lead or my steel (meaning the safety razor). The man who is in charge out there will wrap up these sheets and send them by special courier to the Home Secretary. He will hand them to the Prime Minister, who will pass them on to his wife, who wears the trousers. She will read them in bed for her amusement and talk them over, very discreetly, with Those who Count. There will be a small Cabinet committee with a very large blue pencil. If I decide on the razor blade, well and good; if on the bullet, my style is not so individual but that a line here and there cannot be rewritten.

You will have gathered by now that I am to die for reasons of state.

How did Stavisky die? The inner circle knows, but we don't. Not so long ago, in a café-bar in Paris, I met a shabby down and out and gave him a drink. He begged for another. When that was finished he asked for another and we tossed up whether I should give it him. He won. He suggested yet another, but I said No, I was an Englishman, but not a fool. One more drink, he begged, and I will tell you something. I didn't know what he meant, but I wasn't going to miss anything by being mean over one drink. Perhaps he would tell me what to make out of life. I didn't think he would, but you never know. I thought he was going to tell me about the girls in the quarter. That is information, too. Anyway, I gave him the drink.

When he had finished it I said: Well? He took me by the arm and we walked to the door. There he glanced around before putting his mouth to my ear. I shot Stavisky, he whispered, and ran. I asked the barmaid who he was. A bad character, she said, but he used to be a gendarme. And that is all I shall ever know. He didn't ask for another drink, so

4

I think he may have shot Stavisky. On the other hand, he took me to the door first, whispered it in my ear, and bolted. Perhaps he expected a boot in his bottom. If that was so, he didn't shoot Stavisky. It matters little, but some day you may be handing out drinks at a London bar to a shabby ex-soldier, and wondering if what he tells you is true.

Why do I set myself this weary task? Partly it is because it will take my mind away from what is coming to me, but that is a small part of the reason. I write about this miracle of our days and the mess we made of it because I want you to see it from our point of view. You believe now that it was a dirty mixture of crime and hocus-pocus. That is what the newspapers have told you, not because they have been misleading you, but because they have known no better themselves. There was crime; there was hocus-pocus, but nevertheless this affair has not been what you have been told it was. See for yourselves, and judge.

I sit in this dusty upstairs room of the 'Red Lion' in a lonely Welsh village, writing and writing. It will go on for seven days and then I shall be dead, as dead as the noble browed man whose large sized photograph stares at me from over the mantelpiece. Who is he? I asked the round barrelled landlord. Thomas Charles of Bala, he replied, a very saintly man. Is he dead? I asked. Oh yes, a long time, but he was very saintly. I am not very saintly, but soon I shall have a great deal in common with him.

It began as a laughing matter, and those who have not lost their sense of humour over dogs (there are still a few) will be glad to know that it was a dog started it.

5

Mrs Marsham went to Vienna and parked her dog on my uncle, Colonel Starling, who had a ground floor flat in a big block at Hampstead. On an August afternoon Dobbs, the Colonel's personal servant, took the dog for a walk up the High Street. Dobbs was middle aged, fat, and walked with a slow, waddling movement, like a duck at evening. It was a very hot day, and he had undone the three bottom buttons of his waistcoat. He wanted to get to the water at the top of the hill. It would be cooler up there.

Connected to Dobbs' wrist by what looked like a very long thin brown snake was the dog, That There, a miserable specimen of his kind. Dobbs held that he was mentally deficient, and put it down to the fact that he had lived his life amongst women. 'Like a brat.' He was extraordinarily woolly-minded, mean-hearted, and contrary. 'Can't make up 'is mind fer two minutes together,' said Dobbs. This afternoon he was going through the whole rich gamut of his deficiencies, stiffening his forelegs out in front of him, bunching back in an alarming manner and skidding along the pavement, his head twisted painfully to one side as if he were on a gibbet; giving that up and trotting with a whimpering docility at his master's heels, nose unnaturally low, stricken with sin and unworthiness; and when he grew tired of that, which was often, getting himself into the gibbet position again and trying desperately hard to commit suicide.

'Now 'e thinks 'isself a tug of war,' swore Dobbs. 'Does 'e ever think 'es a dawg? Does 'e 'ell. An' is 'e right? 'E is.'

They came, by and by, to the Pond, the water, the sails, the children, and a breeze. Dobbs stood there for a time absorbing coolness. The Dog, being the kind of dog he was, turned his back mournfully and flattened his ears as the cars whizzed past.

Dobbs crossed the road towards the Heath, and stood for a moment at the pavement's edge, looking with a townsman's surprise at such foreign bodies as trees and green grass and blue skies. Then, with a little sigh (he had his duty to do by the dog) he stepped off the familiar asphalt into alien nature.

But the dog objected: fiercely. He had been brought up in ladies' laps and drawing-rooms, fondled and dandled and kissed on the nose, and he hated all this tugging and hauling. He sat down with such a jerk that it looked as if he had finally succeeded in hanging himself. Dobbs swore and tugged so impetuously that the lead slipped off his wrist and snapped back at the dog's nose. He jumped a clear foot into the air, and set off at a wild gallop over the grass.

'Hi, you,' shouted Dobbs, following at what speed he could and lifting his arms to the sky like a prophet. 'Thinks 'es got an electric 'are in front of 'im nah,' he panted. 'Thinks 'es at the dawgs, no doubt. Stop 'im,' he yelled to a group of children, but they only stared at the beast as it swung past, and even more eagerly at the fat man. Dobbs shook his fist at them. The dog, vanishing over a hillock, stopped, wagged his tail uproariously and set off again. The insulted Dobbs panted to the top of the mound to see his quarry doing a long tireless lope in the middle distance. 'Hi,' he shouted again, but half heartedly. 'You wait till I get yer,' he mumbled. 'You wait.'

He undid the other buttons of his waistcoat and waddled off in the wake.

But the dog was not consecutive. He could keep nothing up for long. Dobbs was still a good two hundred yards behind when the dog stopped short in his flight and turned, crawling oddly, towards a man in brown sitting on the grass. ''Old 'im, Sir, 'old the devil,' shouted Dobbs. Then slowly, getting his breath, buttoning up his waistcoat and mopping his brow, he waddled towards them.

'Sits there easy as a statoo,' he grumbled. 'Sits like a peach on a plate, like he 'ad no legs to gallop on. Let 'im wait!'

The man in brown patted the dog's flanks. 'I've got him,' he said.

'Thank you, Sir,' said Dobbs. 'An' as for you,' turning to the dog, 'I'll see to you in the privacy of the 'ome.'

He sat on the grass and cooled himself by flapping his bowler fanwise in the air.

The man in brown offered him a cigarette. The old soldier touched the rim of his bowler in a military salute. 'Name of Dobbs, Sir, and thank you,' he said. 'Name of Roper,' grinned the stranger. They lit up. Dobbs rolled gently on to his back, tilted his hat over his eyes, and smoked into the air.

He fell asleep.

That is what Dobbs thought he did. That is what he told me he did when I talked to him about it. He must have fallen asleep, but there were dreams. He couldn't remember the dreams but he knew they were uncomfortable. 'Lying on me back in the sun. Nightmares,' he mumbled to me. But he couldn't remember a thing. If he could remember

8

he'd tell me, honest, he would. He wasn't hiding anything. There had been dreams, bad ones. But he could only sort of ... sort of ... it was like trying to remember in the morning what had happened when you had been very, very screwed the night before. It came at you and then went away before you could get your hand round it and hold it.

'Now look, Dobbs,' I said, 'something funny happened then. You know something happened. I don't believe you were asleep. And you don't believe it yourself. Try and remember.'

'I can't, Sir. Not a thing.'

'He did something to the dog.'

'You think so, Sir?'

'Look at what happened afterwards. Of course he did something to that dog.'

'I didn't see 'im do anything.'

'Dobbs, you're not the sort of man who falls asleep if you've got somebody to talk to. About this man. What was he like?'

''E 'ad a brown suit on, but no 'at. 'E was ugly as sin. That's all I can tell you.'

'What do you mean, ugly as sin?'

Dobbs pondered.

''E 'ad knobs on 'is forehead. An' a mouth, that wide.'

'Anything else? Old? Young?'

'Youngish.'

'You've got to remember, Dobbs. You probably talked about the Colonel. You're always talking about the Colonel. You were talking about the Colonel when I was a boy. What about that little speech of yours: "Am I a Indian servant? I am not. Is it what the Colonel would like me ter be? Ah! Ah! An' will I ever be one? Never, not whilst I'm Dobbs. ''Im with one foot in the grave, too!'''

Dobbs looked uncomfortable, but he shook his head dumbly.

'"He expects you to salaam and touch yer forred and do the old kow tow,"' I went on relentlessly. '"An' all fer twenty-five bloomin' bob a week. But do I do it? Do I?" this is where you spit, Dobbs. "Catch me wiv a loin cloth round me little bottom." You must have said that.'

Dobbs' eyes wavered. He, too, knew his speeches off by heart.

'The first thing I knows,' said Dobbs, 'is I was ...'

The first thing Dobbs knew was that he was running, the sweat cruising down his face, and that he had the dog clasped in his arms. He was a good two hundred yards away from the man in brown, and he couldn't remember how he had got up and come that distance, how the dog had got into his arms, why he was running, or what his terror meant. He was trembling all over, and he couldn't remember why. He had not the vaguest idea why. 'I must a been asleep,' he thought. Sleep walking. But even in his sleep he couldn't think how he had come to pick up that piece of leprosy, That There, the dog. He promptly threw him to the ground, and walked rapidly towards the streets.

Funny he had fallen asleep, like that!

But everything was all right again, except, of course, for That There. That There was acting according to his nature. There was no way of knowing in advance what That There would do. Twice, during the short walk back to the flat, he had stood stock still in his tracks, which was usual enough, but he had then sat up like a beggar on his haunches, looking extremely miserable, and had rattled his teeth, scraping at them with a paw. It was something new even for him. But Dobbs wasn't standing any nonsense from a dog, and on both occasions got him on the march again, double quick.

They were back at the flat about ten minutes to four, a ground floor flat. Dobbs slipped the dog loose in the drawing-room, and was busy for several minutes laying the Colonel's tea on a low occasional table near the french window. He plugged in the electric kettle in the kitchen and cut a few thin slices of bread ready for the toaster. Then he went back to the drawing-room to wait for the Colonel. It was a minute or two to four, and the Colonel had said he would be back by four, prompt.

He waited, holding his head in his hands, elbows on the mantelpiece, wondering what had happened to him in the park. To wake up with That There in his arms! He lifted his head to see where the dog was now. It was crouched in the corner. Dobbs felt unaccountably miserable, closed his eyes and held his head in his hands. Four o'clock tinkled from the clock. The Colonel was going to be late. But he was too miserable to take advantage of it. He felt … humble, and Dobbs, to whom humility was a new sensation, suspected that he was a bit off colour. 'I ain't feeling very well, seemingly,' he mumbled, rubbing the back of his hand against his forehead. 'Liver,' he thought, remembering the Colonel's diagnosis of all human ills. This must be liver.

Things were beginning to sideslip. He grasped the edge of the mantelpiece, but did not feel very secure even with the cold wood between the ball of his thumb and the fingers. There was a funny swaying feeling about his legs, like water-cress in a current....

'It's like as if ... as if ...' he began thinking. 'It's like having one's senses stole.' His knees were wobbly as a jelly. There was no strength in them. If he didn't look out he'd be measuring his length on the floor, going wallop. Sure thing, going wallop. Having your senses stole, that was it. He remembered a fellow in a loincloth in the bazaar who had done that to him in India, and he grew very suspicious. 'I been got at,' he said aloud. He was sure of that. He was having his senses stole. Something outside himself was doing things to him, getting at him, making water out of his thighs and knees and ankles and fair flooding his boots. He was clinging now to the mantelpiece, with both hands. The free born Briton in him rose in terrific protest. 'Ah, would you now?' he muttered. 'Would you now?' and he glared round the room. Old That There was still in his corner, but sitting upon his haunches, eyes bulging and glowing, his red slip of tongue hanging out of his mouth, all a grin from ear to ear. The moment he saw the dog's eyes there was a tremendous increase in the wateriness about his knees. Jesus, he was awash, fair awash! It was That There was doing it. It was the dog was getting at him. Old That There....

But he rose into his right senses for a moment again. 'I'm slippin',' he shouted or thought he shouted, and held on grimly to the mantelpiece. The wall was rolling in front

12

of his eyes. He mustn't let go. He must hold on. He mustn't slip into the waters rising about him. He gave one wild last look at the dog, and the struggle was over. He let go. He wanted to. His hands opened, he turned round slowly, and dived headlong to the floor.

The Colonel was five minutes late, hurrying home through the heat, and he didn't like being late. The army had given him the secret of time. You conquered it by sticking to it. Tea, he had told Dobbs, would be at four, and now it was five past four. As likely as not that very difficult man had served it up at four, prompt, to spite him, and now the tea would be cold, and the thin crisp slices of Austrian toast would be cold, and Dobbs would be looking at him as much as to say: Serve you right. If you say tea is at four tea is at four.

By the time he was letting himself into the hall of the flat there was quite a skirl of rising winds about the Colonel's heart. Dobbs was impossible. He would order him at once to make fresh tea, fresh toast. Dobbs! he shouted from the hall. Dobbs! There was no answer. (A troop of Indian servants padded softly along the corridors of his brain, running, and that did not help matters.) It was Dobbs' duty to be in the hall, to help him divest his coat, to take his hat and his gloves, to open the drawing-room door for him; and above all, to make him feel that he was being welcomed, attended to, fussed over. Not that Dobbs ever did that. But if the Colonel could not command love in his own home country (there had never been any difficulty about it in India) he could at least enforce the strict letter of the law. Dobbs! Dobbs!

13

There was no answer.

He must be gone. He had not only made the tea at four but gone out!

Was that a noise? Did that come from the flat?

Good God, this was going too far. Was Dobbs in there pretending he hadn't heard?

Dobbs!

The Colonel took off his coat in a fluster, temper rising, threw it over a chair, flung his hat and gloves after it, opened the door briskly, and stepped in.

Ah, the dog. It must have been the dog he had heard. There was no one else there. Dobbs was either gone out or was hiding in one of the other rooms. The dog came bounding towards him, and he bent over to pat it on the head. But before the dog had quite come up to him the arm chair near the tea table was pushed to one side and a strange creature came galumphing across the floor. Dobbs! on his hands and knees, bounding and leaping in the most brazen, unhuman way possible! His tongue was hanging out; his eyes were liquid with joy and devotion, and he was shaking his bottom from side to side like a ... like a cinder sifter. And now he was making small piping noises in his throat like an animal, giving vent, indeed, to the same extravagant motions and whimperings that a dog does when it welcomes its master. Mixed with his shocked surprise there was a momentary triumph in the Colonel's mind. This, after all, was the Dobbs he had always wanted; and this, the welcome home.

For about as long as it takes to count ten the Colonel felt and fought the emotions his batman had known by the mantelpiece; but he was stricken more quickly, so that at no time did he realise clearly what was happening to him. At one moment, there was the dog in front of him, wagging its tail; and there was Dobbs, going through the same parade in his clumsy, caricaturing human way. Then there was a rift of time filled with turbulent emotions, and the next instant he also had collapsed on his hands and knees and his own square-built rump had begun that self-same cinder-sifting motion.

But with a difference, naturally, the difference, even in this outlandish experience, between the well-bred and the vulgar, between Colonel and batman. Dobbs was behaving like an undisciplined mongrel, with zest and exuberance (he was now trying to scratch behind his right ear with his boot and not doing it very well). But the Colonel sank to earth as impressively as anything at the Dog Show, with a stiff, creaking dignity. He yawned a little and stretched out his hands on the carpet, laid his chin upon them, and closed one eye, keeping the other steadfastly on Dobbs, who was getting more and more heated over that right ear. The day was hot. The Colonel put out his tongue occasionally, and licked his chops before reverting to his Argus-eyed stance. It was very like Landseer's Dignity and Impudence.

As for Impudence, it was impudence with a vengeance. There was that fellow Dobbs (who never had known his place), letting himself go, giving free vent to his abounding spirits, pretending to bite Dignity's paws, launching himself at him in mock attacks, romping round him in circles, sitting up on his haunches, panting, tongue out, and never keeping still a moment. Jumping over Dignity's back and stumbling

15

at it, too. Now he was trotting over to the tea table, taking a piece of cake and eating it off the carpet. Now he was putting a playful paw on the Colonel's head, rubbing against him and once more trying to clear his back. The Colonel had to snarl back at him and show his false fangs. The ridiculous Dobbs yapped about this, at a safe distance, for some time. The Colonel creaked on all fours over to the bookcase and subsided there with a slight clatter. Even Dobbs in time grew quieter and crouched down near the armchair, facing That There and gazing steadily into its eyes, only an occasional quiver and shake of the rump to show that he was ready for a game any time.

There was a restaurant attached to the block of flats. The Colonel took his meals there when he was not lunching or dining out. Because he was pernickety over his food the manager used to send one of the waitresses up to his flat to find out from Dobbs what his master fancied that day. The girl now rang the front door bell, but there was no answer. Knowing, however, that Dobbs sometimes left a note on the kitchen table, she let herself into the hall with a master key. The door of the drawing-room was ajar. Thinking that Dobbs might be there, or perhaps not thinking at all but following her pretty nose, the girl pushed the door wide and peeped through.

She was not a nervous young woman. She had served her apprenticeship in a boarding house and seen (for so young a creature) many strange sights, and what she hadn't seen there she had seen on the films. But what met her eyes now was very much outside her experience, and when the Colonel lifted a regal head and licked at his moustaches,

16

when both the real dog and that underdog, Dobbs, began bounding towards her, she let off a fine, piercing shriek and sprang back as if she were on the stage. But the next instant she too was down on all fours and advancing shyly into the room, looking extraordinarily graceful and young and attractive, blushing prettily, and moving with a kind of easy, sideways cavort. She was, in fact, so delicately reticent that Dobbs was only able to come up with her by pushing over a chair and doubling several times in his tracks. Being the kind of dog he was, he licked her nose half a dozen times and seemingly quite overcome by emotion, leapt into the air and went for a quick gallop round the room. Even the old Colonel paid his tribute to her youth and beauty by stalking in a finely courteous but non-committal manner across the floor, and after collapsing again, regarding her with grave approval from between his paws. It was as if one of the lions had come down from Nelson's plinth and taken a solemn small walk.

There was electricity in the air, as the novelists say. And Dobbs was a good conductor. One does not know what might not have happened if the spell had remained unbroken. But broken it was. The waitress, fortunately for herself, perhaps, had left both the drawing-room door and the hall door open. The dog, frightened by the antics of these humans, scuttled off at a brisk pace towards freedom. At the very moment when it disappeared Dobbs was beginning a second and even more dashing series of licks. Suddenly he stopped, looked at the maid with surprise, looked at the Colonel, and scrambled to his feet. They gazed at one another, first with alarm, and then as the memory of their deeds crowded into their minds, with dismay. The girl looked reproachfully at Dobbs, burst into tears, and ran from the room. The Colonel rose slowly, stiff in every joint, and brushed the knees of his trousers. Then he caught his man's eye, frowned automatically, mumbled something about tea, and with a cry asked for the dog.

Dobbs ran out into the hall, and came back again to say that it was not there. From the sitting-room window the Colonel looked up and down the street. 'There he is,' he said. Dobbs went to the window too, and looked out. The dog was stationed very deliberately at a lamp post across the road. Already, in both their minds, some vague perception of the dog's responsibility had taken shape. Now, after looking at the dog, and looking at the lamp post, they looked at one another, and away again hastily.

There were things which had been spared them.

'Shall I fetch it?' asked Dobbs.

'Not on your life,' said the Colonel. 'Get tea.'

Dobbs went at once, forgot even to remind him he was late. The kettle was boiling its head off. Nothing was said during tea time. The Colonel drank his tea and munched his toast without a word, glancing occasionally at the place he had occupied on the floor, and occasionally at the ceiling, which had stretched so high above his head and was now so low. It was not until Dobbs had lit his cigarette for him that he disposed of the matter, oracularly, once and for all.

'That dog,' said the Colonel, 'was bewitched.'

'Yes, Sir,' said Dobbs.

The last witch was burnt in England two hundred years ago. Neither Dobbs nor the Colonel believed in witchcraft.

The Colonel did not know in the least what he meant by saying that the dog was bewitched. Nor did Dobbs. But both of them found it an absolutely satisfactory explanation. It accounted for everything.

'What happened to the girl?' I asked Dobbs.

'She gave notice, Sir.'

'What, she's gone?'

'Well, Sir, I explained to her as 'ow the dog was bewitched, so that was all right. She's still 'ere if you'd like to speak to 'er.'

'And the dog? Did it get home?'

'No Sir. It was run over rahnd the corner.'

And that, somehow, seemed proof positive that the dog had been bewitched.

I am very fond of England and the English people. I like them. I have travelled all round the world and never come across anything like them. We are Unique.

Well, I have let myself go rather, but the temptation was large. When you begin writing, words get hold of you and run away with you and in no time you are writing things you never meant to write at all. I never meant to let go like that over Dobbs and the Colonel. It was not much more than a funny incident. But when you are going to be dead in a few days you want fun, as much of it as there is. And so, I have let myself go. I wasn't there to see it. The facts are right. But all that about what the Colonel thought and what Dobbs thought is obviously as much me as it is them. But it is what I think did happen. I believe that it happened just so, as I have written it. I know my uncle very well, and there was not much about Dobbs, I fancy, that was hidden.

As it chanced I was to have tea with my uncle the very next day. I was there early and had a long talk with Dobbs. It was he who told me all about it. The Colonel takes his tea at four, but that day he was sitting on some important A.R.P. committee. It was so important that he had ordered tea at five, so I had a long time with Dobbs. I didn't laugh much, because I could see that it would hurt Dobbs, who was very serious. The laughter has grown in me later. Men behaving like dogs ... that is not funny. There are plenty doing it everywhere. But men behaving as dogs, that is different. It seems to me more funny now than it did then.

'If you please, Sir, will you say nothing to the Colonel?'

'Not a word, Dobbs.'

'You know how it is, Sir.'

'Of course I know.'

I had tea with the Colonel, later. After a while he sent Dobbs out to buy a paper.

'Been talking to Dobbs, eh?'

'Yes, a little.'

My uncle looked at me, suspiciously.

'You didn't notice anything odd, did you?'

'Odd? No. Why?'

'Perhaps I am exaggerating,' said the Colonel, 'but still ... very peculiar behaviour. I hope he is all right.'

'What? When?' I asked blankly.

'Yesterday, as a matter of fact. I was late for tea, very unusual, but absolutely unavoidable. I found Dobbs on his hands and knees playing with the dog.'

'There's nothing very odd in that,' I said. 'Most people seem to do it.'

'Yes, quite. But...' he hesitated, 'he took such a long time to stand up again. Just as if he were a dog himself, if you know what I mean.'

'A dog himself?'

'Well he galloped round on all fours.'

'With you there! What did you do, Uncle?'

'Oh, I soon stopped it,' he said hastily. 'Don't stand any nonsense from Dobbs, you know.'

'The dog,' I said slowly and deliberately, 'wasn't bewitched by any chance?'

'That's exactly what I thought,' he exploded. 'My very words.'

Later, when I was leaving, I had another word with Dobbs.

'I have remembered something,' he said.

'Oh.'

'It come out of the blue at me.'

'Well.'

'You know that man with knobs on 'is forehead? 'E told me 'is name.'

'Are you sure, Dobbs?'

'It come at me from the blue. 'Is name was Roper, Sir.'

'Roper? Knobs on his forehead? But I know the man!'

We had been to the same school and had kept in touch, distantly, perhaps, but still, in touch. I had asked him to dinner before I left for the States, and we would no doubt dine together again before I left for somewhere else – if ever that should come about. His father had retired, and young Roper was now running the analytical chemist business on his own. I remembered vaguely a laboratory on the top floor of a shabby building in Hampstead.

Roper had an odd face. It was not odd simply because it was ugly (there are plenty of commonplace ugly faces), but because it was an intense, very deliberate ugliness, ugliness for the sake of ugliness, as it were. The impression he always gave you was that he had chosen it, and chosen it with care. I remember a woman at a party saying – after he had left – that she could never look at him without thinking: As a baby that man drew in a large gulp of air and *blew*. A determined young Boreas, but with his mouth shut. This mighty draught had raised two glistening lumps on his forehead and filled his eyes out, not distressingly, you understand, but more than a little. It had distended and raised the cheek bones, too, although the cheeks themselves looked as if they had been sucked inwards. You felt that his face would be passable if the upper parts could be deflated. The ugliness hung together, though. It was all of a piece, and was not truly repellent. It surprised you but it did not make you feel bad. Women, I believe, got the shudders at first, but men soon grew used to it, and even to like it.

Another curious thing about Roper was that you never knew what he was feeling unless he told you. The ordinary face is an ideal negative on which to snap emotions. One can see clearly enough, usually, whether a man is angry or jealous or envious or feeling right with the world, but it was almost impossible to read anything in Roper's face. That ugliness of his obscured and distorted the emotions.

It was new territory. It hadn't been mapped. The first thing you knew at school was that he was hitting out or perhaps blubbing and no-one had guessed that the tears or the fists were coming. It made the rest of us careful with him.

It isn't possible to have a face like that without the thing bulging over into your character. I remember how shy, how desperately shy, he was when he came to school. Ugly, we called him at once. No other nickname was possible. It stuck, naturally. School was possibly the first place where he had been branded, had the thing pointed out to him. He seemed to take it in very good part; at least, he said nothing. He did not protest or glower. Later on, when his body filled out – he grew into a biggish man – he mauled one of the boys who used the nickname rather dreadfully, and was nearly expelled. It showed an unexpected streak of ferocity.

He was engagingly direct and simple when he came first, but after a while he was no longer simple. He developed an astonishingly complete capacity for unbelief. It was a positive thing with him. He did not believe in the masters, in the school, in God, in the Empire, in himself, in anything, and he had a facetiously mordant way of saying things which repelled and delighted at the same time. I remember how shocked and impressed we were.

In the upper school he was more formed than the rest of us. I felt about him then what I felt about him later, when I used to meet him. I am light metal, myself, a buoyant alloy, but he was (it is difficult to explain) iron. Heavier stuff altogether. (I always sense character in terms of specific gravity.) Even at school I felt myself being moved like a tide by the moon. There was a strong 'pull' about him.

The day after I had talked to the Colonel and Dobbs I ran the car up to Hampstead, but it took me some time to find the shabby small place in which the family profession was carried on. That warren of streets on the Northern Heights is confusing, and I had forgotten the layout.

But I got there at last and rang the bell of the lodging house. It was out of order, so I banged on the knocker. I had hardly stopped when the door opened with a rush, as if the person opening it were trying to catch small boys at their games. It was a woman, and she made me think at once of the Eiffel Tower. She was very tall, and very thin, a spectre with a shawl round its skeleton. The shoulder blades stuck up like an old horse's.

'Mr Roper, please?'

She moved to one side spectrally and closed the door softly behind me. I felt as if I had been captured by an ogre. The hall was dark and I almost blundered into a hatstand so full of pegs that it looked like a harrow turned sideways up.

'Top floor,' said a prim voice behind me.

The carpet on the stairs was hard and worn. My feet made woody noises as I ran up. On the first floor landing a door was open and there was a smell of stew. (Whenever I went to see Roper the smell was still there, as if the stew, like the landlady, were a ghost not very successfully laid.) The next landing was lighter. Another short flight of stairs and I was at the top, under a grimy skylight.

There were three doors. I remembered them vaguely. One, I knew, led to the lavatory and bathroom, another to Roper's bedroom, and the third into the laboratory.

I knocked at the one on the right and went in. It was the

laboratory. This laboratory is a long, low room and the ceiling comes down almost to your head. To the right, as you go in, the street wall is pierced by a window which runs almost the whole way along. On the sill are a number of coloured bottles, and just below the level of the sill is a long, plain deal bench. I know little about laboratories and I was never interested enough to ask Roper the names of things. There were pipettes and bunsen burners, aluminium crucibles, racks of test tubes, balances in a glass case, beakers and so forth, a number of What Nots I know nothing about. There is a gas fire at the end wall and two chairs in front of it. Opposite the bench, along the left wall as you enter, is one of those grow-with-your-income book cases filled with formidable-looking volumes. Most of them are in German. A door immediately to the left goes straight to Roper's bedroom, and another one, near the bookcase, to the spare bedroom.

Roper was working at the bench when I entered, and turned to see who it was. He was wearing glasses, and the light fell full on his face. I was chagrined that he did not come up and shake hands with me or show any signs of surprise. He kept on looking at me.

'Well, how are you, old man,' I said fatuously, somewhat chilled by this reception.

He took his glasses off, looked at me, and put them on again.

'What's the matter, Roper? Am I disturbing you?'

He laughed and walked right up to me.

'Oh, not at all. Not at all,' he said. 'I have a most curious sub-conscious. You, of all people!'

'Well then, how are things?' I put my hand out.

'I am tired of this,' said Roper. He didn't seem to be talking to me at all. It was more as if he were talking to himself. 'I am damned tired of it,' he repeated.

I began to look at him closely.

'You all right, Roper?'

He lost his temper at this.

'He's in America,' he said. 'Of course he is in America.' He looked at me again, coldly, from my head to my toes. 'I could swear... extraordinary,' he mumbled. 'He's in America. Oh, damn this,' he burst out, and caught me a neat back hander across the face.

'I say, Roper...'

He punched me again, hard. I couldn't let that go on. Roper had gone batty or something. I couldn't make out what it meant, but I wasn't going to let him go on punching. I made a rush at him, trying to tackle him low, but missed his legs and sprawled headlong to the floor. I scrambled to my feet again and there was Roper, standing by the door, looking at me. I thought his eyes bulged more than usual.

'What's the meaning of all this...' I began.

'Wait a minute,' said Roper, and I stood there, feeling a fool. He kept staring at me.

'It's gone!' he said. He seemed very surprised. 'It's completely gone!'

'What's gone?' I asked.

'Well, you're not lifting your right leg...'

I was sure he was batty by now.

He came up and shook me by the hand. 'Sorry, Jim. I thought you weren't there. Did I hit you very hard?'

26

'Not very.'

'I've been seeing things. At least I thought I was seeing things. Where there is no vision, the people perish... Good lord, perhaps they weren't.'

He stood stock still, thinking.

'Is it really you!' He pinched my arm. 'You're palpable enough. That's a pun. I thought you were in America.'

'It's me all right. But what does all this mean? Did you think...?'

'I thought you were a vision,' he said. 'What does it feel like to be thought a vision?'

'What was it you said about my right leg? Did that have anything to do with it?'

'Have a drink and I'll tell you. I want to make sure of the time first and then I'll get you some whisky.'

He looked at his watch and entered the time in a fat notebook on his desk. 'Almost exactly five days,' I heard him say.

He got the whisky bottle and the syphon and poured out the drinks. I sat in one of the chairs by the gas fire and he cleared a space for himself on the bench.

'The thing began five days ago,' said Roper. 'I had been working for about an hour...'

Roper had been working for about an hour before his landlady brought up breakfast on a tray – toast, marmalade, and a pot of tea. He nodded absent-mindedly to her and went on with his work, munching his toast and drinking his tea in the in-betweens, as it were. Soon after eight he heard a car draw up outside and after a pause (for ringing the abortive bell, no doubt) the knocker rattling. Footsteps thudded up the stairs and came to a halt on the landing outside. Roper opened the door to find a short, round, heavily-shouldered man knocking at one of the other doors.

'That's the bathroom,' said Roper, in his take-you-down-a-peg way.

'Mr Roper?'

'Yes. Come in.'

The man entered and Roper shut the door.

'Will you sit down?'

'Thank you.'

The man had taken his hat off. The top of his head was bald, with ringlets of crisp brown hair falling over his ears. He was neatly and conventionally dressed. Small town grocer, thought Roper.

'My name is Joubert,' said the man slowly. 'You may have heard of me.'

'Not the painter?'

'Yes.'

'I have seen your work, of course.'

'Kingston, the architect, told me about you. I would like you to do something for me, if you will.'

Roper was leaning against the wall, smoking. He nodded.

'Kingston told me you specialised in drugs.'

'Kingston always gets his facts right. That's probably why his buildings are not so good.'

Joubert laughed at that. 'Perhaps you would care to deal with this.'

He pulled a bottle from his pocket and handed it to Roper, who held it up to the light, and then placed it on the bench.

'What is it?' asked Roper.

'Mescal. Do you know the drug?'

'I have dealt with it once or twice.'

'I take mescal.'

'I wondered if you did,' said Roper.

'Oh!' Joubert seemed surprised. 'I suppose Kingston...'

'No, I knew by the colour in your paintings.'

'Most French painters use it,' said Joubert. 'Some of them take it regularly, but I only use it when I feel empty, when I want to recharge the batteries, as it were.' He smiled slowly.

Roper went over to the shelves.

'I have Havelock Ellis' monograph on it here,' he said, 'Rouhier's *Le Peyotl*, and Ernst Spath on the chemistry of the drug. Ellis advises painters to take it, but it is difficult to get, isn't it?'

'I have a friend in Mexico, a Consul. But there's something wrong with this consignment. Have you ever taken any?'

'No, I have only analysed it. Doesn't the effect differ with different people?'

'I suppose it does, but I get much the same results as those described by Ellis. This bottle arrived yesterday morning, and I took small doses during the day. I asked some friends in during the evening. I generally do, for it amuses them to listen to the descriptions of what I see. The room was in darkness, of course, except for the fire.'

'I remember now. The fire acts as a stimulant for the visions.' Joubert nodded.

'I sat in front of the fire, my friends around. In the ordinary way there is a frieze of moving figures. In my case they move from the right over to the left, a kind of chain belt of men, women, children, trees, landscapes even, and all of them so beautiful, so luminous that...' He hesitated. 'You must take the drug yourself to know. There are no after effects at all. But the best of it is the colour. I did not really know what colour was until I took mescal. It made a great difference to my painting.'

'And this lot?'

'Oh, it worked in a way. The figures were there, but they were blurred. And there was no colour. They looked like mud pies.'

Roper considered.

'Most drugs work queerly. It may be the drug, or it may be you.'

'Me?'

'Your general health.'

Joubert shook his head.

'I don't believe that. By the way, there was a severe headache afterwards, when I went to bed. I have never had that before.'

'It must be the drug then. I'll look into it and put it right for you.'

'That is very good of you.' He got up heavily. 'I must get some sleep. When you've finished with it perhaps you could send it along by District Messenger.'

'It will take a day or two,' said Roper.

Joubert shook hands with him.

'Come and see us when you can,' he said. 'Do you know that you are extraordinarily paintable?'

'There are all sorts of synonyms for it,' Roper growled,

and he banged the door deliberately behind his visitor.

'Most of the really good artists probably look, behave, and talk like grocers,' he thought.

Roper was not able to get to work on the mescal at once, but he started on it that evening and spent most of the next two days over it. It was a complicated business. There were easily separated impurities one could expect in mescal – the stuff was always very crudely produced by the Indios – but this adulterant, whatever it was, clung like a mistress. Eliminating it was the devil, and he was doubtful, when he sent the mescal on to Joubert, whether it would be satisfactory. Joubert, however, told him over the telephone that it worked beautifully, and repeated his invitation to come to the studio.

'Obdurate, as well as tactless,' thought Roper, grimacing into a mirror.

He was left with a white residue which puzzled him. It was complicated and unstable. In the end, after several tests, he began to suspect that this white crystalline stuff was another drug which had somehow got mixed with the mescal. The next morning he pilled most of it, and went on with his analysis of what remained. There were twenty-six pills, and about ten in the morning, exasperated with his failure, he swallowed one of them, entering the fact and the time in his notebook.

The analysis eluded him. The stuff would not even precipitate with any of the usual reagents, and he passed on to his ordinary work – he had to determine the alkaloid content of some ephedra herb. But every hour or so he took his pulse and blood-pressure. They remained constant. It was probably not a drug after all. He must have been wrong about that.

Mrs Melville brought up his lunch on a tray.

And after lunch, as always, Micky scuttled out from behind the carboys of acid in the corner, and sat on her haunches, and cleaned her moustaches, and scurried about the floor in erratic circles, the regular tomfoolery before a meal. By and by, – and how well she knows it! he thought, he would throw her a piece of cheese. She would be frightened and shoot in amongst the carboys again. But after a while – more coquetry – she would peep out, and look at him, and approach the cheese as warily as a diplomat after a pact. It was an amusing and cynical game to watch. She was so very feminine.

He yielded up the cheese and when they had both finished their meals he sat smoking his pipe and watching her. He began thinking what a very fine thing it was to be a mouse, to be any animal but the man animal. A mouse was a mouse, quite complete as a mouse, and didn't want to be anything else but a mouse. It accepted its premise as a mouse, and lived its life as a mouse without any complications about wanting to be a rat. It must be a fine life. Anything that was complete in itself was fine. A mouse had a centre and a circumference and it didn't go outside. Its brain was perfectly adapted to give it what it wanted as a mouse, to keep it alive as a mouse. It had no silly feelings about how an ideal mouse would live an ideal life. All mice were ideal mice and lived ideal lives. They didn't lie awake in the dark weeping for their sins or plucking up courage to die heroic deaths for other mice....

'You don't even say thank you for your cheese, you pagan,' said Roper aloud. 'Come, smile a sweet thank you for your cheese. How can you expect free lunches without using your sex appeal?' He glanced at a long wooden case upended on the floor. 'Come. Run up that case and sit looking at me, your paws together like any enthralled flapper. Now then.'

The mouse went quietly to the case, sniffed the wood, ran up niftily and sat looking at him, its paws raised and placed together.

Roper laughed. 'Just to show what a clever little woman you are, run across to the other corner and the same, again.'

The mouse lowered her paws, touched wood, and scurried over to the corner he had in mind. There, once more, she put up her paws and placed them together.

Roper nearly cried out at this: he was so startled. He stood there, pipe in hand, his mouth open, staring at the mouse. 'It actually does what I want it to do!' he exclaimed. 'But that is so ridiculous, so out of nature. Back to the other corner, Micky, and the same thing over again.'

When Micky did in fact obey he sprang to his feet with an oath and dropped his pipe. By the time he had picked it up the mouse was gone.

Roper sat down. 'There is nothing to this,' he told himself soberly. 'I must be going mad.'

Then he remembered the pill he had taken, and sighed with relief.

The drug was working.

He had not seen a mouse at all. He had imagined a

mouse. Micky had not turned up, but a vision of Micky had. He had been seeing things.

He carried out his tests again, to see if there were any noticeable physical effects. The tests were all negative.

'The mouse I saw,' he argued, 'did not behave like a mouse. It did what I wanted it to do. Therefore it cannot have been a real mouse. I imagined it, and there was a delusion that I could convey my wishes to it. That, naturally, will apply to anything.'

He strode towards the bench and fixing his eyes upon a glass beaker, commanded it to mount to the ceiling. 'Now then, up you go,' he said. Canute did not command a fracture of the forces of nature with a greater confidence that it would happen.

'Up,' said Roper, flicking his fingers.

But the beaker stayed where it was.

'The effect is already wearing off, or... or that mouse was a real mouse. Which is silly.'

Another objection occurred to him. Perhaps the essence of this delusion – he knew the subtle ways of drugs – was a semi-awareness, an absent-mindedness. He had been talking nonsense, with the edge of his mind, to the mouse, at least to begin with. Perhaps it was no good going so baldheadedly for things, no use bullying the beaker. Given the proper conditions, the beaker would mount all right. Micky couldn't obey his orders and the beaker stay put.

He sat down again, lit his pipe, and eased off his mind. When he was in what he considered the right mood of inconsequence, he caught a kettle on the hop and bade it lift itself a yard or so into the air.

'Up you go and make your bow.'

But the kettle, like the beaker, would not play. It stayed put with an obdurate air of not intending to budge.

'The effect is gone,' said Roper to himself, but he must make certain of that.

'Of course,' he considered, 'it is possible that the illusions obey the laws of probability. Drugs are not finicky when it comes to effects, but each drug has a kind of peculiar interior logic. Micky could do all the things I asked of it. I didn't ask it to do anything which was impossible for it in the ordinary way. If I had asked it to fly, for example, it might have refused. A beaker or a kettle can't move. I know they cannot move, and that may prevent the illusion that they do in fact move. I can soon prove if the effect is gone, but I must have some living material to work on.'

The sun was shining through the window. Work could wait and he would take a walk. He put the box of pills in his pocket and went out.

Walking along the street towards the Heath, and watching for an opportunity, his eyes fell on a milkman's pony. He got to within a few yards of it and stopped.

'Now then,' he addressed the pony, 'lift that right foreleg of yours.'

With great docility the pony, batting its eye as if it were winking at him, raised its foreleg.

Roper nodded. The drug was still working. Now for the second elimination.

'A short flight,' he suggested, 'over the tops of the houses and back again. Please.'

But although there was an uneasy stamping of the feet

and arching of the back, the pony did not fly.

'Damn,' said Roper. He had half expected the pony to fly. He was disappointed it hadn't flown. But that only meant that the probabilities had to be preserved.

Now he must get proof that the things he had seen happen did not actually happen, but only seemed to him to do so.

Illusion: that, in one way or the other, was the effect produced by many drugs. Mescal itself, the illusion of form and colour. Suddenly it struck him that Joubert, too, might have had his experiences. But no, it was unlikely. Joubert had looked for one thing, and had been disappointed. It was only by accident that he himself had made this discovery. If it had not been for Micky he would never have dreamt that anything out of the usual was happening. There had been no reason why Joubert should ask horses to fly.

Rounding the corner into a wider street he came to a halt near a small fruit shop. A whistling, tow-headed youngster had brought out a crate of tomatoes, and was distributing them on trestles amongst an array of beetroot, broad beans, apples, cucumbers, and broccoli.

'We'll see,' thought Roper, and walked on a few steps.

'Pick up a tomato. Throw it into the air and catch it,' he ordered the boy, thinking it, but not saying it.

Roper, by now, was not in the least surprised to see the boy throw a tomato into the air and catch it; a neat catch, too, and the boy laughed.

'Again,' Roper willed, and it was done for him.

'That's enough,' he thought. 'I can now go up and ask the lad if he did in fact throw a tomato into the air.'

But surely, there was something wrong with that?

'How foolish of me! If he says, "Yes", it proves nothing at all!'

He looked closely at the lad. There was something improbable about that boy, about his freckles, his tow hair, his trousers. Perhaps there was something improbable about all greengrocer boys. But he had not noticed it before.

'How far does this illusion extend?' he asked himself. 'To words, perhaps, as well as to appearances? To all the senses, probably, the sense of hearing, of smell, and of sight.

'Does that boy exist at all, or have I created him? And devil take it, here I am in Bishop Berkeley's shoes! I create the stuff on which I experiment. Was the pony there at all? And this boy before my eyes? Have I been making them all up? If I ask a passer-by if he sees this boy as roundly in the flesh as I do... No good, I create the passer-by too.

'Here I am, the prisoner of my senses. There is no way of finding what happens outside. No way at all.'

He stopped at that point for quite a while.

'But there is a way out,' he thought. 'The effects produced by a drug come to an end. If that boy is there... and I don't believe he is... I can make him do something he won't forget in a hurry, something pretty dramatic. When the drug has worn off I can come back and ask him about it.

'If he's still there, that is...'

But what would a greengrocer's boy consider dramatic? They led wild lives, he believed.

'Well, here goes.'

The whistling, tow-headed boy, obeying to the letter what Roper wished him to do, turned round to face the street, a tomato in his hand. A woman walked past, home-ward bound from shopping. The boy's hand drew back, the tomato poised.

But Roper thought better of it. If the woman was a real woman; if the boy was real, too, and the tomato...

'I must keep myself in check,' he admonished himself. 'Not that. Certainly not that.'

But here, coming down the street, was the very thing, a taxicab with a fare. ('Quite a creditable invention of mine,' thought Roper.) And this time the tomato was well and truly flung, with a shrill whoop. Roper could never decide whether the whoop, in a real sense, had been his or the boy's. The missile carried away the driver's peaked cap as he ducked. There was a screech of brakes, a wobble, and then the driver came tumbling out.

'I am not willing or controlling anything now,' thought Roper, 'but all the same this is *not* happening.'

The boy doubled back into the shop and the driver, who had not chanced to see him, walked up and down, shouting: 'Who threw that bloomin' stone? Who threw it?'

A small crowd collected from nowhere and the driver grew truculent. 'What I want to know is, who threw a stone at me? If I get my fists on him...' He spat on his hands and rubbed them together yearningly.

Roper crossed over to the far side of the road, and there, smashed in the gutter, was the tomato. What appears to be a tomato, he corrected. He turned to a large eyed little girl who was sucking her thumb and looking at the mess too.

'Is that... a tomato?' he asked her hesitantly.

'Aw naw, it's an egg.'

Roper was shaken for a moment. Did a phantom tomato appear to one of his phantom creations as a phantom egg? But a boy who had listened to the conversation chimed in solemnly: 'Garn, Jine, wot a liar you are. It's a tomater all right, Sir.'

The fare, a middle-aged woman of considerable determination, was rapping the window with a pencil.

'Why do I create such women?' thought Roper. 'As if there were not enough of them already!'

'Coming, lady,' said the taxi driver, but he had still a few things to tell the stolid onlookers. Amongst them, on the outskirts, and still whistling, Roper was surprised to see the tow-headed boy, eager to know what it was about, jostling his way through, hands deep in his pockets.

'That's enough,' thought Roper. 'Come along, my visions. About your business. Time to go.'

The driver went back to his taxi, still talking and gesticulating and wishing he had his hands on him; the boy strolled over to the shop and ('Cheek!' thought Roper) began rearranging the tomatoes. The taxi drove away and the crowd dispersed.

Roper pondered. The illusions were not strictly comparable to those produced by other drugs. Under mescal, for example the illusions were complete enough, the figures solid, but the shapes and the colours were never exactly those to be seen in nature. You would never mistake the women you saw under mescal for real women. They were too lovely.

But this drug... everything seemed real, real mice, real looking people, ponies, taxis, tomatoes. This drug not only kept strictly to the laws of nature, refusing to allow ponies to fly over houses, as women floated through the air under mescal, but kept so firmly to the form and feature and nature of reality that the vision was in no way distinguishable from it.

And there was the rub, the doubt.

It was impossible for him as a rationalist, a materialist, to doubt that what he had seen were illusions. He had commanded certain things to happen. They shouldn't have happened, and they had.

But they *couldn't* have happened.

Illusions, a parcel of illusions. They *must* be.

All the same, there was a sneaking, fearing doubt as to whether they were illusions. They *looked* like truth, plain and bald, without any imaginative fripperies.

Suppose... suppose for a moment that they were not illusions. What would that mean? It meant that he had got through the wall which separates person from person, mind from mind. And he had not only burst through the wall, but actually captured and controlled the will and the mind behind it....

But this wall itself was the toughest, soundest, hardest, thickest, most impenetrable kind of wall ever built. Each mind was a very Jericho. There were, it is true, ways of communicating with the inhabitant through the embrasures – eyes, ears, nose. But to enter and capture? No.

But that, as he remembered, was not quite true. There were ways and means. The fort was not absolutely impregnable.

Hypnotism. That was a way of entry and capture. A dubious, unsatisfactory affair, but possible. It was used daily.

Telepathy? But that was only a way of communicating. And even at that it had not been proved beyond doubt.

He didn't really believe in telepathy. As a man of science he kept an open mind about it, but it was a strain.

If the things he had seen were real, then this drug made it possible to practise telepathy and mesmerism combined, to pass through without speech, and to capture the will.

The which, as he told himself firmly (blast the dubiety) was ridiculous.

By and by, when the effect had worn off, he would seek out that boy. He would not be there.

But if he were!

He hoped devoutly that he wouldn't be.

He wandered about and got to the Heath and sat down on the grass in the warm sunshine. He rested there a while, smoking. And all the time he kept suppressing an itch to go on with his experiments.

There are always some people on the Heath, he pondered. On a day like this there should be a number. The Heath can't be empty, not altogether. It wouldn't be natural. Good. If I command a man within sight to raise his right arm, and if he does, then I can be sure he is my make believe. But if I ask all of them to raise their arms, and some of them do and some don't, then I shall know which are my creations and which... God's!

He chuckled over that. It seemed to him pretty foolproof.

The only objection he could discover was possibility that under the drug he was unable to see anyone who did not live in the world of his imagination.

'But here I am, sitting in the park, and to get here I must see people and houses and things clearly. I can't be

41

stumbling about in a dream. Unless,' and he sat up with a jerk, 'unless all this *is* a dream....

'Am I really in the park or am I at this very instant asleep in the laboratory? Good lord, that must be the explanation....

'I am fast asleep now, dreaming that this is happening. I ought to have thought of that before. Of course! Perhaps Mrs Melville brought up the lunch and found me asleep. Blue in the face. I am no doubt in hospital by this time, snoring on a bed, with two or three puzzled doctors around.'

He had taken the drug at ten. Mrs Melville brought his lunch at one. It was now (he looked at his watch) four. Then he laughed. As if his watch were any better evidence than all the rest!

He wondered lazily which hospital it was.

'Perhaps the drug kills, after a while,' he thought.

'To prove that I am dreaming, I shall now ask the whole boiling to put up their right hands. *And* all of them will go up, you bet!'

And, so far as he could see, up they all went. He released them with a grin.

'Just as I thought! Fast asleep. Dying perhaps.'

It was not a comfortable thought.

It was soon after this that the dog came running past, with Dobbs chasing him in the distance.

'Strange things, dreams,' thought Roper. 'Why a man and a dog, for example? Moon mythology. There's a man and a dog in the moon.'

He willed the dog to come to him, and it crawled

forward, its belly to the ground, a guilty look in its eye. Roper caught the lead and put his hand in his pocket for a packet of cigarettes. It fell upon the pillbox.

'I shall now,' he said, 'give a dream pill to a dream dog. This is getting complicated.'

''Old 'im, Sir, 'old the devil,' the pursuer shouted from a distance.

The fat man came up and sat down beside him, fanning himself with his bowler.

Roper offered him a cigarette. The man touched the rim of his hat in a military salute. 'Name of Dobbs, Sir, and thank you,' he said. 'Name of Roper,' grinned the man in brown. They lit up, and Dobbs rolled gently on to his back, tilted his hat over his eyes, and smoked into the air.

'Wonder 'ow That There came trotting up to you, Sir,' said Dobbs after a while. 'You don't 'appen to know its mistress, do you?'

'Oh no. It came up to me because it couldn't help it.'

Dobbs lifted his head an inch.

'Meaning, Sir?'

'What I say. It couldn't help itself. I made it stop and come up to me.'

'Oh ah,' said Dobbs, and his head went back to earth. For a time he lay perfectly still. Then his head popped up again.

'You said you... what?

'Stopped it. Made it come up to me.'

'Called aht to it. I see.'

'No, I didn't say a word.'

Dobbs slapped his forehead once, slapped it twice, as if it were a watch which had stopped. But even after a third slap there did not seem to be any ticking.

'Beats me,' he murmured, and relapsed on to his back. But a moment later his head was up once more.

'Say it agen, mister.'

'I commanded the dog to come to me.'

'But didn't call aht to it?'

'No.'

'Nah then,' said Dobbs with a profound effort, ''ow do you command That There to come to you withaht callin'?'

'You see,' said Roper, 'I can make living things do whatever I want them to.'

Roper found there was a peculiar and somewhat unpleasant thrill in talking openly to the man. He was a piece of his imagination, of course, but... he looked so confoundedly solid! There was a million to one chance that something truly odd was happening and that the man was a real man.

It was dangerous, but exhilarating.

There was a long pause.

'So you can make a dawg come to you.'

'You have seen me do it.'

'Dawgs is queer fish,' said Dobbs oracularly.

'Dogs, anything,' said Roper.

Dobbs felt for his watch and moved, cautiously, a shade further away.

'Nice day, Sir,' he said by and by. 'Lovely sky.' He looked up and caught sight of the swaying branches overhanging him.

'That tree, for example,' he lifted a fat finger and pointed, 'you could...'

'Living things. Not trees, no.'

'Them kids, then.' Dobbs nodded towards a small boy and girl playing about a hundred yards in front of them. 'Stand on their 'eads, fer example. Easy, suppose?'

'Quite easy.'

One of the children burst out crying, a sudden squall of sound which swept across the grass to them. A nursemaid in uniform appeared from behind a tree, running, a magazine flapping in her hands. She took the boy by the shoulders and shook him.

'You?' asked Dobbs, cocking an eye at Roper.

But Roper shook his head.

The boy was kicking at her shins, and the nurse promptly upended him and smacked.

'Suppose the boy did that to the nurse,' said Roper. 'Suppose *he* smacked *her.*'

'It don't 'appen,' said Dobbs. 'It ain't in the book of words.'

'Watch.'

The nurse let the boy go, stood upright a moment and then bent over, as if she were playing leap-frog. The boy started smacking her for all he was worth.

Dobbs stared, first at the group, then at Roper.

'Ay, kids will play,' he murmured, but he was shaken. 'Friends of yours, I suppose.' It had all been arranged, of course.

'Never seen them before.'

'Better stop it,' said Dobbs jocularly. 'That kid'll get into trouble, 'e will.'

'Just as you like. Now the boy will stop.'

And stop he did.

'What 'appens now, eh?'

'I don't know. They are free.'

'I knew 'e'd get it,' said Dobbs a moment later. ''E's gettin' it good an' 'ot. 'E won't sit dahn for a day or two.' ''Ere,' he asked suddenly, looking intently at Roper. ''Ere, wot you up to?'

'I am not up to anything.'

'You better not, neither.... Garn, I almost believed you fer 'alf a sec.'

'Would you like to see some more? There's that prim little man with an umbrella coming across. Looks like something drawn by Strube. Would you believe me if he went up to the nurse and kissed her?'

'Kissed 'er!'

'Kissed her, or patted her on the head, or sat down with her on the grass with the umbrella over their heads. Anything you like.'

'There's no 'arm in kissin',' said Dobbs with a small gurgle. 'Show me.'

An amusing lunatic, this.

'Watch.'

The nurse was walking back to the tree. She was walking slowly, reading as she went. The man with the umbrella turned round and began walking towards her. They both stopped, facing each other. The man stuck his umbrella upright in the ground. The nurse put her magazine down on the grass. They neither of them seemed in the least flustered or in any hurry. The nurse lifted her arms, the man took a step forward and the next instant they were kissing and hugging, the two children looking on with intense interest.

'Well?' asked Roper.

46

'Stop it,' gasped Dobbs.

'All right.'

A stifled scream came across the grass, and the noise of a resounding slap. Then another little scream and a shout. The man was snatching up his umbrella and running, for dear life, bent half double. The nurse chased after him, but thought better of it and returned to pick up her magazine. Then she took both children by the hands and began walking rapidly towards the streets. They passed close to the two men.

'If you say anything to your mummy...' Roper heard her say. Her face was very flushed.

Roper turned over on to his side and Dobbs jumped.

'You keep quiet, I warn yer,' said Dobbs, red as a fighting cock. 'You keep yer 'ands off of me or it'll be the worse for yer.'

'But I need not move,' said Roper. 'If I want you to stand on your head in White Stone Pond, I needn't move. I order you to go and do it. I sit here, quietly.'

'Stand on me 'ead in the pond?'

'If you like.'

'An' drown,' shouted Dobbs, as the full implication of standing on his head in three feet of water burst on him. 'Not likely!'

'Shall we try?'

'Not arf we shan't. Nah then, no jiggery pokery wiv me. Do you 'ear? You keep yer 'ands off of me.'

'Well, then, some small thing.... Come now, I want you to be convinced.'

'Not a thing. You keep quiet. None of yer tricks on me.

I've 'alf a mind, see, to put the perlice on to you. I'm goin'. It's time fer the Colonel's tea.' He scrambled to his feet and felt for his watch again. 'Cahm along, That There.' He tugged sharply on the lead. 'An' w'en me back is' turned I don't want to kiss no nursemaids.' His voice lost its truculence and became a shade plaintive. 'You won't, will yer?'

'No.'

'Cross yer fored?'

'Cross my forehead.'

'An' drop dahn dead?'

'And drop down dead.'

'Cahm along, you,' he said to the dog, and walked rapidly away. Now and again he turned round, to catch Roper looking steadily after him.

Roper, watching his receding back, was almost inclined to try out some more of his magic. If he were a real man, he thought, he would fix him on the sky-line, firm on one leg, the other stretched forwards over space, a rooted statue of a human who waddled as he walked. He could imagine the expression that would come over the fat folded face, first surprise, a grim effort to bring the dangling leg down, then rage, consternation and shouts....

Even as he imagined what would happen the doubt grew into his mind again: was Dobbs a figment of his imagination, or was he real? Had he an objective existence? If he had, then there would be trouble. 'I've 'alf a mind to put the perlice on to you,' he had said. That would not do at all. If Dobbs were real, so was the nurse; so was the man who had kissed her. It would make a fine kettle of fish if it came out. Dobbs was not the kind of man to keep an experience like that to himself.

Even if he did not go to the police he would talk at the pubs. No, it was no good risking it. It must be stopped.

Dobbs was already a hundred and fifty yards away, moving out of sight. 'Forget it,' Roper willed intently. 'Forget it.'

Perhaps that was impossible. It very likely was impossible. But if he could get people to do whatever he wanted, by capturing their wills, there was a remote chance that he could make them forget, too.

He had been making a fool of himself. Letting himself go.

The dog. Why in the name of idiocy had he forced the dog to swallow a pill? Of all the disastrous fatuities! Where was that likely to end? Inside that dog's belly, at that very moment, was a pill with extraordinary powers, either of illusion or of interference.

What would a dog do with it, if the dog were real?

He cursed himself for a fool.

He glanced at his watch, took his own temperature with a pocket thermometer, timed his pulse. 'Not a sign of the least abnormality,' he murmured. 'Pulse steady. Temperature normal. Head clear. Well, where do I go now? Home?'

But he decided to stay where he was for a while. It was good to sit there on the Heath, listening to the birds, watching children play, basking in the sun with the wind in his hair, letting the green leaves sink home through the eyes. Normal, cheerful things they were, anchors to the everyday rhythm of things. And he needed anchors.

How good it was to keep within the prescribed limits of the everyday!

For a serious scientific worker it had been... sheer mental disarray!

'Incredible. I didn't know I had it in me,' he thought ruefully. 'That smacking. That kissing. But I am not fit to be at large! Even if they are delusions.

'I shall go home now and wait for the effects of the drug to wear off.'

He got to his feet. He was tired.

'This decision to go home probably coincides with some change in my condition. I am coming to in the hospital. Or in the laboratory.'

He walked home through the streets and let himself into the house. He waited in the hall.

'Mrs Melville!'

She appeared at his elbow, startling him.

'Yes, Mr Roper?'

'Did you notice what time I went out?'

'It was about a quarter to two.'

'Well, would you mind – there's a reason for it – writing that down somewhere.'

She looked alarmed at this. 'Nothing has happened, I hope, Mr Roper.'

'Oh no, nothing to worry about. By the way... I had lunch, I suppose?'

'But of course. Don't you remember?' She was now very much alarmed. 'I took your lunch up in the usual way. I saw you go out and I cleared the lunch.'

Roper grinned at her. 'Might as well go the whole hog with the landlady of my dreams,' he thought. 'Well,' he said aloud, 'was I lying on the floor when you came up, by any chance?'

'Certainly not!'

'And you didn't get me taken away to hospital?'

'Mr Roper, there *is* something the matter with you. You...
you quite frighten me.'

'I have only taken one of those drugs, you know,' he
said, and he saw the relief break into her face.

'Have another drink,' I said.

'Don't mind if I do.'

I splashed him out a bumper one, and a fair sized one
for myself.

'What did you do afterwards?' I asked.

'Nothing. I have not been out for three days. I have gone
on working... so far as I know. There was a lot of work to
be done, but I couldn't trust myself to send off the results.
They might have been crazy.'

'And when I came in?'

'Half an hour before you came the drug was still
working. I know that, for I tried it out at hour intervals.'

'How, exactly?'

'Oh, looked out of the window and made people do
things, scratch their necks, lift their hats. Quite small
things.' He laughed. 'Not that it would have mattered
making them do anything, but I was never quite certain. It
got on my nerves, rather. Sorry I hit out. It shows you.'

'How do things stand now?' I asked.

'What do you mean?'

'Do you still think they were delusions?'

'Certainly. What else could they be?'

'You are quite convinced?'

'Of course I am. Strange business, though.'

'Very strange.'

'I must get on with the analysis of that drug as soon as I find time. There must be more experiments, too.'

'How are you feeling, Bill?' I asked.

'A bit shaken, still. It's been rotten, these five days, wondering all the time what was happening. I've been drinking. I'm pretty full now.'

'Have another.'

'I don't think so.'

'To steady yourself. I've got something to say to you.'

He looked at me, then nodded. I poured out two more drinks.

'You are quite sure the effects are gone, now?' I asked.

'Well, I tried to make you lift a leg, and you wouldn't. It's gone all right.'

'Try again.'

'If you want me to.'

He looked at my leg, and I could see him concentrating.

'No, it's gone,' he said. 'You don't seem to do anything, so that's all right. What have you got to tell me? I haven't been doing things I didn't know about, have I?'

'In a way, yes.'

'Out with it.'

'You remember that man and the dog?'

'Yes.'

'Did he tell you he looked after a Colonel?'

'He mentioned a Colonel.'

'The Colonel is my uncle.'

'Oh!'

'They were real enough, Dobbs and the dog.'

'Good God!'

'Dobbs told me all about it.'

'What did he say?'

'Just that he had met you in the park.'

'The slapping? The kissing?'

'No, he did not mention them. He thought he had been asleep.'

'Do you mean it all happened?'

'Yes.'

He drank off his whisky at a gulp and held the glass out for more.

'Good God!' he said again. And then, with a rush: 'Did I give a real pill to the dog?'

'Of course you did.'

'And the dog...?'

'There was the devil to pay. I'll tell you.'

And I told him.

We began to laugh. It seemed very funny, the way I told it. We laughed until the tears ran down our faces. It was Roper who pulled himself together first.

'I don't know why we're laughing,' he said. 'It's a serious matter. What *is* this drug? What *does* it do? There's never been anything like it before. Not that I know of, and I would have heard. Are they suspicious?' he asked.

'I don't think so. In a way they must be, but the dog was bewitched, you know. They'll let it go at that.'

'The mess I might have got myself into,' he mused. 'There's a prim little man somewhere in Hampstead who kissed a girl in the park. The deliberate way I staged that! They hugged quite a lot. He must think he went mad. He'll never trust himself to walk across a park again, without his wife.

'And that boy who flung the tomato. There's no need to go and see if he's still there. It looked horribly real at the time. We'll finish that bottle.'

'There's a lot.'

'Oh, let's finish it.'

I poured out some more.

'How much of the stuff have you got?'

'Twenty pills.'

'That's plenty.'

'For what?' he asked, looking at me.

'How should I know? Experiment.'

'You were not thinking of anything of the kind.' He was getting rather drunk. 'You tell me what you were thinking of. You don't care a damn for experiment.'

'I wasn't thinking of anything.'

'Yes, you were.'

'No, I wasn't.'

'Liar. I know you were thinking of something. Why the hell don't you tell me!'

'Steady on, Bill. Honestly, I wasn't thinking of anything much. Of course you can't help thinking things with stuff like that about.'

'I won't have you thinking things.' His voice was getting thick. 'Give me another drink. I found this and it has nothing to do with anybody else. What were you thinking, anyway? Out with it.'

'Practical jokes, you know. Going along to the Club and making the fellows stand on their heads. That sort of game.'

'Damn silly,' said Roper. 'You get a thing like this and you want to stand people on their heads. You're an idiot, Jim.'

'But what are you going to do with it?

'I shall do what I damn well like with it. You keep your nose out of this. I know what to do with it. I am going to experiment. It will make me famous.'

He was very drunk by now, spilling his whisky, and looking more ugly than ever. I was getting drunk myself.

'I didn't know you wanted to be famous,' I said.

'Of course I want to be famous. Everybody wants to be famous. I shall be a shining light of science. Statues all over the place. William Roper, shining light of science.'

'You're drunk,' I said.

'Never been soberer. Never. Is that bottle finished?'

'Almost.'

'Give me a drink and open another. This is a great day. Let's get tight.'

We drank for quite a time.

'Give me a pill, old man.'

'No, I won't give you a pill.'

'Don't be mean. I want a pill.'

'What do you want a pill for?'

'I just want one.'

'You tell me what you want it for.'

'I want everybody standing on their heads.'

'Damn silly thing, people upside down.'

'Be a sport. Give me a pill.'

I didn't want a pill. I just went on saying he'd got to give me one. He kept on saying he wasn't giving me one, and that he was going to be a shining light of science, with statues all over the place.

We argued for a long time, and then I went home. Drove the car, too, though I can't imagine how. I was very drunk.

I was not up until midday. After lunch there was a telephone call from Roper.

He wanted me to come and see him.

I was there about three. He was working in his shirtsleeves.

'We were very tight yesterday,' he said, smiling wryly. 'You wanted everybody to stand on their heads.'

'Yes, I remember.'

'We must talk about this. Let's sit down. You don't want a drink, do you?'

'Better not.'

Roper was somewhat distant; not unfriendly, but distant.

'I was upset yesterday. That drug does more than... interfere with things. It affects the taker slightly, throws him off his balance.'

'I thought you were queer.'

'What are you doing in this country? You told me you would be away a long time, studying labour conditions in the States.'

That is what I was supposed to be doing. That is what everybody thought I was doing. But I was not, in fact, doing anything of the kind. I went to America because I liked New York, and California, not to work. I have never worked in my life.

When I was a youngster my father gave me a comfortable allowance. He was self made and liked to see his children spending money. But he had also a streak of puritanism in him and wanted us all to do something. I found the kind of job I liked quite early. 'I think I will go out and study snow: there's more in it than people think.' My father, pleased as Punch, let me go. Other people's sons went to Austria or Sestria to ski, to enjoy themselves. His son went there to study snow. There's a lot of difference. I skiied, of course, like the rest.

Later on, there were the political conditions in Germany. Munich is one of the grandest towns in the world to live in. If Germany has a cultural centre, it is Munich. I could have learnt a great deal there about political conditions. I fell in love with an American girl, and stayed six months. When she went home I came back to England. If people asked me about political conditions in Germany I told them what we had for lunch and dinner, and that, so far as I could make out, satisfied everybody about political conditions. There were lots of people in London who took me for a serious-minded young man. Nobody seemed to see through the game.

Once you start on political conditions, there is no end to it. Russia was very interesting. China too (that was after my father died). South America is bung full of political conditions, and I was so fascinated by the United States that I nearly got myself adopted. I don't know why, but when you tell English people that the Americans call lavatories 'comfort-stations', they feel that you have made a contribution to their political knowledge. I felt sometimes that I could have got into parliament as an expert on the United States on the strength of that. There was a story, too, about how I went into a 'rest room' at an American hotel, thinking it was a lounge, which seemed to convince my listeners that I knew a great deal more about America than most people. Several men asked me point blank if I was in touch with the Foreign Office. The more I denied it the more they believed it. I have never been inside the F.O. in my life.

I had come back from the States because there had been a Crash. When the old family solicitor died and the accountants went through his papers, they found that it would have been better if he had died sooner. They couldn't tell me how much was left, but they didn't think it was more than about two-hundred a year. That isn't enough to study political conditions the way I do it. To tell you the truth, I was not sorry. I was tiring. A playboy's life is not all fun. I had reached the yawning stage, when you begin to think there may be something to this work business – putting on striped trousers and going in a Rolls Royce to the City. Only now, of course, the family solicitor had gone away in the Rolls Royce, and taken the striped trousers with him, too. I was thinking (like most idle young men) of something decorative in the way of selling motor-cars behind acres of plate glass. But I had done nothing about it, yet. There was no hurry.

I told Roper how things were with me. Behind his poker-faced ugliness I suspected that he was disturbed.

'I am glad I didn't give you the pill you wanted last night,' he said.

'Why, what do you think I'd do with it?'

'You've been used to money and you'll want some more, quickly, won't you?'

'I suppose so.'

'And any man who wants quick money is a rogue,' said Roper. 'There are criminal possibilities in those pills.'

'Thanks,' I said curtly.

'Well, there are, aren't there? There would be nothing to stop you from going up to the next man and asking him to hand over his wallet.'

'The same goes for you.'

'I know, but I've never had much money, and I don't want any now.'

'That's what you all say until you get the chance.'

'It depends what you go for,' said Roper. 'There's a contempt for money in my make-up, money as such, that is. I don't want to go to a cabaret every night of my life, and I am sure that Ascot and the Riviera and what they stand for would bore me stiff. I don't run after women, either. I've always worked, and liked it.'

'What are you going to do with this stuff, then?'

'Nothing. I shall work on it, analyse it, if that is possible, get to know exactly what it does. I've barely started, yet. At what range does it work? A mile, a hundred miles? We don't know. Does it work always? There may be types of men it does not affect. There's a lot of work to be done.'

'You could have fun with it.'

'Standing people on their heads? Stealing their pocket books? I don't want that kind of fun, thanks. No, I don't see that it can be of the least practical use. At the moment it looks like a freak. There may be uses for it, of course, therapeutic uses; a mechanical hypnotism which could be used by any fool doctor. That's not a happy prospect, is it? What I can see clearly enough are the dangers.'

He looked at me, pondering.

'I want you to promise not to say a word to anybody about it. We are the only two who know so far. The others, the Colonel, Dobbs, the nursemaid and the man who kissed her, they may all suspect there's something curious in the wind, but they cannot possibly guess the truth.'

'Oh, I'll keep my mouth shut.'

'I shall want someone to help me with the experiments. Would you like the job? It's a good job for the indigent rich. It's the kind of thing they're all looking for.'

'I am messed up with this inquiry into the solicitor's affairs.'

'A pity,' said Roper. 'My assistant will have to be here most of the time. He will have to know, too, and perhaps it doesn't work if you know about it. I shall have to find out.'

'Your father?' I suggested.

'He's retired, and I wouldn't like to bother him with it. No, I'll think it out. Well,' he got up, 'I'm rather busy. You don't mind?'

'Can I keep in touch?'

'Come and see how things are going, but mum's the word.'

'Of course.'

'I'll think things out. See you later then.'

He was back in his shell, and on guard, I felt.

A few days later Bert Phillips sauntered, slowly, singing at the top of his voice, down the shabby by-street in Hampstead. A thin drizzle of rain was falling. There's a silver lining, through the dark clouds shining, he sang, his head swivelling slowly from side to side, keeping a sharp look-out on the windows to catch the stirring curtains. Turn the dark clouds inside out and dree... eem of home.

And that, he told himself ruefully, was the end of that

one. Twopence, so far, one from the invalid lady on the first floor of number two, and one clinking at his feet from goodness knows where. The street was never worth more than a tanner, anyway, but they were trickling in very slowly today. Perhaps he was a touch doleful for the day. Well, then, let it be John Peel, a good rousing catch would be sure to shake the shekels out of them.

Not a damned thing. He liked the cheerful ones himself, but business was business, and the poor liked 'em sad. Don't go down to the mine, daddy, that was their style. But even that one didn't bring more than one small girl running out with a penny, and looking as if she'd like to keep it herself, if she dared.

And here he was, at the end of the street.

No, he would be hanged if he was going to let them get away with it. A tanner the street was worth, and a tanner it was going to be. 'You owe me threepence, and you're going to put it in the plate if I have to sing my Adam's apple out of joint,' he told himself. There you are, hiding behind your windows, thoroughly ashamed of yourselves, and we can't have that, you know.' The weather certainly wasn't helping any. He looked at the rain and turned up the collar of his coat, remembering what his father had told him years before on their way to the village eisteddfod. 'Your voice is a shining blade, Bert, and you mustn't let the rain rust it.' That was true enough, too.

Now he would try an old dodge he had invented himself. He had come along the street head up, a man of hope singing to his fellow creatures. Result, threepence! Now he would tear their blooming heartstrings for them, shambling back a poor, broken man dreaming of his own country and the hills, singing (but to himself, mind) the old songs, the fireside chants and the chapel hymns.

There goes a broken heart, they would say, feeling sorry for him. Wonderful how sentimental the English were, especially the middle class. The poor saw through the dodges quicker, and he respected them for it. You couldn't use the broken wing trick too often, though, not even up the wealthy streets, because there was nothing so quick as meanness to see through anything.

Besides, amusing as the game was (and Bert was so pleased with his profession that he was always adding decorations to it) it had its embarrassments. It put you in a false position to jerk yourself out of dreamland to pick up pennies, especially if they rolled about, as the damned things had a way of doing, and you had to chase them. One had to be a good actor then, and even so it was difficult to keep up the pretence and not look like a hungry hen pecking up the corn.

What is there for me in the world
But oppression all the time.

That was a good, long-drawn, morbid old hymn as sung to the tune of Aberystwyth. Let them battle against that one, if they could. He walked up the street, in a dream of vocal self-communing, head low.

Enemy after enemy is
Wounding me by night and day.

Doctor of defeated ones
Quickly come and make me well...

A penny dropped at his feet and startled him. Yes, truly startled, for that was the worst of being Welsh, one got into the spirit of a thing, and though you began by acting, in a moment, quick as anything, you were serious and inside the skin of the song, mournful as midnight and feeling a black sort of ecstasy.

There was that damned penny, very embarrassing, lying in the gutter. At a moment like that, calling on the Great Doctor to come and heal you, it was ridiculous to have to walk out of your way to pick up a penny from the gutter. But it had to be done, and done, too, as if you were Moses picking manna. Drowned in sorrow though you might be, you had to make some kind of vague unhappy gesture to the woman waiting for recognition of her kindness at a window, and no doubt trying to keep your pecker up with a smile which couldn't, the play being *Hamlet*, be answered merrily.

Well, that had been done, and not too badly, he hoped. He must move on now, for there was another two pence in it. But here was another copper tinkling down from the upstairs regions just as he was about to begin the Welsh graveside chant, the one which describes the fine view from the hills of Jerusalem of the twisty track you've been following through the Vale of Sorrows. Twisty indeed! He was but half way back, yet, and five pence already. Perhaps there was going to be a record in it! You never knew your luck. Only he must keep the cockiness out of his voice.

The day was getting darker. Rain was lacing the mist now

in good earnest. Singing would soon be a vanity, for purses shut like flowers in the wet. Bert looked up anxiously and saw, at an upper window, a man's face. Above the head two palms were pressed whitely, like flatfish bellies, against the glass. The man was no doubt supporting himself on them, as one does when peering out of a window; it looked, thought Bert, as if the man was crying Kamerad to him. The face drew away and was dissolved in the shadows. Then one palm went, leaving the other with no wrist or arm to support it. There for a while it stayed, the white belly of a flatfish glued mysteriously to a pane. Then it, too, unstuck itself, and there was only the dark window, the mist and the rain.

Bert, who had a lively sense of the macabre, stopped singing, walked towards the door of the house and rang the bell. It seemed to him a natural thing to do, to stop singing, walk up to the door, and ring the bell. But at the same time, behind hedges in his brain, there was a scuffle, a protesting and a clamour, an astonishment at himself that he should be doing these things. But it was a grappling and wrestling of mists which blurred only very slightly the solidity, the rightness of what he was doing. But he did, as it were, turn vexatiously towards this ghostly dogfight and say firmly to it that there was nothing to be alarmed about. Nothing.

The door in front of him, for example, the door which had once been green but was now a weather-stained blue – how well he knew that door! He had gone through it many a time. And more than that, he knew perfectly well the woman who would answer it, a tall, thin scarecrow of a woman with a shawl round her shoulders. He knew all about the door and the woman. Of course he did.

But all the same, at the back of this certainty, from behind the barricades of consciousness, a voice was crying fire, alarm, a dozen foreboding things.

But that buzzing irrelevance was nothing. The bell was out of action. He should have known that. He banged on the knocker, and the door opened at once. There she was, the scarecrow, just as he had pictured she would be. He nodded brightly to her and walked up the stairs.

I had been with Roper about half an hour, talking. Roper had asked me to come.

'I have decided to take another pill,' he told me. 'I simply can't find out what the stuff is. I've been analysing it for the last three days, but it's unlike any other drug I have known.

'I wanted you to come because I must find out exactly how long it takes to get going. You don't mind if I try and make you lift your hand at five minute intervals, do you?

'I can't find out what it is, but I can find out what it does.

'I'll keep notes this time. I weighed out the stuff when I pilled it. Each one contains the same amount of the stuff.

'I am going to watch, too, what the drug does to me, subjectively.'

'Have you found a man to experiment on yet?' I asked.

'No, but we must get hold of one during the next five days. There's no hurry.'

He swallowed the pill at two o'clock.

'I'll go on with my work, if you don't mind, and try it out on you now and again,' he said.

'What exactly is your work, Bill?'

'Oh, it's percentaging, mostly, and a lot of it is opium. An American buys opium in Bulgaria, Yugoslavia, Turkey or Afghanistan. He gets it sampled locally and the sample is sent to me. I have a licence from the Home Office to import samples, you know. Sometimes the samples come through the post, or they are brought by Continental Carriers. They are all cleared at the Mount Pleasant Customs and Excise Department, and entered, of course, on my licence. I analyse each sample for the morphine content, and it's on that analysis that the stuff is bought and sold.

'That Mount Pleasant business is complicated. Do you know my father's secretary, Mary? She comes along in the morning to do the donkey work. You must meet her.'

'Isn't there any left over?' I asked.

'I keep that, bulk it, analyse it, and sell it. It's a sort of pourboire we get. Of course it isn't only opium. There's ephedra herb from China and India, ergot of rye from Spain, Portugal, Russia, Poland and Germany, ipecacuanha and cinchona bark from South America, scammony root, jalap, belladonna... oh, all sorts of things. And occasionally the fur goes flying between a client and some firm. I spent the morning analysing lipsticks which made a woman ill. I found cadmium, which accounts for it. It destroys the red blood corpuscles if it gets into the blood stream, and it might, if she licked her lips. There'll be a shindy, I expect.'

'The pill not active, yet?'

'No. I have just tried you out. I do a certain amount of research work, too.'

I picked up a book and he went on with his job at the

bench. I had forgotten about the drug when I found myself lifting an arm into the air.

'Twenty past two,' said Roper. 'Let's have that down. It takes twenty minutes to work. That's fairly fast. What happened?'

'I found myself raising an arm.'

'You wanted to?'

'Oh yes.'

'No struggle against it?'

'None. I thought I would raise my hand, and I did.'

'If I wanted you to do something unpleasant, it might be different. Wait a minute... here's a pin.'

'What do you want me to do with that?'

'Oh, nothing. I'll go on with my work now.'

'All right,' I said, and took up my book again.

Suddenly I picked up the pin and jabbed myself with it in the leg.

'Hell, Bill...'

'Did you want to do that?'

'Yes I did, but it was strange. There was a part of me which didn't want to.'

'But not enough to stop you?'

'It was barely there.'

'If I had asked you to jab it in your eye... I wonder. This is going to be difficult. Could one get a man to kill himself this way? It seems incredible.'

'That jab hurt,' I said. Roper laughed.

I strolled over to the window and heard a man singing in the street, below.

'If you want someone to experiment on,' I said, 'why not

this street singer? He's sure to be hard up and to have plenty of time on his hands.'

'That's an idea. Let's have a look at him.' Roper peered out of the window into the rain.

'Yes, I think he ought to do. I'll get him to come up.'

'Have you put the 'fluence on him?' I asked.

He came away from the window and looked at his watch. 'Yes, he's coming up. Let's put the time down. Half past two. We can start the experiment right away. I am *seeing* the door now and trying to pass it on to him. Now he's pushing the bell that doesn't work. Can you hear the knocker rattling? I have tried to convey to him an image of the landlady, as if he had always known her. He's coming up the stairs. Listen. In a moment he will be at the door. Now I am giving him a mental image of this room. But the moment he comes in I shall snap off and see what happens.'

I was watching the door. It opened smartly and the singer came in. I could almost see him coming out of Roper's compulsion into his own self. He started, his hand still on the knob, and his eyes darted about the room.

He was about forty-five. It was an interesting face, the kind that you look round at and want to see again, although it wasn't, in fact, much to look at. It wasn't beautiful, I mean, or striking, but all the same it was a face that stayed with you when it was gone, and came back with ease into the memory. His hair was turning grey, and a quip of it fell almost romantically over his right eye. The eyes were a clear blue, and shrewd. They seemed to know what you were thinking about, and understand why you were thinking that way, and condoning it, too. The face was fine and thin, and as with so

68

many Welsh people, the cheekbones were prominent. It was a shrewd, humorous, easy-going face you liked at first glance, and went on liking, finding more and more in it.

'Sorry, wrong room,' he blurted, and began closing the door behind him.

'Wait, don't go,' I shouted. 'You were looking for another room, were you?'

He came in again and stood by the door.

'Well...' He hesitated, looking at me.

'Can I help you?'

'Don't you bother,' he said heartily. 'I'll find my way about. Sorry I butted in on you like that. I am sure I don't know how I came to make a mistake like that.'

Again he turned to go.

'If you are not in a hurry I would like to talk to you,' said Roper.

'No, no particular hurry,' he said cautiously.

'You look wet. Come in and dry yourself by the gas fire.'

'That's good of you,' he said, but he was still perplexed. He shut the door behind him and I placed a chair for him near the fire. He sat down on the edge of it.

'This is Mr Roper. He works here,' I said.

'How do you do, Mr Roper. It's a grand place you've got.'

'I have called to see him. My name is Starling. I don't know yours.'

'Bert they call me, Bert Phillips.'

He warmed his hands by the fire and looked round.

'This is the room you were looking for, isn't it?' asked Roper in his deep voice.

'Yes and no,' said Bert.

69

'What does that mean?' I asked.

'I've been in a bit of a mix,' said Bert cautiously.

He was very much on his guard. He must be put at his ease. I looked for cigarettes but had run out of them. Roper was smoking his pipe.

'I have run out of cigarettes, but if you would like to smoke...' I said.

'I would like a whiff,' he said eagerly, and pulled out a crumpled packet of Woodbines. 'Not very classy cigarettes,' he grinned, 'but try one.'

I tried one, and we lit up. Roper looked at me, but I didn't know how to get on with the business. He sat there, warily, obviously thinking things and wondering, but quietly self-confident all the same.

It was he who spoke.

'Not a very nice day, is it?'

I almost laughed.

'I suppose it makes a difference to your earnings,' said Roper.

'Well, so long as it does not actually rain cats and dogs, it's not so bad.'

'Do you come along this way often?'

'Every Wednesday fortnight, regular as clockwork.'

'I thought I had seen you before.'

'Shall we say you have been here long then?' asked Bert politely.

'Shall we say...' Roper repeated. 'Oh, I see. You are Welsh, aren't you?'

'That's right. That's what I am, and I suppose we do speak queer sometimes.'

70

'We shall say,' smiled Roper, 'that I have been here about four years.'

'And I've been working the street for three, every bit of three.'

'The usual thing, unemployment?' I asked.

'It used to be, once upon a time, but I can't say it is that now. I like being my own boss, that is what is the matter with me. My voice and me, we get along and we don't quarrel. It brings me in the dibs and I give it a wet sometimes to keep it sweet. Oh, we get on fine. There's no rows between us, and no sackings either, which is more than can be said for most masters and servants.'

'No ambitions, eh?' asked Roper.

'To pick up a bob in the street is about as far as it goes.'

'Still ... you'd like a few things?' asked Roper.

'I don't know, I am sure.'

'Married?'

'Me, married! Who'd marry a chanter, I'd like to know.'

'But you would like to be,' Roper insisted.

'Well, you put me in a forked stick, there. You know what flesh and blood is like, in spite of plenty of warnings.'

This was getting on famously, I thought. Roper was handling him very well. He was sitting back in his chair now, at his ease, smiling at the fun.

'A wife then, perhaps a child or two,' said Roper, puffing at his pipe. 'And money. Come now, you would like some more money?'

'Who in their senses wouldn't,' agreed Bert. 'Give me the money and the wife comes along like a packet out of a cigarette machine.'

'There, a wife, a child or two, more money, and a house to live in,' quizzed Roper.

'And there,' said Bert, obviously enjoying himself, 'you go making a complete stranger of me. That isn't little me any longer, with all those things.'

'Why not? Other people have these things.'

'Ay, but they've got ambition.'

'And no voice,' I said.

'True,' grinned Bert, 'most of them do sing out of tune.'

'I like your Welsh accent,' said Roper, pulling his leg.

'I like it myself,' said Bert. 'It's nice to have a voice that goes over the hurdles instead of along the flat.'

This was really splendid, I thought. Nothing could have gone better. Bert pulled out his Woodbines again and we had one each.

'Why don't you get on with it?' asked Bert suddenly, looking me in the eye.

'Get on with what?' I asked stupidly. Roper laughed and came to the rescue.

'What is it you want to know?' asked Roper.

'A strange thing has happened to me,' said Bert. 'I have never been in this room before, nor in the house, but I've come up to you from the street like I was a train between Cardiff and Paddington.'

'I did that,' said Roper. 'There's nothing to be frightened about. It was just an experiment.'

'Oh, I wasn't frightened.'

It wasn't true. I could see that. He was still frightened, but keeping a hold on himself.

'Could you tell us what happened to you?' I asked.

'I don't want to say anything,' said Bert evasively.

'But you said just now...'

'That was a pack of nonsense,' said Bert, puffing at his cigarette and avoiding my eye.

He looked tight and close hauled as a snail in its shell. I remembered Dobbs, without an ounce of imagination, and the way he had turned tail and run at the first whiff of sulphur and the devil. And this specimen was a Celt, a hundred times more responsive to any suggestion of the supernatural or the diabolic. He would take a deal of calming and reassuring.

Roper stepped in again. He had lit his pipe afresh and was leaning against the mantelpiece.

'I will tell you all about it,' he began. 'I am an analytical chemist....'

'A very good one, I am sure,' Bert interrupted, out of pure unease.

'Of course I do a lot of experimenting,' Roper went on. 'I saw you walking up the street just now and tried one on you. It was a perfectly harmless one. You have heard of telepathy?'

'No,' said Bert, 'I have not.'

'You must have read stories in the papers about some woman thinking or feeling that her son had been killed in Canada at three o'clock in the afternoon, and afterwards she's had a cable to say it had happened. I never believed those stories myself, but now I find they were probably true. It means that thought or knowledge can pass between two people without words. That is what I have been trying to do with you this afternoon, passing thoughts on to you.

I ordered you to come up, that is all.'

'I am sure I did not hear you, whatever,' said Bert with a nervous cackle.

'It would be interesting to know what happened your end. This kind of experimenting with telepathy is new, and we must collect all the facts we can.'

'There's no harm in that,' said Bert slowly.

'No harm at all.'

'Well then, the first I knew after seeing you at the window was that I was walking to the door and ringing the bell.'

'Now tell me,' said Roper, 'did you try to stop yourself from doing that?'

'Can't say I did, exactly. There was a small voice saying don't. It was a kind of echo. It was really like...' he searched for a comparison, 'like when your conscience is worn out but still goes on saying things. It didn't make any difference.'

'Did anything surprise you at all?'

'Not at the time.'

'But now, thinking it over?'

'Yes, then.'

Roper waited. 'Well?' he prompted, as the silence lengthened.

'I knew the damned door and the damned woman who was going to open it,' he blurted out, staring at him.

'Good,' said Roper.

'Explain that,' challenged Bert.

'Well, you see, I remembered the door hard, and the woman, too, and tried to pass the pictures on to you so that you would not be frightened by what you were doing. It worked.'

'Is that what it was!' exclaimed Bert, and I could see how immensely relieved he was.

'Everything was natural as a blackbird on a bough till I came right into this place,' he went on delightly.

'That was when I stopped doing things,' said Roper.

'Tell me now, can you do that to anybody?' asked Bert.

'I think so.'

'You mean you can make anybody do what you want?'

And there he was, sitting on the edge of the chair again, rigid.

'I have only tried a few experiments,' said Roper patiently, 'but on the whole they have been successful.'

'That Canadian who gets killed,' said Bert.

'Well?'

'That's not like this. He didn't make his mother do anything.'

'It is different in a way. There's a little more to this.'

'A lot more,' said Bert excitedly, 'a whale of a lot more.'

'This is telepathy and mesmerism.'

'And what's that thing?' asked Bert.

'Hypnotism. You have heard of that?'

'I have,' said Bert slowly. 'It's men getting girls to do what they want... or so I have heard.'

We had frightened our man once more. For a while Roper had made him feel that what had happened to him was normal, out of the way, perhaps, but normal. Now he was scared again, as indeed, I recognised, he had every right to be. We were back to the beginning. Bert Phillips had been out in the street, singing. The singer was now sitting by a fire, in our room. And he could not swallow that. His instinct warned him that it was anything but right.

Roper moved rather suddenly from the mantelpiece to go over to the bench. I saw Bert start and the knuckles of his hands go white on his knees.

He picked up his cap, which had been drying before the fire, and stood up.

'What's the matter?' asked Roper.

'The matter is, I'm hopping,' said Bert. 'I have been here long enough.'

'Don't go,' I said.

'I want to go now, if you don't mind.'

'Just as you like,' said Roper.

'I suppose you could stop me, if you wanted to,' said Bert, looking at Roper.

'Yes, but I don't want to. You can go when you like.'

He twirled the cap about in his hands. He looked more friendly again.

And suddenly I began to suspect that he was not his own free agent now. I looked at Roper. Roper was entering something in his notebook.

'What did you want with me, then?' asked Bert.

Roper went up to him.

'I will tell you, quite frankly. I have found a new drug, and it's this drug which makes it possible for me to do things. But we don't know exactly what it does, or how it works. I want to find out. I want a man who isn't afraid to work with me and who will let me experiment on him. A man who is afraid is no use to me. And he needn't be afraid. No harm can come to him. I promise that. I see that you are afraid, so you are no use. You can go now.'

'Who me, afraid?' said Bert.

'Yes, aren't you?'

'Well, I am a bit,' said Bert, and we all laughed. I think it was this laughter that settled things.

'I'll pay you a pound a day,' said Roper, 'but I won't take you on unless you want to.'

'And what do I do?'

'I would want you to live here for a few days. You can have the spare bedroom.'

'I'll take it on,' said Bert. 'But look, I am not going to stay in these clothes. They are specially for begging, and if I'm taking a job I want me best suit.' He laughed. 'I have a Sunday best, you know, though I don't look like it.'

'Where do you live?' I asked.

'It's a doss house in Camden Town.'

'I'll take you down in the car and bring you back.'

'I'm game.'

Roper was consulting his watch and his notebook.

'Do you mind if I try one experiment before you go? You have been here twenty minutes. Now I believe I could make you forget everything that has happened. Will you let me try?'

'Fire ahead. But won't you have to talk me round to it again?'

'Yes, that's awkward,' said Roper. He had not thought of that. 'Well, perhaps I shall be able to make you remember again when I want you to.'

'Go right ahead.'

'Forget then, forget it all.'

I saw Bert start and look round him. He looked at Roper

and looked at me, as if we were complete strangers.

'What ... what's this?' he asked, bewildered. 'Who are you. What am I doing here?'

'Why what's the matter?' asked Roper. 'What has happened to you?'

'I was knocking at the door,' said Bert, 'and then... here I am.'

'Don't you remember coming up the stairs?'

'No. Stairs?' he asked, dazed. 'What stairs?'

'I am going to will that he remembers it all again,' said Roper to me. 'I doubt whether it will work.'

But it did work. In another moment Bert had picked up the threads, and was wiping his brow with his sleeve.

'For a bit of magic,' he said, 'you couldn't beat that.'

'You are not frightened now, are you?' I asked him.

'Not much, but it was funny.'

'We'll fetch your suit,' I said, 'but have a look at your bedroom first.'

I showed him the door leading to the second bedroom and he went in.

'When he agreed,' I whispered to Roper, 'was he under?'

'For a moment.'

'That's offside, Bill.'

'Oh, to hell with it. I want this man.'

'We can fetch the suit?'

'Keep an eye on him,' said Roper. 'You must not lose him.'

'It's a grand bedroom. It will suit me,' said Bert, coming out.

'We'll get along, then,' I said. 'You can have a bath when you come back.'

'A bath!' said Bert, as if heaven had opened.

Roper handed him a pound note.

'That's the stuff,' said Bert cheerfully, taking out a pocket-book and adding the note to a number of others. I was surprised.

'You have plenty of money,' I said.

'About ten years' savings.'

On the way down to Camden Town he pointed out street after street to me. 'That one's worth half a crown, taken gently. That one's no good except on Friday, after pay day. That's a ninepenny.' He assessed them as dryly as a rate collector. 'There's a girl over there at number ten,' he said, 'always gives me a bob after I sing her the Miner's Lament for Father and Mother.

'You never know you love 'em
Till the grass grows green above 'em,
You never know their value till they're dead and gone,'

he sang softly. 'She laughs her head off and gives me a bob.'

'How much do you make?' I asked.

'About two pound ten a week in the Spring, but not much in the Autumn. You'd be surprised how mean people get in the Autumn. Thinking of the winter coals, I suppose.'

'But why do you live in a doss house, then? You could live nicely on that money.'

'Oh well. Beggars are happier together. Here we are, near enough. It's just round the corner, number thirty-two. You had better stop here. I don't want to go rolling up in a grand car, like a rich 'un. They would never stop teasing me.'

I pulled up the car and he got out. 'I won't be a jiffy,' he said.

'Look here, Bert, you won't vamoose, will you?'

He came back a step and leant over the driving wheel.

'You do not truly think I would do that, do you!' He looked surprised. 'Oh well, I know what you mean.' He pulled out his pocket-book and threw it into the back seat. 'I will be back in a jiffy,' he smiled, and walked round the corner.

I felt a fool.

He was back in five minutes, with a parcel under his arm.

'I suppose now,' he grinned, 'I did ought to count the money in that pocket-book. That would be a sweet come back, wouldn't it?'

'Sorry, Bert.'

He scratched his head comically.

'And I don't even know how much there is in it!' he said.

Back in the house Roper showed him the bathroom.

'You can say goodbye to me now,' said Bert. 'In half an hour you'll be seeing me in my Sunday best, and I promise you a treat. You won't know little me.'

Whilst he was having his bath I talked to Roper.

'Don't you feel at all different?' I asked.

'Yes I do, in a way. Do I look different?'

'The eyes are shinier, but that's my imagination, probably.'

He nodded.

'How do you feel different, exactly?'

'There's an undertow of excitement, an almost furtive sense of power. An uneasy desire to use it and go on using it, too. I could hardly keep away from the window when you were gone. You'd better keep an eye on me and protest if I get silly.'

'But you will always be able to over-ride me.'

'I shall pull myself together. It's all right so long as one knows. I am probably exaggerating.'

'Well, what do you think of it?' asked Bert at the door. He held his hands out like a mannequin, and turned slowly round. 'It is a beauty, isn't it?'

We laughed. We couldn't help laughing, and he laughed with us.

'I thought you would like my courting clothes,' he said. 'And now, what about a spot of work? Your quid is burning a hole in my pocket and I haven't done a thing.'

'You look grand, Bert,' I said. He winked at me.

We made for the Heath. As we walked along Roper stopped at a greengrocer's. A towheaded lad came out, whistling.

'Hallo! You're the lad who knocked the taximan's hat off the other day with a tomato,' said Roper.

'Wot lies!' said the boy indignantly. 'Wot woppers!'

Roper handed him a threepenny piece. The boy looked at it closely, turned it over, bit it, tried it out on the pavement, and then said 'Ta.'

'I saw you,' said Roper. 'I saw you throw it.'

'Oo, wot a wopper!'

'I saw you.'

'A tomater?

'Yes.'

The boy peered into the doorway.

'It just slipped me 'and like,' he said quickly. ''Op it, gents, 'ere's the boss.'

81

We walked along and when we came to the Heath halted under a tree.

'First, the range at which it works,' said Roper. 'I am not well read in miracles. Have they a range? We must find out. If it is a natural force, and it is, it will probably have a limit. Do you think it a natural force, Bert?'

'No,' said Bert soberly, 'I do not. I think it is the Devil.'

'Well, let's see what the Devil can do. Walk over to that rise. It's about three hundred yards away, I should think. I'll ask you to do something a trifle odd. You will know it when it happens.'

'Well,' said Bert, 'don't you forget I am in my Sunday best. No rolling about on the grass, I hope.'

'All right, I'll remember the Savile Row. If nothing happens, walk towards us, and when something does happen, stop. Then we'll pace out the distance.'

'O.K., Chief,' said Bert, and walked off.

'The Devil!' said Roper. 'That fellow has simple faith. I suppose one would develop simple faith if one did nothing and lived on the fat of the land. Financiers believe in the Devil, too, probably.'

'What are you going to make him do?'

'Pull his own nose out of joint.'

'But it will seem quite natural to him that he should do so,' I objected. 'He won't stop walking because of that.'

'True. I had overlooked that. We must make him do something which we can see. Then I'll stop him dead, myself, for he will be within range. I shall make him throw his hat into the air. Is that Sunday best too?'

'Very much so,' I said.

Bert stood on the rise, looking towards us.

'Are you trying now?' I asked.

'Of course. This stuff *has* a range, Jim.'

Bert began walking towards us.

'He's not more than two hundred and fifty yards off now,' I said.

Roper shook his head. He looked troubled. Bert walked on slowly. Suddenly he threw his hat into the air and caught it. Then he stood still, looking at us.

'Good dog,' murmured Roper. 'I was beginning to think the stuff wasn't working.'

We paced it and made it out to be two hundred and fifteen yards, roughly.

'Was that it, throwing up the hat?' asked Bert.

'Yes,' I said.

'Must have looked a fool, sure,' said Bert. 'There were some women looking.'

'Perhaps it differs with different people,' said Roper. 'Off you go, Jim.'

But with me, too, it was the same distance. We tried the experiment several times, on the flat, down a slope, over water (that was Bert's idea, remembering something about witches). It always worked at the same distance, though.

'Now what happens if you are out of sight, but I know you are there,' said Roper. 'Go to the far side of that copse, Bert. You, Jim, find some place where you can see both of us. Walk towards the copse and me, Bert. Perhaps it doesn't work when the man is out of sight.'

But it did. We tried it several times, and Bert always came to a standstill.

'If a particular person is within range, and I will him to do something, then he does it. Astounding, really. But we must find out if it applies to that person only. It may also work on anyone along the direct line of force. Bert, move away about twenty yards. You, Jim, get into a position between us. Now then.'

He made Bert rub his hands together, but nothing happened to me. He put us close together, and made us rub our hands, now Bert, now me.

'As unfailing and discriminatory as a woman's instinct,' he grinned. 'Well, well.'

There were other experiments.

'I am going to try to pass this power on to you, Jim. I shall will you to will Bert to do something. Using the power by proxy.'

I found myself trying hard to make Bert tweak his nose, but nothing happened.

'That's a blank. Pity,' said Roper. 'But there's one thing we must find out. Can I will a man within range to do something outside the range? Off you go, Bert.'

Bert walked away to the rise, and when he was there, placed his hat on the ground and stamped on it.

'His Sunday hat,' I objected.

'That's the point,' said Roper. 'You see, he is prepared to do something which he hates doing, too. I can't think of any other experiments now, can you?'

'No,' I said. 'This is mad enough.'

Bert came back. He was trying to smooth out his hat.

'Look here,' he said angrily, 'that's plenty of this hanky-panky. What did you want me to step on that hat for? It cost me fifteen bob, every penny of it.'

'I'll give you a new one.'

'It was fond I was of that hat,' said Bert ruefully.

'Oh, if that's all,' said Roper, 'I can make you hate the damned thing.'

Bert threw the hat on the ground and stamped on it. He picked it up and tried to tear it to pieces with his teeth. I didn't like the look on his face.

'Stop it, Bill,' I said. 'This is rotten.'

Bert flung the hat away from him, and came to. There was a dazed look in his eye.

'That's astonishingly interesting,' said Roper. 'I didn't will him to do anything to the hat, you know. I merely passed over a feeling of anger towards the hat. The rest followed. We must go further with that experiment. Let's get back to the flat.'

On the way he turned into a second-hand bookshop.

'Nothing like the poets for emotions,' he said. 'I've bought a Tennyson, two pence and not too clean.'

Mrs Melville brought us tea, and afterwards there were more experiments.

'I shall turn my back to you so that you can't see my face,' said Roper. 'I shall then read one of these poems and you can tell me later what you felt. I shall not try and convey the words or the meaning to you, but only what I feel. The pure emotion. Now then.'

He sat on one of the chairs, in a corner. Bert sat on the other and I perched myself up on the bench.

Roper turned to the index, found a page, and started reading.

I began laughing to myself, not a belly laugh, though, but a snicker, the laugh contemptuous; cynical amusement and a kind of astonished incredulity were mixed with it too. It grew upon me until it was as exquisite as tickling.

I saw Roper drop the book and turn round to watch us. He crossed over to the bench and did some work for about a quarter of an hour. But my laughter went on. It did not stop when he stopped reading. Suddenly it dropped away.

'Well?' asked Roper.

'It made me laugh,' said Bert, 'like I do when someone throws me a copper that's a dud.'

I told Roper what I had felt, too.

'The Charge of the Light Brigade,' he said. 'Noble six hundred. It's the funniest poem I know. But tell me, did you go on laughing whilst I was working?'

'Yes,' we answered.

'I willed that you should. I tried to "fix" the emotion. Do you know, I believe that you would have gone on laughing for the next five days if I hadn't switched you off.'

'That wouldn't have been so funny,' said Bert soberly.

'I would like to speak to my father about this,' said Roper. 'There isn't much in the drug line that he doesn't know. We shall go along after dinner.'

He crossed over to the telephone, and I heard him tell his father that he would be bringing one or two people with him.

'Not me,' said Bert hastily. 'No, not me. I am not used to high society.'

'Afterwards we'll see Joubert,' said Roper. 'I must find out if he can get more of that mescal from his consul. I had better telephone him, too.'

Joubert said he would be glad to see us.

'Can you see any use to this stuff at all?' he asked me.

'None,' I said.

'I can see about five hundred uses for it,' said Bert. 'If I was fighting an election, now, it would come in useful, or...'

Roper interrupted him.

'Can this power be broadcast?' he asked suddenly. 'Could it be used over the wireless?' Bert put down his cup and walked out of the room without a word.

'Where has he gone to?' I asked Roper.

'To a telephone booth outside the range of the stuff. I must try it over the wires. He'll ring us in a few minutes.'

We said no more until the telephone rang. Roper went to it and told Bert that he was going to try out an experiment. He was silent for a time.

'Did you do anything? Did you open the door of the booth two or three times?' asked Roper.

He put the receiver down.

'Nothing doing,' he said, 'but we are dealing with something so entirely new that you never know. Range, two hundred and fifteen yards,' he ticked off. 'Function, telepathy plus hypnotism, and the hypnotic suggestion works outside the range. Transferred emotion can be fixed and prolonged at will. That is all we know so far.'

'And there is your suggestion that the drug affects the taker.'

'Yes,' said Roper dubiously. 'The difficulty with that is that whatever the subject feels appears to him to be normal. Would you like an entirely new experience?' he asked.

'What is it?'

'I could project myself. That has never been done before. No human being has yet known what it feels like to be another.'

'It would be prying,' I objected feebly. I did not want him to do it.

'Oh, I am not ashamed of myself. It's the kind of thing lovers long for: complete union with the beloved. I don't suppose it would be a healthy experience.'

'Well then, don't,' I said.

'Still, it would be interesting. How normal am I, now, from your point of view?'

'The Charge of the Light Brigade has never struck me as funny.'

'But that wasn't the drug.'

'Well then, I didn't like the hat tearing business.'

'That's what I mean. I may be abnormal, even for me, under this drug. It doesn't show, does it?'

'No.'

'But then, I repress severely at the best of times. We'll try it.'

'I would rather not,' I said.

'We have to find out.'

And then I had the most extraordinary experience of my whole life. In a way it was fascinating; in another, horrible. I became two people. They were not mixed, but quite separate and distinct personalities. The 'I' that is me regarded the other that was Roper and now become myself too. I had never imagined that someone else could feel so different, that his 'being' should vary so profoundly from my 'being'. The mystery of personality has worried me ever since.

How shall I express it? The differences tremble on the verge of expression, but are not to be captured. Some things are clear enough. There was, for example, that 'weight', or 'specific gravity' which I have already mentioned. Roper felt heavier, more solidly based, and at the same time livelier, sharper, more intent than I am. There was an odd sour feeling about his 'being', a sourness with a flash, a cynicism, a resentment which arose out of complicated depths. What was even more apparent was a sense of being in bondage, of being swathed round and of a desperate stretching against the bandages, as though he were buried alive. A subdued and constant strife. The Roper 'I' did not know the compunctions and evasions of my nature. I felt that it could be cruel and unjust and vengeful with a complete absence of conscience.

But these are words, and words mirror only faintly the true nature of the experience. A bold, dark, striving spirit, constantly disintegrating and re-cohering. That is the best I can do as a summing up.

It was over. I must have looked dazed.

'What does it feel like to be me?' grinned Roper. 'You look as if you had received a shock.'

'Who, me?' I evaded.

'Is it as bad as all that, my soul?'

'Don't talk rot, Bill.'

'Well, what was it like? Tell me.'

'It was fine,' I said. 'Interesting.'

'Had you expected it?'

'It was just like you, Bill.'

'You are twisting and jibbing. What was it like, man?'

'It was funny, but you're all right.'

'Nothing abnormal? Nothing that struck you as not like me?'

'Not a thing. It was fine, Bill, all plain sailing.'

'All the same it made you sweat. You're sweating now.'

'It's hot, that's all.

'But you'd probably have sweated any time if you had known what stuff I was made of.'

'You know what you're like. What's the use of saying anything.'

'Do you know what the Aztec princesses did to their lovers when they'd had 'em?'

'Worried them to know what it was like?' I said bitterly.

'No. Killed them. There's a privacy of self which works curiously. I can understand nature imposing the penalty of death for violation. The drone has known the Queen. He must die.'

'You handed yourself over. I couldn't help myself.'

'So did those princesses, quite ardently, I suspect. And probably the poor lover didn't want them either, knowing the consequences. I think I shall always bear you a grudge for this rape.

'And you're so bloody inarticulate, too,' he went on. 'The only man who's ever had this experience can say nothing more than "It was fine, Bill, it was funny." Can't you be more explicit? Isn't there anything more?'

'Not a thing, Bill. Honestly.'

'Old school tie to the last, even in the matter of souls,' said Roper, and left it at that.

There was, and there remains, a furtive sense of shame in that experience. I do not pretend to know why it should be so.

'What happened to Uncle and Dobbs and the dog, do you think?' I asked, trying to divert him.

'I have been wondering about that. The dog could hardly have willed his own projection, but probably a dog is so fiercely and whole-heartedly dog that he radiates the dogginess of him to those in the immediate vicinity. Whereas I... well, I am a mere human being, a faint echo compared with the intensity of being a dog. A noble savage would probably affect everybody round him in the same way. See what we lose by our civilization and culture!'

He was hugely pleased with that. 'Diminished little emasculates, that's what we are...'

Bert came back, and Roper began to talk about his family.

'You must meet my father. He's younger than you would think, not much over fifty now. My grandfather found him a wife in his twentieth year, never even asked him whether she was suitable or not. He was a great man, in the old overbearing style, my grandfather. He knew what was good for his boy. My father was working at this bench one day and the old man brought up a nice looking girl he had never seen before. "You have been wasting time lately running after the girls," he said. "I have found one for you. She's my tailor's daughter and I have promised him you will marry her. I'll give you till tomorrow morning to make up your mind, and no damned nonsense."

'They were married within ten days, and I was born nine months later, to the day. She died in child-birth. M. & B. 693 would have saved her.'

Why did Roper glance at me when he said that?

And now his father was living in a large Victorian house in Kensington. 'There's something Chinese in his make-up,' said Roper, 'a sense of proportion, a precision over small details, a fatalism which will interest you. He knows exactly what he wants from life, never asks more of it than it can give, and is always prepared to find that it gives less than he expects. He doesn't shrug his shoulders even, never makes the least protest. If things are like that, then the more fool you for expecting them to be different. Give way easily to everything, and nothing can go wrong. He's the only complete realist I know, and the only genuine visionary.

'A handsome man, with a bushy black and white beard.'

I looked at Roper – couldn't help it – and he caught the glance. He was an uncomfortable man, in many ways. I wondered how sensitive he was to his ugliness.

'He's writing a book on the history of drugs, and Mary helps him with that. Not that he needs a secretary but he likes having her round and looking at her just as an oriental likes sitting in the garden gazing at the cherry blossom. Mary is the schoolgirl-complexion-all-over-and-all-through type, very sweet and simple and devoted. What the middle class girl was like before she went to Oxford and discovered sin. There's never a cloud in the sky for her and they get on famously. I can't understand why he doesn't marry her. I have often wondered how long it will take her to arrange it. She wants to, I think.

'Then there's Flo, my father's cousin, Miss Shere with the bunch of keys. She's the hen, to me. You can almost hear her clucking over her work. She's forty-two, in the tough spinsterish stage now. I can remember the time when she was a ball of fluff with wings. A tragic thing, to watch youth draining and seeping drop by drop from a woman. The ardent little yellow chicken grows into a hen, and the hen gets tougher and tougher. Of course it lays eggs, which is something. Cousin Flo lays them for father now, the golden eggs of a noiseless, unflustered house. She pecks at Mary, but she would hardly be the human hen if she didn't. Mary is lost youth, tender chicken.

'We had hopes of the Vicar once, I remember. The Vicar is not quite the gentleman, not quite-quite, and she's so much the combed lady that he's never dared. Father said the Vicar would be there tonight, for a while. You'll see him.'

Roper stood up and stretched himself.

'Buy a hat, you two. I am going on with my work, now. Be back in time for dinner. I shall order for three. We can have it here.'

And almost before we realised it, Bert and I were walking downstairs.

After dinner I ran them down to Kensington, but when we got to the house Bert refused to enter.

'No, really, Mr Roper, I could not think of it. Just because I am in my Sunday best you have forgotten that I am a chanter. That is what I am, though, a street beggar. I wouldn't know what to say any more than you would if you met the King.'

'But listen, Bert...'

'No, honestly, Mr Roper, fair do's. It would give me prickly heat all over to go in there. I'll hop round the corner and have a game of darts and a pint or two at the Rising Sun. You come and fetch me afterwards. That will make everybody happy.'

'I'll make you go in, Bert.'

But Bert looked so unhappy that we were forced to let him escape to the Rising Sun. I felt like following him.

They were in the drawing-room, Roper's father, Miss Shere, Mary and the Vicar. Even as we were announced I saw Cousin Flo press a bell by the mantelpiece. Coffee, I thought. The Vicar, a short, thin man with glasses on his nose, jumped to his feet as if he had been stung, and rubbed his hands together, smiling. Mary walked quietly to a corner and began pushing a chair towards the group. The Vicar raced to help her.

'My dear young lady...' he stuttered. 'Excuse me.' He pushed the chair along with immense exaggeration, as if he were Sisyphus rolling his stone up the last grade, and then stood rubbing his hands, smiling benevolently at his great work.

'Trouble, Vicar,' said Mr Roper, 'a father never sees his son these days unless there is trouble.'

The Vicar seemed to consider that a capital joke, and laughed very heartily.

Coffee was brought on a Benares brass tray. Cousin Flo watched the maid attentively from the moment she came into the room until she left. I saw the maid flash a nervous eye at her.

'She is shaping well, that girl,' said Cousin Flo.

'Shall I pour?' asked Mary, in an aside.

'No, I can manage, thank you,' said Cousin Flo, as precisely courteous as if she had been a complete stranger.

'We were talking about the annual outing for our poor children,' said the Vicar, folding one leg over the other. 'There are so many of them, so very many. There seem to be more every year.' He unwound his legs again. 'And the better off parents, they *will* try and get their children on the list, too, though it is really meant for the *very* poor.' He beamed at us, and seemed quite unable to stop himself from talking. 'Last year, my word, there was a scandal. There were two motor cars, one quite a smart car,' he made a gesture in the air and nearly lost his coffee cup, 'waiting for the children. We felt so upset about it.'

'It is downright dishonest and must be stopped,' said Cousin Flo.

'This evening, this very evening,' said the Vicar, looking round wildly for somewhere to put his empty cup, 'the Smith woman – but perhaps I should not call her that – told me that she simply must have her little girl on the list.'

Mary took the cup away from him.

'Her husband gets three pounds a week,' said Cousin Flo. 'I'll talk to her.'

'I really don't know what I would do without you, Miss Shere. Quite invaluable,' gushed the Vicar, crossing his legs again and grasping the toe of his shoe, only to let it go as if it had bitten him.

Roper was sitting beside his father, on the settee. 'I would like your opinion,' I heard him say, and his father nodded.

'I am sure you would like some music, Vicar,' said Mr Roper. 'Shall we go up to the music room?'

Cousin Flo looked tart and pressed the bell. Mary gazed reproachfully at her employer, and Roper grinned maliciously. The Vicar said he would be delighted, delighted. It was quite a long time since he had had the privilege of listening to the new gramophone. Quite a time. Cousin Flo told the maid who answered the bell to prepare the music room.

As we were trooping upstairs Roper whispered: 'The Vicar doesn't know God Save the King from Pop Goes the Weasel. He won't be able to stand much of it. He's being thrown out and Cousin Flo doesn't like it. Typical of father to use Beethoven to exorcise a Vicar.'

We went into a long parquet-floored room unfurnished save for a few chairs at one end, and the enormous horn of an E.M.G. gramophone at the other. Along one side were the cabinets for holding the records.

Mary busied herself with the needles, the Davey cutter twinkling in her hands.

'Mozart?' she asked, a little imploringly, I thought. Even to the tone deaf Mozart makes a cheerful noise.

'Shall we have the B Flat Major?' said Mr Roper. 'Yes, Mary, the B Flat Major, Op. 133, with the original Grosse Fugue.'

'You will be interested in that last movement, Vicar,' said Roper. 'Beethoven was induced to write a substitute because his contemporaries found the Fugue so difficult. But he said that the world would insist upon getting it when it was ripe for it.'

'Ripeness is all, isn't it,' said the unhappy Vicar. 'I know so very little about music, but it would be pleasant to hear the original, I am sure.'

Mr Roper stroked his beard and smiled faintly.

The quartet took about twenty minutes to play. Mary changed the records deftly, slithering like a ghost back to her seat. Cousin Flo followed the music with a score, glasses severely on her nose. The poor Vicar wound and unwound his legs under the chair, his arms folded and his face lifted towards the ceiling, eyes closed. I had never heard the Fugue before, but I thought it a puzzling racket of noise, a slap in the face after the three glorious movements which preceded it. It came to a sudden end.

'Wonderful. Really very wonderful,' beamed the Vicar. 'Dear me, it is getting quite late. I must be going. Well, good night, good night. No, please, Miss Shere. I can see myself out. Yes, quite well.'

And the Vicar was gone.

'There are not many musicians who can stand that Fugue,' said Roper. 'Perhaps it is easier when music means nothing to you.'

'It was somewhat cruel,' said his father.

'Well, he's gone, anyway,' said Roper, 'and that's the main thing. You must hear about this new drug I have discovered. No, don't go, Mary. Shall we talk here, Father? It won't take long.'

We sat in a circle and I heard the story over again. Mr Roper said nothing until the end, did not even look very surprised. But Mary gasped several times, her pretty eyes rounding. Cousin Flo sat bolt upright, a monument of disapproval.

'What do you think of it, father?'

'It is interesting, from a scientific point of view. It cannot, of course, serve any purpose, but then I have a weakness for useless things.'

'It frightens me,' said Mary. 'I feel sure there is something wrong about it.'

'It is certainly not a thing to be left lying about for all

and sundry,' said Cousin Flo. 'I hope you keep it under lock and key, William.'

It was odd to hear him called William.

'I have them here,' said Roper, and produced the pill box.

We all looked at them, nestling in the cotton wool, like eggs in a bird's nest. Cousin Flo raised them to her nose, smelt them, and put the open box on her knees.

The door opened, and a maid entered.

'The telephone, Madame.'

Cousin Flo stood up hastily and the box fell upon the floor, the pills scattering far and wide over the parquet.

'Mary, please, the telephone,' she said, and Mary went. The rest of us got down on our hands and knees and collected the pills. They had rolled all over the place.

'How many were there?' asked Cousin Flo.

'Nineteen,' said Roper. 'There is still one missing.'

We hunted everywhere, but we could not find the missing pill. We went along the skirting on our hands and knees, looked in the turn ups of our trousers, took off our shoes, shook out the one small rug near the gramophone, but nothing came of it.

'You must have been mistaken, William,' said Cousin Flo.

'No. We must find it.'

It was a wearisome game, hunting for a pill which each of us was convinced had been stolen by one of the others. I saw Roper looking at me with a challenging eye.

'I haven't got it,' I said hotly.

We stopped searching at once, as if we had been waiting for this.

'You are not suggesting, William,' said Cousin Flo tartly, 'that one of us has secreted the pill!'

'Yes I am,' said Roper bluntly. 'Not father, of course, and I don't see what you could do with a pill. So it's you, Starling.'

'Enough of this ridiculous scene, William,' said Cousin Flo, and flounced out of the room.

'It does not matter, my boy,' said Mr Roper.

'But it does, father. They are extremely dangerous.'

'You exaggerate. A pill can only give you what you want for a very brief period. It would be a salutary experience, but hardly, I think, one that could be called dangerous.'

'It could not have been Mary...' Roper began.

'What would Mary want with a pill? Besides, she went out of the room at once. We saw her.'

'All the same...' muttered Roper. He looked at me threateningly as we went down to the hall. Cousin Flo had disappeared, but Mary was there, waiting for us.

'One of the pills has disappeared,' said Roper. 'You haven't got it, Mary?'

She flushed warmly.

'How could you possibly think it!' she said, deeply distressed.

'We will search again in the morning,' said Mr Roper. 'It is sure to be there.'

We left and got into the car.

'Now then, that pill,' said Roper.

'I haven't got it, I tell you.'

'You have.'

'Honour bright.'

99

'Produce it, and in double quick time. I am going to make you. You realise that I could have willed you to hand it over in the house, but I didn't want to embarrass you. Now then.'

I felt the injunction to produce the pill flash into my mind, but I could do nothing about it.

'You haven't got it!' said Roper, with some surprise.

'I told you.'

'Then who the devil... not father, surely!'

We drove round the corner towards the Rising Sun.

'By the way,' I said, 'when you want someone to do something he can't do, he feels beastly. I nearly let go of the wheel.'

'One of them pinched that pill,' said Roper grimly. 'I know there were nineteen, and now there are only eighteen.'

We picked Bert up at the Rising Sun. He had been winning steadily at darts, and had consumed his victor's trophies in whisky. He was feeling merry.

'No more pubs this evening,' said Roper, 'or we shall be losing you. You're coming along with us, this time.'

'Where are we going then?' asked Bert.

'To a studio.'

'That will be more like the doss house, if all I hear is right,' said Bert.

We cut across to the Fulham Road and turned up a side street. There were a number of cars parked in front of the studio.

'I have that prickly heat again,' said Bert.

'You come in with us,' said Roper.

There was a piano pounding in the studio and a small party in progress. Some were in evening dress and some were not. They were talking at the tops of their voices. There was a small hush, like a wind wave in wheat, then the noise went on. Joubert came to meet us, stocky, round, and quietly good humoured. Roper introduced us to him.

'You are a painter, I hear,' said Bert.

'That is right.'

'And I am a Welshman,' said Bert. Bert had drunk one over the eight.

'Sounds like a whole time occupation,' said Roper.

Joubert led us up to his wife. She was as big and warm and round as a sunflower.

'I have never been to a party before,' said Bert. 'What I am is a street singer. That man can play the piano, I must say.'

'You must sing to us,' said Mrs Joubert jovially. 'Come, I shall take you over to the piano.'

'What do you think, boys, shall I do it?' he asked us, his eyes dancing.

'Of course you must sing,' said Mrs Joubert. 'You *must.*'

'No, really, Mrs Joubert. Whatever shall I sing? In the rich streets they like the Collier's Lament for Father and Mother.'

I heard him ask the pianist, a young man in ribbed corduroys and a purple tie, whether he knew this Lament.

'But it does not matter a whit,' said Bert, 'I can smack the ivories about any time.'

Shortly afterwards Bert, pounding at the keys, was singing us the famous 'Lament.'

You never know you love 'em
Till the grass grows green above 'em
You never know their value till they're dead and gone.

He taught them the chorus; everyone sang. They crowded round him. He gave them 'Don't Go Down to the Mine, Daddy,' and after that I saw him being led off to the buffet, flushed and happy, by an astoundingly beautiful girl.

'I have wasted my life, completely wasted it,' I heard him say as he went past. 'This is what I was born for.'

Roper was asking Joubert about the mescal. He got it, said Joubert, from a Consul in Mexico who went hunting in the hills and was in touch with the Indians. All the consignments had worked perfectly before this last one. Yes, he would get some more, if Roper wanted it. No, it was no trouble at all. He would let him have the consignment the moment it arrived.

'I am interested, chemically, in the residue,' said Roper. 'Not enough work has been done on these vegetable alkalies. Would you mind cabling your friend for some more? I shall, of course...'

'I'll cable in the morning,' said Joubert. 'Come and see my latest.'

We went to a stack of canvases behind the piano. Joubert turned one of them round, and stepped back. The three of us looked at it.

It was almost a full length painting of a young girl, the girl I had seen taking Bert off to the buffet. She stood facing us, naked, looking at us and through us and beyond us into the distance. Her arms were hanging down by her side, the hands turned towards us. She looked as if she were saying: Behold, this is I! But she did not seem to be saying it to us but to whatever it was beyond us, away in the distance. It might be a lover, it might be God that was there. It was difficult to say, there was such a starry look of ardent unself-conscious disclosure in her eyes. 'Look, you made me, here I am. I have nothing to hide. The beauty is yours, all is yours.' She seemed to be saying that, and glorying, too, that the beauty was there to bestow, utterly, without reservation.

'I don't know what to call it,' said Joubert. 'I'll have to give it a name. They always want a title. Do you like it?'

'Yes,' I said.

'The moment of truth,' said Roper, in a strange-sounding voice.

Joubert looked quickly at him, as if he were learning him anew.

'Of course,' he said. 'The moment of truth. *Le moment de la verité*. That is what it is.'

'You looking at me?'

I turned round to see the model grinning mischievously at us. Bert was with her and his eyes were goggling.

Joubert took her hand and drew her towards him.

'I think I've got that lustre on the skin, this time,' he said, slipping her dress down over one shoulder until the breast showed. 'It's almost better than the original.'

She made a monkey grimace at him and rearranged her dress.

'What do you think of it, Bert? That's me, you know.' She pulled him forward and placed him in front of the painting.

'I think it's horrible,' said Bert, looking away hastily. 'I didn't know you let them do that to you.'

'I get well paid for it, silly.'

'But it isn't right,' he said seriously. 'I don't like you doing that.'

'You make me laugh,' she said, taking his arm. 'Come and have another drink.'

I didn't like looking at the nude painting of a girl who is standing fully dressed beside you much more than Bert.

Roper, the muscles of his face pulsing strongly, was still staring at the painting when Joubert turned the canvas round and stacked it.

'What is she?' asked Roper.

'The girl?'

'Yes.'

'She's been my model now for two years. A nice girl, but... well, does any woman deserve a body like that? She has a good heart, though, and God knows she needs it! Her husband is a ne'er-do-well, a bookie's runner. She's not happy, but you know how plucky they are and how much they can stand. There have been bruises, now and again, but she hasn't said anything.'

'Bruises on that body!' said Roper.

'Yes, strange, isn't it! You'd think such beauty would be untouchable. I don't suppose the brute notices it. It isn't the sexy kind.'

'Oh, it's that too,' said Roper.

'Yes, but there is a severity, a chill. There always is in true beauty. I couldn't hit that girl, myself.'

'No,' said Roper. 'It would have to be death or love.'

I moved away into the heart of the party. It was warming up. The corduroyed young fellow was at the piano again and they were dancing a dance I had not met before. The partners faced each other, tapped their hands, clapped their knees delicately, bumped hips, put their hands on their hearts and bowed. Then they waltzed for a while and went through the business again, singing:

Hands, knees, and BOOMPS-A-Daisy!
I like a bustle that bends.
Hands, knees, and BOOMPS-A-Daisy!
What's a BOOMP between friends?

Bert was having a great time. He was bumping the model for all he was worth.

The party broke up early. Several people had to go and the rest of us drifted away.

Mrs Joubert took Bert by the arm. 'You have been the success of the evening,' she smiled.

'Have I?' said Bert. 'I didn't know I had it in me, and that is a fact.'

Roper was talking to the model; then he crossed over and spoke to me.

'We are giving her a lift home,' he said.

'Right. What is her name?'

'I don't know. Bert, what does she call herself?'

'Anita, but I do not know what else.'

We said our goodbyes and the four of us got into the car, Roper and Anita in the back seat, Bert beside me.

'Take us to Notting Hill,' said Roper. Bert was nodding with sleep, and I could hear them talking in the back seat. In the mirror I saw that Roper was clasping her hand with both his.

'Come and have dinner with me tomorrow evening,' I heard him say.

'What a quick worker you are!'

'But you will?'

'Say please?

'Please.'

'But I can't. I am not that kind of girl. Don't you know that I am married?

'Yes, but...'

'Then you shouldn't ask me, you naughty man.'

She laughed a great deal, too.

'I shall call for you at half past six. We'll go to a small place in Soho.'

'Yes,' she said tonelessly, and I pricked up my ears.

'Be ready by half past six,' said Roper curtly, and I was sure of it now.

'Yes,' she said again in that queer, stilled voice.

They said no more, and I drove on. I hated him at that moment.

'Half past six,' said Roper again. She got down and went in. Bert was fast asleep.

'You forced her,' I said. 'You used the stuff on her.'

'What if I did?'

'It was a rotten trick.'

'Mind your own business.'

'It is my business. This is criminal. You can't use that beastly drug on girls.'

'She's only a tart,' said Roper.

'She's nothing of the kind, and you know it.'

'You are driving too fast.'

I slowed down to thirty.

'What you said about the drug acting on you... It must be

true,' I said. 'You wouldn't do a thing like that normally.'

Roper laughed.

'I didn't know you were interested in women, anyway.'

'They are not usually so beautiful. I want this one,' he said dryly.

'It's pretty caddish.'

'What, to force a girl to come and eat a first rate meal? Don't be a fool. I shan't rape her, if that is what you are thinking.'

I was, in truth, thinking of something of the kind. I shut up and drove them home.

'You should have gone in for the Church,' jeered Roper.

I drove back to my flat, depressed and disturbed. I had a feeling that things were going to be bad.

Yes, I had a feeling that things were going to be bad. This was the first time I had ever known Roper interested in a girl, and so far as I could see, the girl was not reciprocating. She and Bert, now, they seemed to get on splendidly. She was simple and natural with Bert. They understood one another, but with Roper she was different. She was cheap with him, used her eyes, laughed immoderately, coquetted, put on a kind of false mincing manner distressing in a girl so beautiful.

'I want that one,' Roper had said. And I didn't think she would want him. But he could get her all the same. He had the drug in him.

I tried to calm my fears. After all, Roper had a good many obstacles of habit and breeding to hurdle over before he did anything quite so despicable as that. We say that all's fair in love, but no other game is so circumscribed and limited with commandments. And the first of them is: Thou shalt not force a woman.

I had to visit an aunt in the west. In the ordinary way I would have put it off and put it off and then written an apologetic letter explaining that I had been called upon to go to Manchuria or Paraguay or wherever it was. But now that the money had vanished she took on a different complexion. She began to wear a halo. I don't think this was very foul of me. I was honestly quite fond of her. There was nothing unnatural about it. I merely discovered that I liked her more than I thought I did.

I telephoned Roper before going away. It was lunchtime but he was not in. Bert answered and almost uprooted my ear with his bellowing.

'Is he in?' I asked. 'And don't shout. Whisper.'

'I am not used to these things,' yelled Bert. 'Can you hear?'

'Whisper,' I said, 'for heaven's sake whisper.'

'He is not in then,' said Bert in a more normal voice. 'I don't know where he is gone. Come up and have a chat, Mr Starling. It is against nature to speak into a thing like this.'

'Was he out last night?' I asked.

'Aye, he was. But what do you think of this? I am taken on for good now. Can you hear?' He had started bellowing again.

'Do whisper, Bert, for the love of mike. What do you mean, taken on for good?'

'I have a job here, going to Mount Pleasant Customs House and other things. That girl does not come any more.

I have a card and put Lloyd George stamps on it, like a gentleman. Can you hear?'

I could bear it no longer, said good-bye, and rubbed my wilting ear.

Roper had been out with the girl the night before. I had no doubt of it. And now he was with her again, lunching.

I felt that I ought to stay around. He had once asked me to check him if the drug worked upon him in a noticeable way. The drug was doing that already, I knew. I still had a vivid memory of the half minute when he had projected himself and I was sure that what I had experienced was not Roper, unalloyed. But I had to make my salaams to the aunt. I had to.

Deep in me, too, was the sense of calamity on the tip of the tongue; imminent. Something was stirring down wind, a faceless evil. And I was going away. I felt in my bones then that it was wisdom to be going away, before the thing without a face came rampaging down upon us.

I sent Roper a postcard, gave him my new address, and told him I would be away twelve days.

On the very morning I was to leave my aunt there was a letter from Roper saying that he would be down that afternoon at a small market town not more than ten miles from where I was staying. Could I meet him with the car at three o'clock? He would be waiting for me at the entry to the town, by the road-side.

It sounded extraordinary to me. What was Roper doing down west? He must be coming specially to see me, and I could not imagine the reason. Why wait for me by the side of the road instead of at one of the hotels? He could easily have obtained the name of a suitable hotel from Baedeker.

We were having breakfast. I threw the letter aside and was going to tell my aunt about the change of plan when a postscript on the back caught my eye. 'Don't say anything to anybody,' I read.

That seriously alarmed me, but whatever thoughts were beginning to stir were nipped by my aunt.

'Another murder in London,' she said, with that pleasure which country dwellers seem to take in the wickedness of the metropolis.

A woman had been shot in Hyde Park three days before. That had interested her because the description fitted herself so exactly, even to the height and colouring. 'It might have been me,' she said with relish. 'White hair, fresh complexion.' But the next morning's papers were disappointing. It had been a suicide.

'Shooting again?' I asked. 'Another suicide?'

'Killed with a blunt instrument, poor man,' she said with gusto. 'You must read it. It happened just as he was going into a police station, too. It is really very horrible,' she went on, her eyes glued to the paper, a piece of toast suspended in the air. 'It says here that the gutter was swimming in blood. I do think they might leave out the details.'

'Where did it happen?' I asked still thinking of Roper's letter.

'Hampstead,' she said absently, turning to page six.

The paper crinkled in her hand and her eyes widened excitedly as she looked at me.

'Colonel Starling,' she said. 'Surely that is your uncle!'

'Has he been murdered!'

'It was his man, Thomas Dobbs.'

'Dobbs! Good God!'

'It is almost like a murder in the family,' she said, her eyes bright as a bird's. 'Why, you must have known the poor man.'

'Of course I knew him,' I said. 'Dobbs, of all people! Who on earth...'

And it was then that a horrible suspicion floated into my mind. It was Roper who had killed him. I knew it was Roper. He had clubbed Dobbs the evening before and was now fleeing from justice.

I took the paper from her and read the account. A policeman coming back to report at the station had seen a man lying in the gutter, doubled up. He had bent over him and found that he was dead.

The murder had taken place at twenty-five past nine.

I looked at the envelope by my plate. The time of posting was given as 6.30. It had been written before the murder then, and I sighed with relief. Unless Roper had planned it, unless it was a deliberate, cold-blooded, foreseen affair, his visit to the west had nothing to do with it.

And immediately I was not so sure that it was Roper who had done it. The certainty I had felt a moment before burst like a soap bubble. But I was still shaken.

'Now, my dear boy, you must see your uncle the moment you are back in town,' said my aunt. 'It must have been a most dreadful shock for a man of his age. It is such a terrible thing to happen to anyone one knows, even a servant.'

'They were always at loggerheads,' I said, 'but the Colonel was really very attached to him. He'll be quite lost.'

111

'And you will write me all the details,' said auntie. 'I don't mean the horrible things they put in the papers but the things which don't come out. I am sure that in every murder a number of things don't come out at all. The police are very secretive.'

My aunt's avidity, which had been amusing enough up till now, began to pall.

'And what is your letter about?' she asked brightly. Life in the country is very dull.

'An appointment,' I said, and crammed it into my pocket.

'With the solicitors?' she asked hopefully. The country is not only dull. It is dull with precision.

'No, the dentist.'

'Everything, remember, *everything*,' said my aunt as I drove away that afternoon.

I left her house about a quarter to three and cruised slowly towards the town. The countryside wore the faded look of August. There was no spring or lustre in the grass. The leaves hung heavily in the trees, without a breath of wind to ruffle their listlessness. The heat brooded, as if the sun itself were sulking. Only the occasional small river glimpsed from the road had any life or joy in it. Even the car ran badly and noisily.

Roper was waiting for me a good mile from the town, sitting on a gate at a right hand turn which gave him a full view of any oncoming traffic. He waved to me and I stopped.

'You are early,' he said. He was wearing a wide awake hat which seemed to cover a good deal of his face.

'Am I? You had better get in. I want to talk to you.'

He got into the seat beside me and took off his hat.

'If you are going to talk, and I can see you are – you have a nasty loquacious look in your eye – we'd better do it up a lane somewhere. You will know by and by why I don't want to be seen more than I can help.'

I swung the car round and after a mile or so turned up a lane. We stopped at a gate and got out.

'You killed Dobbs,' I said. I found that I was shivering with rage. The moment I had seen him my suspicions had returned in force.

'What was that?' He was looking at me with genuine surprise.

'You murdered Dobbs, damn you.'

'Who's Dobbs?' he asked, 'and why should I murder him?'

'The man with the dog.' He looked so surprised that I was no longer sure.

'Yes, I remember. Has he been murdered then?'

'Don't you read the newspapers?'

'Not the murders.'

'He was killed last night.'

'A stupid man,' said Roper lightly. 'If I were a murderer I couldn't think of a more fitting subject to practise on. But there you are: not guilty.'

'Sorry, Bill. I thought he had recognised you or something and that you had finished him. The drug was affecting you, you know. Look at the way you carried on with that girl.'

'Is the drug bad for me?' he asked innocently. 'Let's see,

you went away twelve days ago and I had taken a pill two days before you left. I have taken two more since, one of them last night.'

'What for?' I was flabbergasted by this news.

'Addict,' said Roper lightly, looking at me.

'Do you mean that?'

'Yes I do. It gets you quickly. The moment I am rid of it I feel beastly.'

'How, exactly?'

'Empty, like a house to let.'

'You must stop it.'

'I will try to, after this one.'

'Throw the rotten things away, or give them to your father.'

'There are not many left, anyway,' he said gloomily.

'Enough to make it bad for you when they come to an end. You haven't been doing anything with the pills you've taken?'

'Only playing about. Don't look alarmed! When you are under it is difficult not to use this power, but I've kept myself in check. Merely small things.'

We said nothing for a while.

'Have you seen Anita again?'

'I've seen her every day,' he said soberly.

'Don't tell me... look here, Bill, you haven't been using the stuff on her all this time?'

'Not after that first time. She likes the dinners. You should see her. She's developing tastes. She knows a guinea fowl from a duckling and spots a second growth in Medoc blindfold. Astounding how adaptable females are. She trips up the restaurants as an ambitious man mounts the clubs. I'm through my cash already.'

'Give her up. She's no good.'

'She's the loveliest girl on earth. I can look at her until the cows come home. I never listen, merely look. She's a worse addiction than the drug.'

'You're making a fool of yourself. She's married.'

'I am in love with her, so frantically....' He stopped.

I looked at him in surprise, and there it was. He was fumbling for a cigarette and his face was working as I had seen it working at the party, looking at the nude.

'There will be trouble if you don't chuck her.'

'How am I to do that?'

'Go for a holiday... or something,' I suggested lamely.

'Golf, cold baths, the companionship of nice women, pig sticking in India, which would you like it to be, Jim? Personally I favour pig sticking as a way of getting over love. It sounds so atrocious and thorough. But even you must know,' he went on, 'that the only cure is a hair of the dog that bites you. A woman for a woman, ad infinitum. It is this curing of love which makes the amorous dipsomaniac. Better ruin one than a dozen.'

He put a leery emphasis upon the 'ruin', and looked at his watch.

'Time we were pushing along,' he said.

'Back to town?'

'There's work to do here first.'

'Oh, what?'

'I told you I had run out of cash.'

'Well?'

'We're going to get some more.'

'How?' I asked, beginning to get alarmed.

'Robbery. What else?'

'I don't understand.'

'We're going to raid a bank.'

'I won't have anything to do with it,' I protested, the alarm mounting to full flood. 'You can count me out. That kind of thing is completely mad. They'll catch you, give you five years.... No, I'm going back to town, now.' I moved towards the car. 'You can come if you like, but I'm going straight back.'

'Wait a minute. Be reasonable. You don't expect me to hold up the citizens one by one, do you? It would take too much time. Better get it all in a lump and the only place where they keep it stacked is in the banks. Very well, then, a bank it is.'

'It is mad,' I shouted. 'I won't have anything to do with it.'

'There's no danger, none at all,' he went on. 'I am bung full of the drug. They'll hand it over like lambs. They'll want to hand it over, they'll press it upon us, carry the stuff into the car for us, as much as we want. There's going to be lots of it. It's market day, and the farmers have been shovelling it in since morning. We'll go now. I've already put the 'fluence on a porter.

'The bank shuts at three thirty. Ten minutes later we'll walk in through an open door.'

'For God's sake, Bill...'

'If you refuse, you know what I'll do, don't you?'

I looked at him as if I had seen him for the first time, with a kind of amazement. He meant it. He meant every word of it. I remember recognising a new quality in his face, something which may always have been there, but had never been disclosed to me before. It was sinister. I turned and ran, pelted down the lane as if the devil were at my heels. I heard his laugh ringing out behind, and the next moment I had stopped and was walking back towards him, hand outstretched.

'Okay by me, Bill,' I said.

We were going to rob a bank. Of course we were going to rob a bank. It was the most reasonable thing in the world. I was all for it. I was entirely with him. It was going to be fun, walking into a bank and walking out again, bulging with banknotes. There was no danger of any kind. It was going to be one long laugh. And I would be going to America in the autumn, as usual.

'Let's go,' I said eagerly. 'We've only got five minutes before the door opens. Where do we leave the car?'

'Round the corner. There's a parking place.'

'Splendid. Come along then.'

We got into the car and made for the main road. The traffic had thickened. Farmers were trotting home in their dog carts, lazily whipping the flies off the flanks of their ponies.

Roper closed the roof. 'We don't want to be seen more than can be helped,' he explained.

When that was done he threw a piece of black cambric into my lap.

'What is this for?' I asked.

'I can only make them forget the past for twenty minutes. We proved that, and we may take longer. The porter, in any case, will see us plain as we enter, but I shall blot that out

117

of his memory. There's a tiny hall inside, and when we get in we put these on. It will be safer.'

I laughed. I could not help laughing. It was fun.

'There are eye-holes and mouth-holes cut in the cambric,' he said.

'You've thought of everything.'

He took a few pound notes out of his pocket-book and produced his petrol lighter.

'What is that for?' I asked.

'Quiet for a moment.'

He put the edge of a pound note in the flame and watched it burning. He did it again with another one.

'What on earth...' I began.

'I have to get into the proper frame of mind,' he said. 'I want to develop a first class contempt for money, and that is difficult, when I need it so badly.'

He burnt another, and another, and began to laugh.

'Silly stuff, money, when you come to think of it. That is all I shall do to them, make them feel about money as I feel at this moment and wipe out their sense of duty. Well, I am ready.'

We were in the pinched and twisting streets of the town, its houses stone built for the most part, with grey lichened roofs bending under the weight of years. We came to the quaintly timbered square and saw the hucksters' booths clustered round a large bellied equestrian statue. People were strolling along the pavement under the hot sun, broad-beamed country-women mostly, carrying their crammed shopping baskets.

Roper burnt another note as we parked the car. 'I make it three forty,' he said.

We left the car and walked confidently round the corner towards the grey stone building.

'Open sesame,' murmured Roper, and indeed, as we reached the step, the door did open.

'Good afternoon, gentlemen,' said the porter, a broad country grin slitting his big red face. He had the spiked and waxed moustaches of an ex-sergeant major.

We went through the door and the man shut it behind us. We were in a small hall. I heard the clanking of chains behind us, at the door. Roper put his mask on, but I had some difficulty with mine. The porter helped.

'You stay by the door,' said Roper. The porter saluted.

'Would you like me to let go now?' asked Roper.

'It would be more fun,' I laughed.

A slide was withdrawn across my mind, the way one slips a slide out of a magic lantern projector, and another was substituted. It was an entirely different picture, for I was myself again. We were walking into a bank; pushing a door open; yes, we were walking in. I found my knees shaking and my heart pounding. I remembered an American film I had seen of a bank robbery, a masked man waltzing towards the counter like a toreador advancing to kill his bull, a sub-machine gun's snout poking out from the folds of his cloak. I had a blank white moment of hesitation, turned round with a gasp, to see the porter twirling his moustaches and smiling benevolently at me. I think he winked. I am sure he winked.

Behind the counter was a cashier, an elderly man with a peaked nose, a thin pursed mouth, the dewlaps of a lawyer, and a high circle of baldness above the horizontal furrows in his brow. When he saw us he wiped a hand slowly across his mouth and sank like a stone. There were two people in the well, a young man and a woman. The young fellow had a bright tie; his hair was lustrously plastered. He looked a masher, a blood of the tennis courts. When we came in he sprang to his feet, a heavy ebony ruler in his hand. He looked as if he were about to die for his school. (I have cribbed most of these descriptions from Roper.) The girl was round-faced and apple red, with heavy glasses and frizzed up hair. When she saw us her mouth fell open abruptly, and stayed open. She reminded me of a goldfish.

The manager's room was on the near side of the counter. He had just come out, and had that very moment whisked a handkerchief from his hip pocket and taken up the stance of a man on the verge of a large, satisfying, cathartic sneeze. The handkerchief was held six inches in front of his mouth, and his face was contorted with the inexpressible delights of the coming explosion. He saw us and fell back a step. The sneeze was caught short as though by death.

All this lasted but a second. The next instant the manager, a small spry man with quick, darting eyes, was coming towards us, rubbing his hands and smiling. The cashier's head rose slowly above the counter, each individual hair stiff as a porcupine's. The girl's teeth shone like a dentifrice advertisement, and the masher waved us a cheerful welcome.

'How you startled me!' said the manager. 'I thought for a moment that it was a hold-up.'

His jerky body movements reminded me of a cock sparrow. Until he spoke I had been tremblingly anxious. The drug might not work; Roper might not be able to put across the proper emotion; the unforeseen might come plunging at us calamitously. But now, when the little man accepted our presence so calmly, I sighed with relief and wiped the sweat from my forehead.

'What can I do for you?' asked the manager, his head tilted to one side, his hands behind his coat tails.

'We have come to fetch the money,' said Roper.

'Ah yes, of course, I see. How much would you want?'

'But all of it,' said Roper with ingenuous surprise.

'Certainly. Certainly,' said the manager. 'You... you really want it?' He seemed as surprised as Roper had been.

'If you don't mind.'

'Not at all. Very good of you to take it, I am sure.'

I looked closely at him and wondered. Were there no traces left of the feelings which would have been proper to the occasion? I thought I did glimpse a whiteness, a strain, at the back of the eyes, but that may have been my imagination.

'Widden, how much is there?'

The cashier bent over his papers and said that altogether there was seven thousand three hundred and thirty pounds, sixteen shillings and twopence.

'Ah, we shan't bother over the twopence,' said Roper.

We laughed at that. The masher looked particularly jocular and spun a penny in the air with a waggish suggestion of double or quits.

'I only want the pound and ten shilling notes,' Roper amplified, 'those whose numbers you haven't noted.'

'Just as you like,' said the manager. 'The client,' he laughed, 'is always right, you know. But we don't keep much reserve here in any case.'

'Fine,' murmured Roper, 'fine.'

'How shall we pack it for you?'

'I leave that to you.'

The manager turned to the cashier. 'Brown paper packages.'

'And how,' asked the cashier, looking very like an owl, 'do I enter the transaction?'

The manager cut a short sharp swathe in the air with his hand.

'Between friends, entirely between friends,' he said. 'Don't enter it.'

The masher and the girl were busy heaping up notes and slipping elastic bands over them. The place rustled like a cornfield.

'We shall not detain you long,' promised the manager.

'Shall we have a drink?' asked Roper.

But the manager was sorry. There was no drink on the premises. 'I don't take it,' he said, 'but we could send the porter out for some.'

'Porter!' Roper called.

The man came in, twirling his moustaches.

'Three bottles of gin, some french vermouth, and seven glasses,' said Roper. 'Throw me over two pounds, will you?'

'Catch,' cried the masher, who had crunched up the notes into pellets. The manager caught one and I caught the other.

'Caught, Sir!' the girl shrilled, and was then covered in confusion.

'Cricket in the office!' the manager laughed, rubbing his hands again. 'There is a very pleasant feeling about the place today.'

'Don't play the fool, hurry,' I whispered to Roper. I was

nervous about the porter.

The cock sparrow was over by the counter, watching the cashier packing the notes. He drew a hand from under his coat tails and felt one of them curiously, rubbing it between his fingers.

'Widden,' he said, 'how long have you been here?'

'Twenty-two years, Sir.'

'I've been here twenty-eight. And what,' he asked with a comically perplexed look on his face, 'have we been doing all that time?'

Mr Widden was nonplussed by this and did not answer.

'We've been taking these things over the counter and handing them out again and entering them in books,' the manager went on. 'Why, Widden, why?'

'I don't know, I'm sure.' Mr Widden looked melancholy and utterly at sea.

'Nor do I,' said the manager. He rested his head on a hand and stared perkily at the pile.

'Why, Widden, why?'

But Widden could only shake his head.

'They don't mean anything,' the manager went on, ruffling the notes with a careless hand. 'They don't mean a thing. *Why* have we been counting these things?'

Widden had stopped packing and their two heads were close together.

The manager swept the notes away with a flourish. 'Autumn leaves are far, far more important,' he said. 'Do we count them, Widden?'

'No, Sir.'

'Why not?' asked the manager. 'Why not, Widden?'

The porter came back with the bottles and the glasses. He was sweating with the heat and the hurry.

'Dull work,' said Roper, 'packing up all that stuff. Let's waken things up. What do you say to a drink, everybody?'

The manager swivelled round. 'I am a teetotaller, myself, a life-long abstainer. But on a special occasion like this...'

Roper ranged the glasses on the counter and poured out the drinks. The cashier, the girl and the masher came forward. The porter stood at our elbow.

We lifted our glasses.

'Speech. Speech,' cried the masher suddenly. The girl beamed through her heavy glasses, and even the cashier's brow cleared.

'Drink first, speech afterwards,' said Roper.

''Ere's 'ealth,' said the porter, opened his mouth and poured it down in one gulp.

'Looking towards you, Sir,' said the masher with a little bow. 'All the best.' 'Good health.' 'Here's to you,' we chimed, and drank. The manager choked and his eyes swam. 'My very first drink,' he apologised. 'Most invigorating but somewhat... um!'

Roper filled up again.

'Spee... eech,' intoned the masher in a deep, low voice.

'Just a word or two,' said Roper.

'Well, if I must...' said the manager.

'Ladies and gentlemen,' he began, looking strangely solemn for him. 'We have been honoured this afternoon with a visit from our two friends. They have come, they tell me, to take away with them these...' he picked up one of the notes, 'these pieces of paper. Why they should want to do so

I cannot imagine. It is, if I may say so, very good of them.'

There was some vigorous hand clapping at this.

'Pieces of paper,' he went on, 'silly little pieces of paper with pictures on them. Gentlemen, you are welcome to them. (Cheers.) Take them all. (Cheers.) Leave not a wrack behind. (Loud cheers.) We are sick of the sight of them. (Hear hear, from the masher.) I myself shall empty my pockets of them. (No no, from me.) I want the place cleaned up, like the whatever you call them stables, you know,' he finished lamely.

He lifted his glass high. 'Gentlemen, my thanks and humblest apologies that there is not more of it.'

We drank. I laughed, for I could not help it. So did Roper. So, for the matter of that, did everybody.

The manager looked happy and washed his hands a great deal. The glasses were filled up again and we clinked them once more.

'Went down quite well, don't you think?' said the manager.

'Capital speech, capital,' I said.

'Our car,' Roper told the porter, 'is round the corner, the first in the parking place. Take these packages out and stow them in the back seat, will you?'

'Yes, Sir.'

The packing went on, and the moment a parcel was ready the porter carried it out to the car. It seemed to me to take an age. Roper was talking politics with the manager, filling his glass and getting him to empty it. The man was beginning to glow.

The last package went out to the car.

'I shall never forget your kindness,' said the manager,

his eyes swimming. 'Any little thing I can do for you at any time... Any time you are down our way, you are heartily welcome.'

We shook hands all round, took our masks off in the hall, and went out to the car. The porter closed the door behind us.

'Suppose someone sees us,' I said as we went through the door.

'Well, look,' said Roper.

Everyone in the square had their backs turned to us. There was a policeman not twenty yards away.

'All the same,' said Roper, 'we might as well get away as soon as we can. There's no sense in lingering. Take the London road. Those people will be there a long time, at least as long as the drink lasts. They won't remember anything about the car. I blotted out the last twenty minutes.'

'I hope it works,' I said. 'Why didn't you will them to stay there until midnight?'

'Would that work after we were out of range? I can get someone within range to do something definite outside the range, but I don't know how long a generalised emotion would last. I concentrated at the last on getting them to finish those bottles. They'll pass out, but the porter looked as if he could stand a lot.'

'I wish you hadn't thought of this,' I said bitterly. 'It's bound to get us into trouble.'

'I don't see how. Everything went off beautifully.'

'I never wanted to do it.'

'Don't you want any of the autumn leaves?' asked Roper.
'No.'

'That's all right. I can do with it all.'

We sped out of the town and along the London road.

'I made them feel that we were garbage collectors. Like dustmen. If we called at Christmas, we'd get a tip. That is what people are like when they have a contempt for money. Uneconomic man is charming, don't you think? The manager was most generous, wasn't he? Quite let himself go in that speech. Lucky for me that I "fixed" the emotion the moment I got in, for I could never have held the attitude as they went on packing. The more the manager ran the stuff down the greedier I got. There's enough there,' he looked round at the back seat, 'to take the girl to the Berkeley once or twice.'

'The masher,' I said, 'will be singing Rule Britannia after a few gins, and the police will hear.'

'But what have they to go on? They find a staff that is soused in a bank that has been rifled. All they can say is that two masked men came in and took away the money. The police won't know what to make of a staff that goes on the spree when a bank has been looted. It will keep them guessing long enough for us to get away. We shall be in London before midnight.'

'It won't work like that,' I said. 'Once they are in they will telephone the station to report the robbery. A police net will be thrown over the roads automatically.'

'But it will be thrown out behind us,' said Roper. 'They will naturally think that the raiders have only just left and will fix their traps accordingly, fifty miles out at the most. We'll be further than that before the alarm is given.'

That is, in fact, what did happen. We learnt later that all

cars had been stopped at a town a few minutes after we had passed through.

On the outskirts of Salisbury Roper asked me to stop and buy a paper.

'But there won't be anything in it yet,' I objected. I wanted to press on as fast as we could.

'No, of course not, but I want to read about Dobbs.'

We bought a paper and went on. Roper read attentively for a while, then threw it into the back seat. I drove for another hour, getting every ounce I could out of the car, but I was tiring.

Roper took the wheel. He was slower and more cautious than I was, but that did not matter so much. After half an hour's rest I would take on again and make it fly. I leant back and closed my eyes.

But it was no good. The moment I closed my eyes my thoughts went racing. I picked up the paper and opened it. The Dobbs murder was all over the front page.

I read it through, and by the time I had finished there was no shred of doubt left in my mind. The murderer was sitting beside me.

'Ready to take the wheel again?' asked Roper.

'Not... not yet,' I said faintly.

'Why, what's the matter?'

'Nothing. I'll be all right in a few minutes.'

'Been reading about Dobbs? Ghastly, isn't it.'

I did not say anything to that. Roper looked at me. I looked at him. He grinned cheerfully.

And here is the curious thing: I felt like grinning back at him. (No, I am sure he was not using the drug on me.) I have always had an extra-peculiar horror of murder. I get it worse than others. I cannot, for example, read a murder yarn. Contemporary literature is almost a closed book to me. This exaggerated feeling dates from my boyhood. There was a lurid case in the woods near my home when I was five, and the nurse was much too explicit. This feeling swept in full flood through me when I realised that I was sitting next to a murderer. The horror of it prickled my skin and numbed my brain. That was according to expectation, but it ebbed away quickly, and that surprised me. I should have thought that a murderer who was a friend would be worst of all, but after the first spasms of automatic reaction I became quite calm. It wasn't a murderer who was sitting by me, but Roper, a friend. I ceased to feel bad about it. I felt miserable, and sorry, and anxious, but there was no horror. If he had touched me, or leant against me, I would not have minded. A friend who murders, it seems, is not a murderer. He is still a friend.

I took the wheel once more and kept the accelerator as hard down as I dared. We said nothing for a very long while.

'Why don't you say it?' asked Roper.

I swung out to pass another car and went on.

'Say it,' said Roper again, but I did not answer.

'The idiot had to be killed.'

'Don't tell me about it,' I said in a burst.

'You are doing seventy. Slow down, or we'll be over the hedge. Slow down and I'll tell you.'

I did not want to hear what he had to say, but I had to slow down. You must have your wits about you when the needle swings high.

Roper picked up the paper and looked at it again.

'You never realise how inaccurate the newspapers are until you commit a murder.' He was grinning sardonically. 'Here's a fine hot-pot of fact and fantasy.'

He put the paper down.

'It was the drug. I knew the dose I had in me would wear off about nine that evening. I can gauge it now to within a few minutes. At half past eight I went for a walk on the Heath. I wanted to break myself of the compulsion, if I could. This time there wasn't going to be another pill the moment the last one had stopped working. I took a pill with me, for fear – addicts are always doing that – but I was going to walk about until I was tired and then go straight to bed. I thought I would be able to face the morning without succumbing. I didn't like the way they were getting hold of me.

'Friend Dobbs was on the Heath, at the edge of a cluster of bushes. He was sitting on the grass, reading the evening paper, his waistcoat buttons undone. I should have turned away at once, but there it is. I didn't. I couldn't resist the temptation.

'You remember what you told me about Dobbs trying to scratch behind his ear with his boot? If you hadn't told me that, nothing would have happened. There was no one in sight. It seemed quite safe, and I tried it on him.

'It was certainly amusing to watch. He tied himself up in knots, got into the most frightful and impossible postures. I have never seen a human being look so like a fish on the grass. He fair whipped about. I kept him at it, too, until the sweat was pouring down his face. Then I cut off.

'He was scared stiff, and the moment he saw me let out a yell.

'"You!" he gasped, tumbling to his feet. "Nah then, you drop these 'ere gimes or I'll go strite to the perlice."

'"I promised to stand you on your head in Whitestone Pond," I said.

'He let out another bellow and came for me, head down. I side-stepped, but he came again, and I tripped him up. He went headlong.

'I sat on the grass a few feet away from him and began to ask, in a chivvying sort of way, what exactly he was going to do about it. "Don't you know that I am the devil? There's a tail stowed away in these trousers, and the feet are cloven. You know I am the devil, don't you?"

'"I'll put the perlice on to you," said Dobbs.

'I made him tweak his nose pretty sharply. He yelped again. I have never seen such fear and resentment in a face before.

'"You've led a pretty bad life, Dobbs. Especially in India. Now you're for it."

'"I don't believe in 'ell," said Dobbs. "It's all me eye."

'I tweaked his nose again and I saw his lips moving. He was mumbling something. A prayer, perhaps.

'"You're going to be my servant now."

'"You wait till I put the perlice on to you," he threatened.

'He had plenty of spunk. I liked him, but could not stop myself playing with him. It seemed as if I had to go on.

'"It's Whitestone Pond for you. I want to see you standing on your head in the Pond. Up you get."

'He swivelled over to his belly and held on to a bush with both hands.

'"I've come for you, Dobbs," I said in a deep churchyard

131

voice. He let out a great yell at that. "Help!" he shouted. "Help!"

'That was dangerous, on an open place like the Heath, so I took control again. He let go of the bush and stood up. "To the Pond," I said, and we walked towards the top of the hill, myself about a dozen yards behind him.

'By and by we came to the streets and I increased the distance between us. He waddled on slowly and stolidly and I made him button up his waistcoat. It was thoughtful of me.'

Roper snickered.

'You were a rotten brute,' I said.

'Take care of your own nose,' said Roper. 'We walked on until we came to the Pond. There was a small crowd round the water, looking at the sailing boats. I released him for a time. He was standing by the edge of the pool, then. He cried out and began to run away, but I took control almost at once. Everybody was looking at him. I made him walk towards the Pond again. I really intended him to walk in – it is quite shallow – and make him forget everything, for I knew we had been under the necessary twenty minutes together. He would wake up and find himself knee deep in water, and he would not have the faintest idea how he got there.

'Then things went wrong. I was still impelling him towards the water when I saw him wave his arms and shout. It took me a few seconds to realise that the effect of the drug was over, and by that time he had seen me.

'I sensed at once the danger I was in and ran. I heard the first strokes of nine striking from the church clock as I slipped the pill into my mouth. It was the paper's description of that scene at the Pond which gave the game away to you, wasn't it?'

'Yes,' I said.

'Fortunately for me the people around must have taken Dobbs for a harmless lunatic. When he cried out and started running after me, only a few kids followed. I had to do some quick thinking. The pill would take twenty minutes to work, and even then I could not see what could be done. Nothing could now wipe out his memory. He would remember clearly everything that had happened during the walk to the Pond. He could go to the police and report it. And I detested the idea of police interference.'

'But why?' I asked. It was getting dark and I turned on the lights. 'You had nothing to fear from the police.'

'No, of course. The police would believe he was touched. They would believe that for the moment. But I had already planned this bank-robbery – I had written to you before I went out for the walk. The police have a nasty way of putting two and two together and getting the sum right. It seemed to me very important at that moment that the faintest suggestion of the truth should be kept from them. I was wise, I think.

'All I could think of at the time was the need for getting Dobbs under control again. I didn't know what I could do with him once I did get him under control, but I would worry that bone at my leisure. There is always a way out, if you have enough time to think of it.

'At the moment there was only one thing to be done. I must lure Dobbs along, play the will-o'-the-wisp with him. That wasn't going to be too easy without attracting

133

attention to myself. I kept out of his way, but only just. He was a slow mover and it was not so difficult. I dodged about those short streets, and you know how quiet they are. By the time he had reached one corner, I was at the next, looking back at him. On he would come in pursuit again, and I would dodge into a passage and let him get to the next corner. He would look round, see me, and charge like a bulldog. I don't know what he thought he was going to do if he did catch me. He probably wanted to get his primitive hands on me, to wipe me one over the eye. It was almost as if he had guessed I was powerless.

'About fifteen of the twenty minutes had gone when I lost him. I went to the end of a street and he did not appear. I waited for a while, then started to walk back. He was not there. He had vanished, and I was seriously alarmed. Where had he gone, and what was he doing now? Perhaps he had found a policeman and was telling his story. It was a horrifying thought and I started to run. I could only run, of course, when there were no people to see. But I could not find him. He had vanished completely.

'I stopped at the corner of a street and did some thinking. Suppose he had found a policeman. What would happen then? The bobby would no doubt take him back to the station. Dobbs would be pretty obdurate. Perhaps he had already gone to the station? I should have thought of that. If he had, it meant cancelling this bank business, and I didn't want to do that.

'I walked towards the nearest station, and as I went along I tried the stuff on several people. It must have been a good twenty minutes since the chase began. A small boy twirled round and I knew it was working.

'The station is down a side street and it was getting dark. I walked past the blue light and wondered if he was inside. The place was very quiet. At the end of the street I turned round and there, coming past a lamp, I saw Dobbs waddling along with a constable. He was talking and gesticulating.

'I am afraid that I lost my head.'

'How did you do it?' I asked. I could barely recognise my own voice. 'The papers say that it was done with a blunt instrument.'

Roper laughed.

'A puzzle, isn't it?'

He lit a cigarette. I watched the flicker of the flame across his ugly features.

'Truncheon,' he said. 'I made the bobby do it.'

'Good lord!'

'It was all over in a minute, and the instant it was done I realised how badly I had lost my head. All I had to do was to make them both forget the conversation they'd had. But I never thought of it.'

'And the bobby? He knows, then?'

'Oh no he doesn't. That's the beauty of it. I made him forget all about it, the blow, the conversation, everything.'

'You must be mad,' I said, and I meant it.

'As a murder, purely as a murder, it was neat,' said Roper. 'But I don't pretend that I am proud of it. I lost my head, and I don't like that. I did something which could have been avoided if I had kept cool. But still, Dobbs was a problem. I won't pretend that I am not relieved he is out of the way.'

135

'Good God, Roper, a life is a life. You murdered him. You killed him. He was a decent fellow, there was no harm in him at all. You killed him.'

'Yes, I suppose I should feel it that way,' he went on easily. 'That is the conventional attitude towards murder. Nearly all murderers feel it themselves. They are willing to admit that they have done something which justifies a hanging. Very few of them have a grievance when they take the drop. But if they caught me and hanged me for Dobbs I would be one loud protest at something absolutely inadmissible. It would be an outrage. You mustn't hang a man unless he feels that he should be hanged. The final bar is a common sense of sin. The hangman and the hanged must agree. I don't feel a bit that I have done something which needs defending.'

I was astounded by the way he rationalised his crime.

'But that's the way all criminals argue,' I said. 'It was necessary to me, so why bother about him. You've travelled a long way in a very short time. Three weeks ago you wouldn't have said a thing like that. Now you've got the vanity and the pride and the low cunning of the criminal, all complete. You're going downhill just as fast as any man could. Three weeks ago money didn't mean anything to you. All you wanted was work. Now you've robbed a bank. You've got several thousand pounds in the back seat, and you're going to swill in the trough like a hog. You've killed a man, and you don't care a damn. I don't say that your morality was ever conventional, but it wasn't as crooked as all that. It's this drug. It's eating into you and corroding you. You've got now to where the average cocaine addict gets after years of doping. You've lost your feeling. You've turned liar. You're lecherous, and you've Satan's own pride. I've seen people go this way before, but never at such express speed. You are not really sane. Compared with what you were three weeks ago you're mad as a hatter.'

'What are you going to do about it?' he asked. But he was smiling complacently. I hadn't even scratched the surface.

'It isn't what I am going to do about it, it's what you are going to do about it. You've got to give up this pill taking. They're turning you into a danger to yourself and a menace to others. You must stop it, Bill. For God's sake, stop it. It seems all right to you, I know. The beastly drug makes you feel like that. But I can see you from the outside, and it isn't a pleasant sight. That business with Dobbs, for example. I don't mean the murder but the teasing and the Pond. It struck you as amusing, I could see that whilst you were telling me. But all the same, it was unpleasant. It was worse than that. It stank. And that is not like you.'

'Best style of English horseplay. Eton and Harrow cricket match,' he murmured.

'Not at all. But we won't argue it. If you were clear of the drug you could see it yourself. I want you to do something.'

'Well, what?'

'You must give me the pills.'

He laughed loud and long.

'I have been waiting for that for some time,' he said. 'So that's it. You want the pills, do you?'

'Yes, I do.'

'And you, what are you going to do with them?'

'Destroy them.'

He laughed again.

'I am afraid that I am a very cynical brute. You've been leading up to the pills all the time, haven't you?'

'Of course I have. The pills are the core of this business.'

'And with you they'd be safe. It sounds like Hitler's argument for taking away the colonies. Don't be an ass. As if I couldn't see what you wanted! So you'd like the pills, eh!'

I gave it up.

We reached Hampstead soon after midnight. The landlady had gone to bed, and we carried the parcels upstairs. I don't think we were seen by anybody. Roper stowed them away in a large portmanteau, locked it, and pushed it under his bed.

'You are sure you don't want any of the loot?' he asked me.

'Yes,' I answered curtly.

'If you run short, let me know.'

'Where's Bert?' I asked.

'He's been given two days off. He'll be here in the morning. Have a drink before you go.'

We had a whisky and soda each. Then we had another, and another and several more. He promised me he would never take another pill in his life. We had some more. He went to the portmanteau and unlocked it. 'Take a hundred,' he urged. He had a parcel in his arms. I refused. We had another drink. 'Take a thousand, then,' he said, but I wouldn't touch any of it. We had one more drink and then I stood up to go.

'Take half, man. Don't be a fool.'

I shook my head.

'I'll tell you what I'll do. I'll leave you some in my will.'

Next morning I felt very bad about the whole thing, about Dobbs, about the bank robbery, about my own affairs, about everything. I sat up in bed reading the newspapers. Dobbs was fading out. The police had a clue, or so they said. They wanted a short, stocky man who slouched. They also wanted to interview those who had seen Dobbs running away from Whitestone Pond. But there was not much of it, and what there was, was tucked away on the inside pages. Roper wasn't short, and he didn't slouch, and in any case I knew that the police themselves were the actual murderers. I didn't see how they could get a line on Roper.

Poor Dobbs had been ousted by the affair at the bank, and I must say I rubbed my eyes. I could hardly recognise it. It was the porter who had given the show away. He had come out into the square and collapsed on the pavement. 'Tight,' I thought, but the police said 'drugged'. The police had entered and found the manager, the masher, and the girl more or less unconscious. The manager, after treatment by a doctor, had been able to make a statement. Two men had entered as the bank was closing. They were masked, and had guns in their hands. 'Hands up!' they had said. One of them had then forced the staff, at the point of a gun to drink gin and french.

'I explained that I was a teetotaller, but they laughed and told me to drink it down. I had only one drink. After that I knew nothing.' He did not know what gin and french should taste like, but it had tasted bitter. He thought it must have been drugged.

Both men had been firm but dangerously courteous. (Yes, he said that!) 'Obviously gentlemen,' according to the manager. 'They spoke with an Oxford accent.'

'Poor Oxford,' said Roper when I saw him, 'between the accent and the groupers it is pretty well done for.'

Several, but not all, of the papers said that the porter had been detained. The police must have heard of his visit to the pub, and suspected that he was an accomplice.

I felt sorry for the manager. The apocalypse had not lasted. A stomach pump had cured him of his peculiar valuation of autumn leaves and bank notes. His happiness had been brief. He was back in his old self and lying his way out of a difficult situation with some adroitness. I hoped the rest of the staff would not let him down, for his sake as well as for mine. He had to lie. What else could he do? 'I felt for the time being that money was really of very little importance and urged them to take it away.' No, the truth was too fantastic (as the truth often is) to be believed. Any policeman would recognise that as the boloney. Masks, Oxford accents, guns, drugged drinks, that's the stuff which wears the face of truth today. The police know their onions.

There was only one thing which caused me any misgiving. We had gone and left our finger-prints large upon the glasses.

But what, I reflected, does a finger-print matter? Ours were not on file. We had neither of us been in trouble before, and I, at any rate, was determined that I never would be.

If it were illegal in England to bury a person without taking finger-prints there would not be such a large list of unsolved mysteries. Every man has a book and a crime in him, and many people commit both, once.

I began to think about Roper. Something had to be done about Roper. He was becoming a danger to himself and to me. Sooner or later, if he carried on as he had been doing, the police would be passing an inked roller over his thumb, and Roper's thumb was a signpost pointing straight to mine.

If there was anyone who could bring Roper to heel, it was his father. I remembered that quiet-faced, handsome man with the bushy beard living with his womenfolk in the large Victorian house in Kensington, remembered the tolerant amusedness in his eyes. I would talk to him, tell him everything. He would be helpful and know what to do.

'Come and have tea with the women,' he said over the telephone. 'They are excited at the moment but they will tell you about that. After tea come into my study, and we will talk.'

I found Mary alone in the drawing-room. She told me the news at once with gushing simplicity.

'Miss Shere and the Vicar are engaged!'

'No, are they really?' A man finds it difficult to strike the right note. Fortunately, the women are ready to accept the most blatant banalities as warm-hearted truth on these occasions.

'I am so glad,' I said, feeling a fool.

'So am I,' said Mary simply, with a quite different intonation. She truly was glad. The gladness was swimming in her face.

'It happened quite suddenly, yesterday,' she said, and went into details, as if it had been a round of golf played on the elysian fields. 'He's coming to tea this afternoon,' she ended with a joyous burst.

Women, on the whole, have always defeated me. There were good reasons why the girl should be glad. The acidulous pecking would stop; the austerity and the somewhat constrained efficiency would disappear via the altar. In another home, what Avatar? But she was not thinking of that. She certainly was not thinking of that. A man had capitulated, and she was rejoicing whole-heartedly with her sister in the masonic lodge of her sex.

Cousin Flo came in, a maid following behind with the tea. She was radiant. A tide of youth had washed back into her and was lapping about in her eyes. She was almost beautiful. She smiled at Mary, the sister in conspiracy, smiled perhaps with a touch of condescension, but that could be understood. One woman's triumph is always a little another woman's poison. But there was no sting in the smile.

I went up to her and said the usual things.

'He is late,' said Cousin Flo, 'but we shall not wait. No, certainly not,' she said to Mary as the girl protested. 'The sooner he learns to come to tea at the proper time the better.'

The monitorship without which no happy marriage is complete had already begun. I thought of what a good wife she would make to that somewhat indecisive man, the Vicar.

But the Vicar was only late by a minute or two. The door opened as I was receiving my cup of tea, and I turned round to look at him. And immediately I smelt a rat.

The Vicar was not himself.

I remembered the short, thin man with the glasses on his

nose; that indefinable quality of not being quite-quite; the way he fussed and fidgeted, fell over his toes, laced his legs, and never knew what to do with his cup; his serialised conversation, going on and on....

The Vicar was not himself. I saw it at once.

The Vicar was a gentleman, and what a gentleman!

He came in with assurance, walked the intervening distance like a courtier at Versailles. Cousin Flo lifted a hand. The Vicar bent over and kissed the tips of her fingers. He made a little bow to Mary, the semi-jocular bow of the intimate, and turned to me and shook my hand with a male valour and whole-heartedness which was perhaps the only false note that he struck. He accepted my congratulations with the right masculine mixture of embarrassment and pleasure, and thereafter sat modestly out of the conversation. He was easy, at home, and steady as a rock. Not once did he fidget with his feet, not once did he wave the cup about as if it were a cobra which had unaccountably got into his hand. The correctness, the nonchalance, the consideration of the manuals of etiquette, all were his without an effort. It struck me, perhaps, as a little too studied, but it was the goods, all the same.

What hit me most of all was his manliness. There was hair on this new Vicar's chest. The insipidity was gone. This was a man's man. It was even more a woman's man. At any rate it was a Man with a capital M. It was astounding.

I wondered where Cousin Flo had found him. For I knew by now, without a shadow of doubt, that this was not the Vicar as the Lord made him, but a recreation of Cousin Flo.

The lost pill was working. Cousin Flo was remaking her world whilst the going was good.

She had bagged her man at the last minute, and incarnated her dreams. I watched her, flushed and happy; admired her, too. I looked at the Vicar and wondered at the dreams locked up in the hearts of our elderly virgins. That kiss of the finger-tips – the touch of old-world Spanish hidalgo courtesy; the male vigour, straight out of Ethel M. Dell. Who would have thought that the secret desire of efficient, eight-cylinder Cousin Flo was for conquest and capitulation! The Vicar, I must admit, was a fascinating creature. There were few women whose hearts would not melt in their mouths at sight of him.

This Frankenstein would only last five days, it is true. After that the Vicar would revert to type. The feet would shuffle and the legs would twist. He would wake up to find himself engaged, too, and no way out, not for a Vicar. Five days! But five days are a long time. One hour of glorious life is worth an age without a name.

I glanced knowingly at Mary, but she appeared quite unconscious of the metamorphosis. She was a simple girl. Perhaps she thought this the natural result of passion declared. I looked at Cousin Flo, too, with a certain satirical amusement, but she returned the look from clear guileless eyes. It was I who was abashed.

The women, and God Bless Them....

After tea Mary took me to Mr Roper's study. He was sitting back in an armchair, a book on his lap. Mary left us to ourselves.

'I wanted you to see the Vicar,' he said, with a faint smile.

'He is a great deal changed,' I said cautiously.

'That will pass. How long did William say that the effect lasted?'

'Five days.'

'No harm is done,' he said gently. 'They have both of them wanted this a long time, and they will be happy together. Have you seen anything of William lately?'

'I want to talk to you about him,' I said.

I told him about the way the drug was affecting him, told him about Dobbs and the bank robbery. I told him everything. I even mentioned Anita and his obsession with her. When I had been thinking it over in my mind I had not meant to tell him about the bank and the murder. I had meant to keep to generalities. But he was so calm and contained that I found no difficulty at all. I told him everything.

When I had finished he asked me if I would take a whisky and soda. I accepted gladly, and he poured out two drinks.

'He is not to blame,' he said. 'People are hardly ever to blame, but we must save him from himself.' He pondered for a moment. 'I know him well, I think, and there is no harm in him. There is, perhaps, a slight perversion, but he would always keep it in check. The drug would get hold of that and amplify it. What we have to do is to get the pills away from him, by hook or by crook.'

'So long as he has the drug in him, he is in control,' I objected. 'He can always prevent us by using his will.'

'He is not likely to agree,' said Mr Roper. 'The pills must be stolen. You can do that, or you can ask the new man, his servant, to do it. There should be no difficulty.'

'I do not know where he keeps them, though.'

'The drug cupboard is the only place which is kept locked in the flat,' he said. 'I have a key to that myself.'

He rang the bell and Mary answered.

'Could you find the key to the drug cupboard at the laboratory, Mary?'

She went to a desk and got it. He handed it over to me.

'Now you must come out into the garden and see the hollyhocks. We are very proud of them. Mary, come with us.'

I was astounded by this calm way of taking murder. It seemed to make very little impression upon him. We walked about the garden and I left after about twenty minutes. He never referred to the business again.

Next day I told Roper over the telephone that I would be coming up to see him that afternoon. 'But I don't want to see you,' he said. 'I am working. I am taking Anita out to dinner tonight, but we'll come here afterwards, if you like. Bert is back. Suppose you turn up about half past nine. I shall be here if she agrees. If she wants to go on somewhere, you can talk to Bert till I'm back. I shan't be later than midnight.'

That was cool, I thought. It was cavalier treatment, but then, he had always been like that. He had never put himself out for others.

So that evening I motored to Hampstead and was there by quarter past nine. Roper and Anita had not turned up and Bert was there on his own.

'Quite a working-chap, I am now,' said Bert. 'Here's little

me with a spanking good job and that wife and family well on the way. They'll turn up any moment now. When are we going to have another party? You can have a drink if you like. There's plenty of drinks here and he won't notice a glass or two gone.'

'Have you been trying any more experiments?' I asked him.

'No, thank goodness. He is very busy these days, always out in the evenings, at the Institute, no doubt.'

I realised that Bert knew nothing about Anita.

'Do you remember that girl we met at the party?' I asked by and by. I wanted to make sure.

'Who, Anita? Don't I just! She is the nicest woman I ever met. Pretty as a picture, too. It was with her and her husband I spent my holiday. I don't know about him, but she's a corker. We get on like a house on fire.'

'Oh. Did you tell Roper that?' I knew I was doing it clumsily, but I wanted to be clear.

'Well,' and Bert scratched his head dubiously, 'the truth is she does not care for him. You know what women are, when they get fancies in their heads. She took against him at that party and she asked me specially to say nothing about staying with her.'

'I see. What is her husband like?'

'Well, I lent him a pound but I don't know about him, to be sure.'

I dropped that and started talking to him about the drug. It was difficult work, but I had to do it, whether I liked it or not. (My class has silly prejudices.) I told him that I had known Roper a long time, over twelve years. I knew what Roper was like before he started taking this drug. And now he was changing. He would not notice it, perhaps, but the drug was having a bad effect upon him. I had noticed it, and his father had noticed it. We had talked together about it and come to the conclusion that it had to be stopped.

'He has his temper,' Bert admitted, 'but that is what comes of working for a living. I shall go that way too, I expect, now I've got a job.'

'I want you to get hold of the pills.'

'I can't do a thing like that!' said Bert. 'No more quod for me. I was there twice for a bit of lifting in the old days.'

I looked at him in amazement.

'Yes, a gaolbird, that's what I am,' said Bert.

'But it is for his own good,' I urged. 'They are having a very bad effect upon him. You don't know everything. You can do what you like with the pills, throw them down the drain or give them to his father. But you must take them away from him.'

'Sorry,' said Bert. 'But I am a reformed character.'

I tried again, told him that Roper had become an addict, that he was trying to break himself of the habit but couldn't.

'His father thinks that if he goes on taking them something is bound to happen. He will commit a crime. Where does he keep them?'

'In his pockets, I should think.'

'Not in the drug cupboard?'

'I don't know, I am sure.'

I produced the key Mr Roper had given me.

'His father has a key to the drug cupboard, too. Here it is. He asked me to give it to you.'

That shook him. The drug cupboard was sacred. Roper

alone was allowed to lock and unlock it.

'We'll see if they are there. If they are I shall take the pills myself, and you can watch me flushing them down the drain.'

'Of course, a man's father is his father,' said Bert doubtfully.

I unlocked the cupboard door and rummaged. But the pills were not there.

'Search for it,' I said, but at that moment we heard a taxi draw up outside. I looked out of the laboratory window. It was Roper.

'He has a pill in him now, Bert.'

'I don't believe it, Mr Starling!'

'I know he has. You must try and get them. It is important.'

'I will keep an eye open,' said Bert unwillingly.

We heard them laughing as they came up the stairs.

'Someone is with him. Sounds like a woman's cackle,' said Bert.

Roper swung the door open. He was in evening dress. Anita stepped in. She was still laughing. Her beauty took my breath away. I had remembered that she was beautiful, but no one could keep such beauty in mind for long. The mind refused to believe it and denied it. Each time I saw her she was a fresh revelation.

Bert was staggered, and not by her beauty.

'Hello, Bert!' she said. 'I've come to see you.'

'Well, that's nice of you,' said Bert lamely.

'We've been out to dinner and he was mean over the drinks. I feel so thirsty. Isn't there something for little me,' she grinned impishly, 'to swallow?'

'I have a lot to swallow, anyway,' I heard him mutter. But Anita only laughed.

But Bert soon cheered up, put out drinks and polished the glasses. He tied an apron round his waist and pretended to be a wine waiter at a bar. It was quite funny. I noticed again how happy and natural the girl was with him. It was good to watch. The mincing affectation fell away from her. She was the girl of the painting, of the moment of truth.

I asked Roper in an aside whether I could speak to him privately. He nodded and stood over Anita. 'Happy?' he asked. 'Yes,' she said, eyes smiling up at him. He put his hand on her shoulder and squeezed it. Her head rolled sideways and she caressed his hand with her cheek. She was looking straight at Bert, as if she were doing it to him by proxy; a suggestion of denied intimacy, as it were. Roper went into the bedroom and I followed him. I shut the door.

The first thing I saw was the box of pills on a table by the side of his bed. A pang of mortification shot through me.

'Come for the boodle?' asked Roper.

'No, I've told you....'

He laughed. 'Well, what then? Nothing about the bank, is it? You see how well that went off. The manager himself put them off the scent. The finger-prints don't mean anything. It was silly of us, but it doesn't matter.'

'I'm bothered about you, Bill,' I said bluntly.

'I am my brother's keeper, etc., etc.'

'If you like.'

'What in particular?'

'The girl. That's not like you.'

'Why not? Have I not hands, organs, passions, etc., etc.'

'It's bad for you and bad for her.'

'Well, my little Luther, well? You've taken on a large sized

150

job. About three-quarters of the adult male population of the world is in love.'

'Not with other people's wives.'

'I'll cut my figures. Say ten per cent. It's still a goodish job.'

'You know what I mean quite well.'

'No I don't. What do you mean?'

'You're sleeping with her, aren't you?'

'I'll cut my statistics again. I'll cut them down to five per cent. I won't go further, Lot. I stand at that. What is our little nosey parker reformer going to do about it?'

'Oh, shut up, Bill. It's damn mean to use that drug on the girl.'

He changed his bantering tone abruptly.

'I have not slept with her. I mean to, but I haven't. She refuses. She plays a game. Well, she can go on playing, but the cards are in my hands. She'll give way sooner or later. I can wait.'

'Is that true?'

'Yes, it is. I haven't used the drug on her and I don't mean to.'

'Thanks,' I said. 'That's all I wanted to know.'

'I'm an idiot not to use it, all the same,' he said slowly. 'It's a sentimentalism, the last wisp of the pukka sahib still clinging. The drug would only fool her. She's being fooled anyway. What is the difference between food and wine and the drug, when it comes to that? She's an empty-headed, cheap bit of baggage. But I love her, meaning that I am not quite sane about her. I don't pretend that it is a high class love. It doesn't lead to the altar.

151

'If Caliban had got hold of Prospero's wand he wouldn't have used it on Miranda. You can be sure of that. Caliban wants the girl to come to his arms of her own free will. It is most frightfully important for him. That's the one way he can heal himself of his Caliban complex.

'You people who have been born with faces like shop window manikins can't be expected to understand that.'

There was a strong undertone of passion in his voice and I believed him. He broke off abruptly and said that he was going to change into something easier and roomier than a boiled shirt. I went back into the laboratory. Bert and Anita were talking quietly. I said that I was going.

'I will let you have one more drink, Anita,' said Bert, 'though you know it is not good for you. It is not right for women to drink at all, and if I was your husband you would have to sign the pledge tomorrow. Look now, I want to talk with Mr Starling, but I will come back.'

We went down the stairs together. In the hall he clutched my arm.

'He is using it on Anita,' he said. 'I know he is. I got it all out of her, about her seeing him every day.'

'Did you tell her about the drug?'

'No, I did not, but he is using it on her. Did you see him putting his hand on her shoulder, and what she did? It makes me mad as starlight. It is not right. She is a nice girl if she is left alone. I am damned if I will stand for that.'

He was indeed very angry. I was about to reassure him when I thought better of it.

'Get hold of the pills,' I said. 'They are on the table by the side of his bed.'

'That I will,' he said, squeezing my arm until it hurt.

He skipped up the stairs again, three at a time, and I went out to the car.

But I had not finished with the night's adventures.

I was stepping into the car when a man crept out of the shadows.

'Hey, Mister! Yes, it is Mister Starling, isn't it?'

'What do you want?' I thought he was a beggar.

There was a street light near the door and we were standing under it. I did not know the man. He was tall and lean and was rolling a toothpick about in his mouth, as an American rolls a cigar. His bowler hat was thrust far back over his head, and there was something shifty and mean and sly about the face. The eyes were far too close together.

'You just come down from Mister Roper?'

'Yes, what is it?'

'Now don't you take on,' he said with a weak ingratiating smile. 'I'd like to have a chat with you.'

'I am going home,' I said curtly, and opened the door of the car again.

'And Anita? Is she up there too?'

'What the devil do you want? Who are you?'

'Only 'er husband,' he said with a faint snicker. 'I just want a word with you, Mister Starling. Bert told me all about you, and I just want a word. There's a little café round the corner. Couldn't we go there for just a minute?'

'I haven't the time,' I said.

'It would be better all round, that's what I think.'

There was the faintest suggestion of unpleasantness in the words.

'I'll give you a minute then. Where is this café?'

'This way.' And we walked along together. 'Hot evening, isn't it?' he said, but I did not reply, and we said no more until we got into the café and sat down at a small bare table. It was a shabby place, and there were only a few people there, loafers and street walkers, mostly.

I looked at the man again in the light. His teeth were rotten and gapped, and he was using his toothpick and contorting his face as he excavated the most distant holes. The waitress came along and I ordered two coffees. He winked knowingly at her and made some sign.

She brought me a coffee and something which was not coffee to him in the same kind of cup.

'What have you there?' I asked.

'Whisky,' he whispered. 'You don't know the game.'

'Well, what do you want?' I asked impatiently.

'Anita's been going about a lot with your friend lately,' he said, smiling at me. 'But we understand one another, don't we?'

'No, I don't understand.'

'What is wrong with me is I got a broad mind,' he went on complacently. 'I got it ever since I was a kid. But there you are. I am too old now to have it cured. Some people 'ave narrow minds. I got a broad mind. I don't mind admitting it,' he added generously.

'What does all this lead to?'

'Some people are very narrow,' he went on, throwing away the toothpick. 'They're agin everything. They're agin a swipe at the pub or a tanner on a 'orse, and they keep their wives like they was in a harem. But I got a broad mind, myself I like a spot of fun. I don't mind it. I don't mind anything. Always like that, I was, broad as a bean. There's Anita now....' He gulped down most of the whisky.

'Well?'

'There's 'usbands would keep her like a parrot in a cage, but not me. I got a broad mind. I don't mind gentlemen 'aving a bit of fun. I like it. I like a bit of fun on the side meself. Savvy?'

He winked at me. 'It comes expensive, though,' and he shook his head.

'All this has nothing to do with me,' I said roughly.

'Now there's no need to be so up and coming about it,' he protested. 'A gentleman is a gentleman. He's got to have a bit of fun. Life ain't natural without a bit of fun. I don't want scenes, like some hubbies. Do things the genteel way, that's my motto. I got a broad mind, I tell you, but I got my feelings too, naturally. Everybody got their feelings, haven't they? Compris?'

He wanted money. That had been patent for a long time. He wanted to be bought over. He was a loathily little beast.

'How much do you want?' I asked.

'What do you mean, how much do I want?' he asked, his eyes wavering at this direct attack.

'You had better talk to someone else,' I said, and got up. But he put his hand on my shoulder and pressed me down.

'A man of the world like you,' he said, 'must know how touchy you gents are about your bit of fun. And I don't want scenes. It isn't my way. You 'ave a talk with him and I'll talk to you. Let's be men of the world about it and no fuss.'

I said nothing to that.

'I am in a bit of a 'ole, as a matter of fact. The 'orses

155

been running sideways lately. You couldn't, between friends, let me 'ave twenty, could you? A loan, o' course. I would repay you as soon as I got the money.'

I called for the bill and paid it.

'Good night,' I said.

'Well, ten then,' he pleaded.

I picked up my hat.

'If you won't play,' he said softly, 'I got other ways of putting salt on your tail. Perhaps Mister Roper thinks he can get away with it....'

'Good night,' I said, and went out of the café. As I walked past the window I saw him stub his cigarette viciously on the tin tray.

Roper must do his own dirty work. I wasn't going to do it for him. I would tell him, and he could do whatever he thought advisable. But I wasn't going to touch that pitch myself.

I told him, next morning, over the telephone.

'Why didn't you give him a tenner?' he asked coolly. 'She's worth that.'

I rang off.

I was out for the afternoon and evening and had dinner at the club. It was probably, I reflected, the last time I would dine at the club. Money was already running short. I would have to give up the club, the car, and the flat. The sooner I gave them up the better. There was, of course, money under Roper's bed. Half of it was mine, if I cared to take it. But I surprised myself by the passion with which I rejected it. (I suspect now that the passion was in inverse ratio to the temptation.) I did not like the life ahead, did not like it one bit.

I got rather panicky and ordered an exceptionally good dinner.

I was toying with a liqueur (the last, I swore to myself) when the waiter told me that I was wanted on the telephone.

It was Roper, and even over the wire I could sense that he was in a towering passion.

'Where the hell have you been? I have been telephoning you everywhere.'

'I am dining at the club, just finished,' I explained.

'I thought you had no money... Bring the car up at once. You'd better hurry.'

I did hurry. On the way I wondered what it could be. I thought of the skeletons in the cupboard – Dobbs, the bank, Anita, but it was only as I approached Hampstead that I remembered that Bert was trying to get hold of the pills. He had probably been caught at it.

Roper was waiting for me at the door, his face like a thunder cloud. I had never seen him look like that before. He opened the door, jumped in before the car had stopped and slammed the door to.

'Is it Bert?' I asked.

'Bert? No. Turn round and drive to Notting Hill. You can't get there too fast for me.'

'The husband?' I asked.

'I took Anita out to dinner this evening,' he said. 'She could barely walk for bruises. Had a black eye, too. He beat her up like a maniac when she went home last night.'

'But you can't interfere in that!' I protested. 'She can go

to the courts.'

'Courts be damned. Step on it.'

'He's a nasty customer. There'll be the devil of a scandal.'

'Don't talk to me,' he shouted. 'Take me there and keep me from pounding the life out of him.'

'Is Anita there?'

'No, she's gone to her mother's. Shut up, will you, and get there.'

'If there's going to be a row,' I said, 'I am not going to leave my car in front of the door.'

I turned into one of many alleys to the south of the High Street and we crossed the road towards the man's home.

'Be reasonable,' I urged. 'The fellow is her husband. He's got the whip hand over you. Tell him off, if you like....'

'I'll deal with him.'

I stopped short, startled.

'You haven't a pill in you?'

'Of course I have. Come on. Must I make you?'

We got to the man's house and rang the bell. He came to the door himself, and I thrust myself hastily between him and Roper.

'You know what you said last night,' I babbled nervously. 'Well, we've come for a talk.'

'Come right in, gents. Come right in. My wife is out, but she won't be long, I expect.'

I took hold of Bill's arm and led him through the hall into a dingy sitting-room. The man closed the door behind us and we turned to face him. He was rolling another toothpick softly between his lips and beaming at us.

158

'You bloody swine, what do you mean by beating Anita about like that? I am going to bang the guts out of you.'

Roper sprang forward as I flung myself upon him. I heard the man gasp and saw him jump towards the door. Roper hit me on the jaw and I rolled over. As I rose to my feet I heard footsteps racing along the street. The room was empty.

I got out as soon as I could; heavy boots were rattling down the stairs. I shut the street door behind me and went after Roper. He was disappearing round the corner, towards the High Street. I ran for all I was worth.

Roper was lighting a cigarette a few yards round the corner. I could see the lights of the High Street at the bottom of the street we were in.

'It's all right,' said Roper, but his hands were trembling as he lit his cigarette. 'Let's get the car.'

We walked along towards the High Street. The traffic had come to a stop and people were running and shouting.

'Something's happened,' I said. 'Where did he get to?'

'I lost him,' said Roper.

'What's happened?' I asked a man on the edge of the crowd.

'An accident,' he said. 'I saw him. He was running like a madman across the road and a bus went over him. The driver didn't have a chance. He's killed all right.'

I tried to push my way forward, but Roper grasped me by the arm. 'Don't be morbid,' he said.

'I want to see who it was.'

The suspicion had already gripped me, but I wanted to make sure.

'It was he all right,' said Roper lightly. 'I saw him dash

across. Good riddance, if you ask me.'

We walked back to the car. I had grown limp and white, as if I had been bled. When we got to the car I asked Roper to drive.

'So you killed him,' I said.

'My dear fellow, how suspicious you've grown! An accident, a pure accident. But why bother your head about it? All's well that ends well.'

'This is the second time you've murdered.'

'Anita won't give a damn,' he went on, disregarding me. 'She'd give me a medal, if she knew. She's free.'

When we arrived at the flat he asked me to come up and have a drink. I refused, for I was still feeling limp and wretched.

'You're a sweet little packet of false humanitarian notions,' he jeered.

'You did kill him,' I mumbled.

'Of course I did, the rat. Go home and forget it.'

I did not sleep much that night.

At four o'clock next day he rang up.

'Seen Bert?' he asked.

'No. Why?'

'He's not here. He's vamoosed.'

'Was he there last night?' I asked.

'No, he wasn't.'

'Any money gone?'

'No. Hop along to that doss house and see if he is there.'

'All right. I'll let you know.'

He rang off. I had not dared ask him the one question

which I was burning to ask. Had the pills gone?

I did some calculations. Roper had taken a pill on Wednesday evening, about nine o'clock. Next day, Thursday, we had cracked the bank and come back to town. On Friday I had seen Anita's husband. Saturday, Roper had got him run over. This was Sunday. The pill's effect would vanish around nine o'clock on Monday night.

I went to the doss house and asked for Bert. The hunchback who ran the place told me that he had not seen him for some time.

'He is not there,' I told Roper over the telephone.

'It doesn't matter.'

I didn't think he had missed the pills yet.

'Can I come round tomorrow evening for a drink?'

'I am not taking Anita out. She's not very well. All right, come round.'

I was there about eight, but he was out. I rang up his father from the flat and told him that Bert had disappeared, possibly with the pills, but I was not certain yet.

'Was it you who sent the key of the cupboard to me?' he asked.

'No. Was it sent by post?'

'Yes, but no word with it.'

'I shall know this evening if the pills are gone,' I said. 'I'll ring you in the morning.'

Roper was not back until about half past nine. I had a few whiskies, waiting for him, and searched quietly for the pills. I could not find them anywhere.

'Where have you been?' I asked.

'Walking,' he said, 'walking like mad. But it's no good. I am taking one more. Just one. Like any other addict I am taking one more. Then, like any other addict, I shall stop. Oh yes,' he jeered, 'this is the last, the very last.'

He took his bunch of keys and opened the cupboard door. I watched him searching, but he said nothing. After a while he straightened up and walked over to the bench. He was white to the lips. He poured out glass after glass of neat whisky and tossed them down.

'What is the matter, Bill?'

'They are gone,' he said flatly. 'Bert's taken them. But how the devil did he get into the cupboard?'

'He told me he had been in prison, twice.'

'Why didn't you tell me?' His forehead was beaded with sweat.

He drank another tumberful of whisky and began to laugh.

'It's all over,' he said. 'All over now. They are gone. We had a hell of a good time, didn't we.'

But he had hardly said that when he was rushing to the telephone directories.

'I want Joubert. Look him up for me, there's a good fellow.'

I gave him the number and he dialled. I heard him ask Joubert about the mescal from Mexico. He was trying to speak normally.

'What did he say?' I asked.

'It's coming over by Deutsche Lufthansa, but it won't be here for two or three days. Not that it will be any good. It will be the usual stuff. No good to me. I want another drink.'

'You'll be getting tight,' I said.

He poured the whisky out with trembling hands.

'I'll never get over this,' he moaned. 'You don't know what it's like. It will drive me crazy. Another drink.'

'You will take soda water with this one,' I said, pouring it out for him.

'Thank God that rat is dead. She's mine now. There's still the money. Oh damn Bert,' he shouted, getting up and walking about. 'Blast him. Blast him.'

He came up to me and put his hand heavily on my shoulder. His eyes were glassy.

'We must find Bert,' he said. 'Do you hear? We've got to find him. These beggars know each other. They'll know where Bert is. We'll turn London inside out, but we'll find him. We've got to. I shall go mad if we don't.'

'All right,' I said, 'we'll try. But keep calm, old man. It's no good raving at me.'

He shook his head dismally and drank a good deal more. I drank a lot myself, too.

'What can *he* want with those pills,' he said, and then stopped short, glaring at me.

'You!' he said, and stood up unsteadily.

'What do you mean, me?' I got up too, and recoiled a little before him.

'You always wanted them,' he said thickly. 'It wasn't Bert, it was you, you... What were you doing here before I came in? Burgling the cupboard, were you?'

'Don't be an idiot, Bill. You know I wouldn't do that.'

'I wouldn't do that,' he mimicked. 'Turn out your bloody pockets and let's see. Come on, turn them out.'

I did turn them out. I thought it was the best thing to do under the circumstances. He had to be calmed, somehow. He helped me, feverishly, plunging his hands into my pockets.

He nearly collapsed when it was over.

'More drink,' he said hoarsely. 'I must pass out.'

We finished that bottle and opened another. I drank about half as much as he did.

'Anita,' he said, 'is mine. The loveliest girl in the world. She's coming to live here now. With me.'

'A silly arrangement,' I said.

'Of course it's silly, but she's coming here. I am going to bring her here. Here.'

Soon after that I put him to bed, and left.

I kept out of his way on Tuesday and refused to answer the telephone when it rang. I was still in bed on Wednesday morning when he came round.

'How goes it?' I asked.

'Better,' he said, and he looked better. He was in control again, more or less. 'I rang you several times yesterday. Were you away?'

'Yes,' I lied.

'I chartered a taxi and looked for him all over the place. We're going out again today. Some of his cronies must have seen him. We'll take the car.'

All Wednesday morning and afternoon we hunted Bert over London. We asked match sellers and singers, organ grinders and pavement artists if they had seen him, but it was not until late afternoon that we had any news. An old man who was selling somersaulting negroes at Holborn

Viaduct told us that he had seen him on Monday in Leadenhall Street. He was walking along towards the market and was peddling boxes of matches, collar studs and boot laces on a tray. He had been very surprised, because he knew that Bert was doing the 'Heights' and stinging 'em like a wasp. 'We bought half a dozen of the tumbling blacks and gave him half a crown extra.'

'He's run away, you see,' said Roper grimly. 'But it's only a matter of time. 'We'll get him yet.'

After tea we went down the Embankment, and there again we had news of him. A pavement artist told us that Bert had bought his pitch from him on Monday evening. 'There wasn't half an hour of light left,' he said, and he had thought it strange he should have been working so far south. 'He's one of the northern men,' he said. 'Got fed up with chanting, I expect.'

'How much did he pay you for the pitch?' asked Roper, throwing half a crown into the hat.

'That's telling,' said the artist.

Roper made towards the hat. 'Oh, if you won't tell...'

'Don't be mean, Bill,' I cautioned. 'He's told you what you want.'

'Why did you want to know how much he had paid for the pitch?' I asked when we were back in the car.

'He's working the pills on the pavement,' said Roper. 'It's obvious. That fellow would not have sold him the pitch if he hadn't offered more than it was worth.'

He was very gloomy.

'Where now?' I asked.

'To her mother. She lives down World's End way. That's

not far from here. I'll take Anita out to dinner. You can come too, if you like.'

'Thanks. I'm going home. Tired.'

'I'm getting that drug out of my system, bit by bit,' said Roper as we went along the Embankment. 'I'm not gasping for the pills, now. I don't quite know why I am chasing Bert like this. I think I'll give it up. It's Anita I am after. I'm taking her home tonight.'

'If she agrees,' I said.

'I've played her long enough. She plagues me worse than the drug. I can do without the drug, and fortunately there is a cure for that insanity, too....'

'A week,' he went on cynically, 'a week should be enough. Then I can forget this business and get back to work. "I am the Captain of my Soul."' He laughed. 'So long, that is, as I can keep clear of morphine, cocaine, and desire. But it's coming to an end. I shan't be hag ridden long.'

Anita's mother was at home, but she did not ask us in. She was a large, vague, blousy woman with vestigial remains of her daughter's beauty. She looked embarrassed when she saw us.

'I am taking Anita out to dinner,' said Roper.

'Oh yes, but she's not in, you know.'

She passed a hand over her hair and smiled vacantly.

'We'll wait until she comes back then,' said Roper.

'But she is not coming back! Didn't she let you know?'

'Know what?' asked Roper.

'Mr Phillips came to fetch her yesterday afternoon. She said she would telephone you, or perhaps she said she would write. I forgot.'

166

'Who is Mr Phillips?' asked Roper.

'Bert,' I said.

'Where have they gone to?' asked Roper.

'I am afraid I have no idea. I understood that Mr Phillips had found her some work, or something.'

Vague as she was, I thought that there was some fairly precise determination and relief in the way she faded back into the hall and closed the door.

'Let's have dinner,' I suggested. But he paid no attention to me. He hammered on the door until the woman appeared again. She looked cross.

'How did they go?' asked Roper.

'In a taxi, if you must know,' she answered, tartly enough.

'Did you know the driver?'

'Now don't be silly, young fellow,' and she banged the door in our noses.

'I'll find the girl if I have to drag the Thames for her,' he muttered through his teeth.

For three more days we scoured London high and low, scouted the suburbs, combed the streets. There was no sign of either of them. At the end of the third day the business had become so pitiful that I decided to say what I had to say to Roper.

'He's gone,' I said, 'and she's gone with him.'

I thought he was going to hit me, he looked so savage. But I was too weary to care about his feelings. I'd had enough.

'That holiday you gave him,' I said, 'he spent it with her and her husband.'

'You did not tell me.'

'No.'

'Any more?'

I was taking him home to his flat and we were nearly there.

'They got on very well together. Didn't you notice?'

'No. Any more?'

We had come to his house.

'No, nothing more,' I said lamely.

He stepped out without a word and went in. His face was devilish. But I didn't care. I was too weary to care.

I took a wrong turning somewhere and found myself at the top of the Heath, near Whitestone Pond, that ganglion of light in the dark body of the surrounding parks. I stopped the car, got out, and walked a few yards along the Spaniards. There, sitting upon a bench, I looked over the patch of darkness towards the warm glow of the London sky and the sparkles of light in the London streets. After a while my weariness fell away and serenity came into me.

I tried to cast up an account.

I am, as I have told you, a light fellow, easy going by nature and inclination, without ambition, without care. I like comfort and cosiness, banter with easy-hearted friends, travel and foreign faces, good food, pretty women, wine, a little music. I don't go to see *Lear* if I can help it. I am all for comedy and the light surface of things. Hello Joe, Hello George, Hello Bully, come and have a drink. That is my style. How about a show tonight, a spot of tennis tomorrow? We talk, we laugh, we drink. I tell them stories about the places I've been to. They let me into the gossip. We go for a week to Scotland, a weekend to Paris. There was not an ounce of harm in it, or in me. I may not have been any good, if you judge me by the men who build bridges in Nigeria or the men who watch the shares skipping up and down in the City. But I was not bad either, at least not by intent. Shall we leave it at that?

But ever since the drug had come into my life the world had been different. I'd been ridden on a hard bit, done things and felt things alien to the old transparent life. Sitting there on the bench, a caricature of the 'Penseur', fist under my chin, looking over London, I remembered what my first ideas had been about the drug. I had wanted to use it on the fellows at the club, to make them stand on their heads and do comic antics. I hadn't wanted to rob banks and kill people. I hadn't desired any unpleasantness. But to Roper, my kind of fun was so much damned silliness. He had his own ideas....

I should have cut and run then. But in my own weak, indecisive way I had hung on. And things had happened.

Unpleasant things. Murder. Robbery. The change in Roper.

Was it too late to cut adrift now?

What had happened to Bert? To Anita?

I swore then that it was over, so far as I was concerned. I would cut Roper out of my life. I would refuse to criss-cross London with him in the car, looking for a needle in a haystack. At the merest whiff of the drug I would turn tail and run.

How blind one is to oneself! As if I had not made a thousand resolutions in my time and broken ninety-nine per cent of them! I should have known.

169

Within ten minutes I was to blunder into the drug again. And I sat pretty as a hen mesmerised by a fox.

I got up from that seat feeling that morning was at seven, the snail on the thorn and all well with the world. I was a free man.

I ran the car along the Spaniards. I don't know why to this day. Perhaps it was the enticing darkness of the Heath; it was certainly not the shortest way home. But there it is. I went along the Spaniards to Highgate Village, down West Hill, past Parliament Hill Fields. At the lights I turned west to Gospel Oak Station, then south again into a labyrinth of streets. If I strike right here, I thought, I shall find my way home by and by.

I remember going along a broadish street and hesitating at a corner, not quite knowing whether I should turn left along a narrower street. I decided suddenly that I would, turned to the left, and pulled up within a few yards in front of a small shop selling sweets and tobacco.

I wanted a packet of cigarettes.

How shall I put it? I wanted to go into that shop and buy a packet of cigarettes. But I knew, all the same, that I had plenty of cigarettes already. Nevertheless, I was going into that small shop to buy cigarettes.

Two people were coming out and I stepped aside for them. Then I went in.

Behind the counter was Anita.

I was not startled. It seemed quite natural to me. But she was.

'Mr Starling!' she said.

'Packet of Player's, please,' I said. I had to get that off my chest first.

I handed her the money and she gave me the cigarettes.

'Bert!' she called through a door behind the counter. 'Bert! Come down at once.'

'This is a surprise!' she said to me. 'Who do you think is here?' she called through the door. Footsteps were tramping down the stairs. Bert came in and stared at me.

'Well, I'm blessed!' he said. 'Mr Starling!'

But his surprise lasted only a moment. He came round the counter and shook me by the hand, shook it up and down as if I were a pump.

'No, you are not going away,' he said in his familiar sing-song. 'You are coming right upstairs with me. Oh yes you are. I am not taking any denials. I am as full of talk as a bone is of marrow, as we say down in Wales.' He lifted the flap of the counter. 'Now in you go and up the stairs. Anita will look after the shop. We'll be closing in half an hour anyway, and then she'll come up and we'll have a good old pow-wow.'

I walked up the narrow stairs to the first floor and was told to enter the room on the left. It was a bed-sitting-room in the best shiny pay-by-instalment style.

'Comfortable, isn't it?' said Bert loudly, and closed the door.

But once the door was shut his manner changed. He put his hand on my shoulder and held me at arm's length.

'Well, of all the things! I saw your car at the end of the street and said to myself: There's a little fly for the spider's web. Have a packet of cigarettes now. That won't harm you. Come right in. And here you are. Of all the things! And I didn't know it was you? That's the joke. I didn't know.'

'You used the pill on me,' I said.

171

'That I did,' said Bert.

'Are you using it now?'

'Mr Starling,' he said soberly, 'I promise you I am not. I would hate to do a thing like that to you. Now sit down and make yourself at home.'

'What does all this mean? How did you come here?' I asked.

'You won't tell Anita about the pills, will you?'

'I promise.'

'You see, she doesn't know anything about them. What do you think of this?' He waved his hands towards the room in general.

'It's grand, Bert.'

'Staggering for little me, isn't it?

'It's grand.'

'Have a fag on the shop.'

He pulled his chair up, sat down, leant forwards, placed a finger on my knee, and said:

'It was like this, Mr Starling....'

When Roper went out in a towering passion to wait for me at the door Bert knew that something serious had happened. He suspected, too, that it had to do with Anita. He had never seen Roper like that before. It frightened him. He would do anything short of killing now, he thought. He had seen it the moment he came back, white and hard, and wordless, and he was not surprised to hear him say over the telephone to me that I had better hurry.

Our car had hardly disappeared up the street when Anita telephoned.

'Is Roper there?' she asked.

'No, he is this moment gone out with Starling. What is the matter with him, Anita?'

She began to cry. He could hear her sobbing over the telephone.

'Such a dreadful thing happened, Bert...' but she could not go on.

'What is it, my dear? No, don't you bother about that. You tell me where you are and I will be with you in a jiffy.'

'No, Bert, I don't want you to see me like this. Really, Bert, I don't want you to. I am with mother now.'

'You don't mean you've left your husband, Anita?'

'He beat me about... last night,' and again she started sobbing.

'I'm coming over this very moment, Anita. Yes, I am. I'll knock his block off when I see him.'

'You mustn't come,' she said, with something of her old spirit. 'I won't see you. There. I'm going straight to bed. Bert, you would laugh. I've got a black eye.'

'It's not so funny,' shouted Bert. 'It's not so damned funny.'

'You would laugh, Bert. You honestly would.'

She rang off.

Bert, angry as he was, could not help feeling a sneaking sympathy with the man. Husbands should not knock their women about. No. But wives shouldn't go out to dinner with other men every night, either. Not that it was Anita's fault. It was Roper's. She couldn't help herself. Roper was using the drug on her. He was sure of that. Anita was a nice girl, a little flighty perhaps, but there was no harm in her.

173

She would stick by her husband all right, given the chance. But Roper didn't give her a chance. He had seen her caress his hand with her cheek, and he knew. It was that drug which was accountable for everything. Anita would be all right once he got his fingers on the pills.

But he couldn't find them. He had looked everywhere the day before, and he couldn't find them. Here was Roper gone again and he must search once more. They must be somewhere in the flat. Perhaps he had put them back in the drug cupboard. He had certainly seen Roper take them out of the drug cupboard once.

He fitted the key to the cupboard door and opened it. And there was the pill box.

He put the box in his pocket without opening it. He must get away at once, before Roper came back. He might be back any minute; he didn't know. Cramming his few things into a small suitcase he walked downstairs and out through the door.

He was afraid of Roper, now that he had stolen the pills. Roper was everywhere. If a man came walking along the street, he knew it was Roper, and dodged into passage ways. All cars, at a distance, looked like my car. For the first half hour of his flight, until he was clear of Hampstead, he expected to see us at any moment, kept dodging down side streets and into doorways. Roper would kill him, if he found him. He was certain of that.

Bert had never been afraid in the streets before. They were home to him. He had come out brightly into them in the morning and left them lingeringly at dark. But tonight they were strange and alien, and he would be glad enough to slink through a doorway.

He ran out from a side street and jumped a train for Tottenham Court Road, holding a newspaper before his face in a back seat of the upper deck. At the terminus he disappeared like a rat into the maze of mean alleyways to the east of Charlotte Street, and slept that night, wallet and the pill box clasped in his hands, in a worse doss house than usual.

His instinct was to sink out of sight. Roper would have no mercy.

But when morning came his fears were not so urgent. His native cockiness reasserted itself. He sang as he washed. Anita would hide him, but could he see her? Should he go to her? Roper would think of that, watch for him there, perhaps. Better let the breeze blow over a bit, better at least let Roper be drained of the drug.

He must keep out of his way till then.

But that, he reflected, shaving in a cracked and blistered mirror, was not going to be so easy. Of course he could hide. No one knew the bolt holes better than he. But the police? Roper would trump up some charge, and they would be after him like bloodhounds. There was no escaping the police. It was 'Hello, Bert!' and 'How's things, Bert!' until they were unleashed. Then it was 'Phillips, I want you.' Years before, when he was young and cocky, he had sneezed at the police and tried his luck. Blue eyes and a bang of hair over the brow, that was all the scent they'd had to go on, the merest whiff, amongst eight million strong-smelling people. But they had found him, nose down on the trail, before evening. No, there was no escaping the flatties. He believed, now, in the omnipotence of the police as he believed in the omnipotence of God. The two forces were, indeed, hardly distinguishable in his mind.

Bert spent the morning playing cards at the doss house, but in the afternoon he ventured out with a newspaper into Regent's Park. He lay there on his belly reading, mostly, about the clever way the police had trapped this man and that. Sunday was the day the police came into their own....

The day was passing, and so far, so good. Perhaps Roper had not missed the pills yet.

He felt for the box in his pocket. Something must be done about that, too.

He would go to sleep for an hour now. He began spreading the newspaper out on the grass, as others in the crowd of people around him had done. All this was not too good for his Sunday best, but it could not be helped.

He was shuffling about to find a comfortable position when he saw the plain clothes man. Even at fifty yards a plain clothes man was unmistakable. 'Bloodhound,' he whispered. The man was sauntering slowly over the grass, between the bodies, nosing around for somebody. And Bert knew that that somebody was himself.

He flattened himself out and drew a sheet of the paper over his head. Not that it was any good. If the cop was looking for him he'd find him. He would take a few minutes longer about it, that was all.

An idea so startling shot into Bert's head that the whole paper rustled with its impact.

He would swallow a pill. Why hadn't he thought of that before? It was obvious. It was the one way out. If he could lie doggo for twenty minutes he would be safe.

He poked a hole through the newspaper with his finger and watched. The plain clothes man was moving steadily in his direction, but slowly. He was taking an age about it, but coming. At last his shadow fell across the newspaper. Bert hoped the paper wasn't shivering as much as he was.

Saved. He hadn't spotted him yet. The fellow was moving off. Now his back was turned and he was a good thirty yards away. Perhaps he could do a bunk.

Bert drew the paper slowly down his nose. The bloodhound slewed round sharply. Who said the police couldn't see out of the backs of their heads?

He'd lie doggo then and wait, pretend to be asleep and snore a bit. Twenty minutes was only about twice as long as eternity. He could stick it.

The stuff wasn't working yet....

The fellow had turned round now and was coming back at a snail's pace, peering and poking. All right, let him come. He wasn't going to play bo-peep any more. Any moment now the stuff should be working, and then....

He tried it out on a large florid lady who reminded him of Mrs Joubert. And by God, it was working!

Bert rose boldly to his feet.

The cop came along at quite a speed. Bert faced him calmly. The cop wasn't certain yet or his feet would be twinkling over the grass, but he would be once he was close enough to see the colour of his eyes.

Bert strode over a body and walked up to him.

'Looking for me, mate?'

'What do you mean, looking for...'

'All right,' said Bert. 'Like a race?'

The cop stared at him, frowning.

'Hop it,' said Bert sharply. 'D'ye hear? Hop it, double quick.'

It was astounding and also alarming, the way the fellow went. 'I put too much vim into that,' thought Bert. 'Altogether too much vim.' Everyone sat up to see what was happening. 'Okay, children,' murmured Bert. 'Just a cop fleeing from yours truly. Lie down again and be good.'

And down they all went, like corn before the reaper. Bert strolled over to the lake and until nightfall watched the boats, chewing blades of grass, meditatively.

There was a noticeable swagger and squaring of the shoulders when he left the parks for the streets. He wasn't going back to the doss house, not he! He was going to visit the Corner House and put away a slapbang one and sixpenny meal to celebrate his victory over the flatties. The police? They'd better look out. Not that he wished them any harm. They were doing their job, but he wasn't going to stand any nonsense.

'Hop it. D'ye hear? Hop it.' That was the way to deal with them.

It warmed the cockles of your heart to order the police about. But he mustn't do too much of it. They always came out top dogs, in the end.

The Corner House, to Bert, was Mecca. He had never dared face it before. It was too munificent. He walked in, with a secret tremor in his heart. He had meant to do it in style, walk right down one of the alleyways bang into the core of the splendid sun, but at the very periphery his legs gave out and he sidled in a panic into one of the side tables. Even here it seemed to him that he was conspicuous, that each shining light in the ceiling turned and focused its beams upon him. He glanced round cautiously. They were not staring so much. In fact, they were not staring at all. Too well bred for that. Or was it that the Sunday best had done it? Good old Sunday best.

Once the tremulous agonies of ordering the slap bang meal were over he leant back in his seat. It wasn't as bad as all that. He was feeling more at ease now. But what a place it was! 'I dreamt that I dwelt in marble halls,' he hummed under his breath. The pillars, the domes, the gorgeously coloured marble, the band on its dais, the waiters in evening dress hurrying to and fro amongst the tables.... This was the goods all right. This was old London at its best.

'Not bad,' Bert whispered to himself, 'not bad for little me. Class, this is. And this is me, sitting here like one of the royal family. One of Them.'

The waiter entered into the conspiracy. 'He knows,' thought Bert, 'but he is not letting on. All right, I'll give him a whacking big tip when I go.'

There were a hell of a lot of knives and forks!

It went down, that meal, it went down, somehow. He was not certain he had got the cutlery right, but there had been no outcry. He hadn't been chucked out, anyway. A man with his wits about him could get through anything....

The exhilaration of the new experience began to fade and he looked around him with a more critical appreciation. He began to watch the others.

And suddenly it was borne in upon him that they were not taking this in the right spirit.

There wasn't enough joy, not half enough joy.

'They don't seem to know how lucky they are,' he thought. 'They have never begged in the streets, that is what is the matter with them. Glum, and they ought to be ... sparkling. It should be a Night Out. Why don't they let themselves Rip....?

'They don't even join in the choruses.'

He hummed a bar or two of the rollicking stuff the band was playing and watched a woman sitting at the next table. She had received her bill and was totting it up and looking into her purse. She didn't look too much above the weather.

He could change all that, if he wanted. He could make this eating into a Feast, a Banquet, a Revelry by Night.

They were too respectable, that was what was wrong with them. Why didn't they sing a bit with the band? They would feel better for that. They should put their heads back and open their mouths and sing. That would lift them out of their boots. Surely they wanted to sing? It wasn't natural not to sing.

Should he give them just a touch of the pill? There wouldn't be any harm in a little decorous singing. No banging of forks and spoons on the plates. Certainly not. But there should be a touch of jollity. Just a pinprick, then, the tiniest touch. Come along, boys, sing.

A humming noise came to his ears, like the hiving of bees.

He felt like the conductor of an orchestra. He was doing all that. Louder please. Take your foot off the soft pedal.

Roll it out as if you meant it. Crescendo, boys, crescendo. He sang himself. This was famous. They were singing like a Rhondda Choir. He caught the rattle of a spoon on a plate in the distance but he wasn't having that. This was a high class place, and no nonsense. The rattling stopped.

Here was his waiter, coming with the bill. Bert had a moment of utter consternation.

Surely the waiters should not be singing too? But this fellow was, and he had lungs like bellows in a smithy.

Well, he had shown them how to enjoy themselves. He had to go now. He picked up his bill and paid at the desk. The dark eyed cashier had a very sweet soprano voice, but she wasn't quite in tune.

'High jinks, tonight,' said Bert, and she laughed up into his face. There was nothing to stop people being happy, if they only let themselves Rip.

He took a bus down to Chelsea and called on Anita.

It was Anita's mother who came to the door and asked him in.

'She's upstairs, but I'll ask her to come down if you like.'

'Yes, I want to see her,' said Bert.

'You have heard, I suppose?'

'No, I have heard nothing. What is it?'

'Don't you know that her husband has been killed?'

'No! You don't say! Killed?'

'He was run over or something,' she said vaguely. 'I'll get Anita to come and talk with you.'

Bert was stunned by the news. He had not liked the man, but there, death was death. It always came at you like

181

a blow from a fist. Worse things might have happened to Anita, but she wouldn't be thinking of that at the moment. The feeling would grow in her later. Now she would be all broken up. He supposed he ought to go. Anita would not want to see him now, with her husband lying dead. Poor girl! The accident must have happened in the middle of a quarrel, too, and that always made it worse.

He felt uncomfortable. He ought to go, really.

Anita came in and he stood up. She was holding a handkerchief in front of her face.

'Bert, you mustn't look,' she said hurriedly. 'Turn your back at once.'

'What for should I turn my back, Anita?'

'I told you I had a black eye. You simply mustn't look.'

'I have only just heard,' said Bert, trying to put on the proper lugubrious expression for the occasion. 'Poor girl, it must be dreadful for you.'

'Didn't you see it in the papers?' she asked.

'No, or I would have come sooner.'

She did not reply, and Bert realised that she did not want to talk about it. She dropped the handkerchief.

'There. I told you that you weren't to look. Isn't it dreadful?'

She put a pink finger nail under a slight abrasion below the eye. Bert didn't think much of it for a black eye, but perhaps it was a good deal blacker under the powder. Her face was done up to the nines, and there was no sign of crying.

He could not understand it. In Wales you mourned for the dead, you wept, you could not forget. It did not matter to the wife and the children if the man was a bad man, when he turned still in death you wept. A body that had been alive was limp and still, and you cried. The man might be a brute, but the accustomed thing in him, the movement of life, the known thing, a fist in the face perhaps, was departed. A strange, terrifying thing had happened. You wept at the terror, even if you did not weep for the man. Life, even in a bad man, was life, and life was unique. It was inconceivable that it should be quenched, and when it was, you wept, you mourned, you were not to be comforted.

'What are you going to do now, Anita?' he asked gently.

'I can get plenty of work as a model,' she said. She looked hard and resolute, not as if death had touched her with his wing.

'You mustn't do that,' said Bert. 'It isn't a proper life for a girl at all, not a nice girl like you. I don't like to think of all those men looking at you. I know what men are like. They can't help it.'

'There's nothing else to do,' she answered.

'There must be some other way.'

'Mr Roper would help, I suppose,' she said dubiously. 'He has plenty of money.'

'Oh, if it's money,' said Bert. 'But you are teasing me, Anita. You don't like him. You told me so yourself. You wouldn't take help from a man you don't like, would you?'

'But what am I to do, Bert? I have to do something. I can't always live with my mother.'

'Anita, suppose I found you a job...'

Her face lit up as she looked at him.

'But that would be lovely, Bert.' Her eyes darkened again. 'But you haven't a job. What's the use of talking.'

'I'll get you a job,' said Bert. The idea had come into his

183

mind like a flash. That is what he would do. He would take her under his own wing, look after her for a while, until she could look round for herself.

'Suppose I was to buy a little shop somewhere, Anita.'

He was on his feet, the excitement of the idea playing in his face.

'But you haven't the money!'

'Money! Who said I had no money! I have lashings of it put away in a stocking. Look, I'll buy a little shop...'

'A sweet shop,' she said.

'All right then. A sweet shop. How would you like to help with that, eh?'

'Behind the counter?'

'Behind the counter.'

'But I would love it, Bert. Honestly, I'd love it.'

'In two days,' said Bert, 'I'll have that shop for you. We will run a little shop, you and me. You have to behave yourself, mind!'

'What do you mean, behave myself?'

'No cheek to the boss, see?'

'No, Sir.' she saluted smartly.

'That's right. No sucking of the bulls' eyes. I shall weigh the bulls' eyes every night.'

'Not one little one?'

'Well, not more than one.'

They were grinning at each other.

'Bert, you are a dear. Do you really mean this?'

'Every word of it, Anita. It's Sunday today. Tomorrow I shall be busy. Next day, Tuesday, I shall come to fetch you. Five o'clock.'

184

'And you are doing this for me, Bert?'

'What, buying a whole shop for you, you baggage? Of course not.'

'You are. I know you are.'

'I would no more buy you a shop...'

'Why are you doing it?'

'I like you, you know,' he said awkwardly.

Her eyes were swimming with tears.

'Now, Anita, for God's sake, don't you cry, my pretty one.' He took her by the shoulders. 'What is there to cry about, you silly?'

'I am not crying,' she sobbed. 'I'm not. I'm not... It's because I'm happy.'

When would the funeral be, he wondered? It would be before Tuesday, anyway.

'Five o'clock, Tuesday, mind. Sharp's the word.'

'Kiss me, Bert,' she whispered.

Kiss her? What was that? Kiss her? But a man doesn't kiss a woman when her husband is in his coffin!

'Now look, Anita....'

'Kiss me,' she said imperiously, and lifted her beautiful face to his.

Bert kissed her. She clung to him.

Out in the street he stopped and wiped his forehead. What had he let himself in for now? Women were the devil; even the nicest of them. If he had been in love with her, that would have been different. But he wasn't. She was a nice girl. He was sorry for her. They got on famously. He liked her, but he didn't love her. She was in a hole, and he was going to help her. But love... that was a different pair of shoes.

185

He had never thought of her in that way. Did she think he was going to marry her?

Worse still. Perhaps she wasn't thinking of marriage....

Little by little, as he tramped over the bridge to a lodging house south of the river, the passionate kiss transmuted itself into the paternal blessing of a man for a woman who mourned.

'I certainly like her,' thought Bert. 'She's a nice girl.'

He was up early in the morning, for it was going to be a busy day. He made a few enquiries as to the nearest place where he could hire a tray of matches, studs, and bootlaces, but decided finally to buy one from the man he had dossed down with. If there was any trouble the police would be sure to comb out the hiring places. Getting a tray without giving your name and address would be simpler and safer. He gave the man ten shillings, and even so the fellow suspected he wasn't going to use it for legitimate begging. Bert could see that he suspected he was keeping watch on some house or other.

The City was the place where you could make most money in the quickest time, and he was there soon after nine.

He walked slowly up Leadenhall Street, keeping his eye open for the directors as they stepped out of their rich cars. Here was an old man, stopped almost at his elbow. The chauffeur had opened the door and was helping him out, a rug thrown over his arm. The face under the shiny top hat was withered and yellow like a winter apple, and the hand on his stick shook as if he had the palsy. 'And he's still making money,' thought Bert. 'Why can't he leave it alone?

He must be dripping with it.'

The chauffeur was waving him aside.

'All the best,' cried Bert. 'All the best. Sir,' stepping boldly in front of him with his tray.

He was sorry for the old man. It must be dreadful to be as old as that. Not even a Rolls Royce and a chauffeur could make up for being as near death as that.

He knew what the pill could do. He and Roper had carried out dozens of experiments. If the old man could be made to feel as sorry for him....

The chauffeur waved him aside again, but the old man stopped and fumbled in his breast pocket. His hands were shaking so much that he could hardly open his pocket-book, and the note he held out to Bert trembled like an aspen.

'God bless you, Sir.... All the best.'

The chauffeur was aghast. This was a new experience for him.

Bert looked at the note and whistled. It was for fifty pounds.

A little shop for himself and Anita, a little shop with bottle-bottom panes. How's trade, Anita? Fine Bert. Have a bull's eye, Anita. Not bad for little me, eh? Not bad. Fifty pounds! What a foundation stone for dreams!

'There's a good time coming,
It's almost come,
It's been a long long time on the way,'

he hummed. Up and down the street he went. 'All the best, Sir,' cried Bert. 'All the best.' He wasn't troubling with the

187

small fry today. No, thank you. He wasn't after the clerks' money. He was only milking jerseys today, the cows with great swinging udders. 'All the best, gentlemen,' he cried at the domed entrance to Lloyds, his back flat against the stone which records that the building was opened by His Majesty King George the Fifth. 'All the best,' he called to the brokers as they went in. Charity, generosity, love, that is what he was sowing today, great fistfuls of them, and not a grain falling in the stony places. Crops of pound notes, five pound notes, ten pound notes. 'All the best, gentlemen, all the best.' He was round in Throgmorton Street after lunch. 'Best of luck, gentlemen.' He met one or two flatties there. 'Hop it. D'you hear. Hop it.' But that was part of the fun. 'Bootlace, Sir?' to a man who hadn't seen his boots for years. That was part of the fun, too. He had lost count of the money long ago. An old gent with a port-wine stain on his face had written him out a cheque on the spot. He hadn't even looked to see how much it was for. 'All the best. All the best.'

What a day it was! What a harvest!

But towards teatime he tired and wandered off towards the Embankment. He had a meal of ham and eggs near Charing Cross Station and then slept on a seat by the river for two hours on end. It was strange and laughable to find that someone had put two clods in the cap he had placed by his side. The twopence affected him more than all the rest of the money. People were not so bad. They were still willing to help a down and out.

He walked slowly along the Embankment towards Chelsea and as evening fell slumped down beside a screever. They were the usual pictures, of dogs, mostly.

'Want a nobber, mate, to help you?'

'A nobber's no good here,' said the man. 'I can collect the clods myself.'

'How much do you want for the pitch?' asked Bert.

'How much have you got?'

'It's almost dark. There's not much more coming your way today. I'll give you a tosheroon for it.'

'What the hell do you want it for?'

'Don't worry. I have my ideas. If you want a tosheroon you can have it.'

'All right, mate, I'll deal.'

Bert handed over the half-crown.

He could count his money, sitting down there on the pavement. There was still enough light left for that. It took him some time, figuring it out with a pencil and a scrap of paper, moving the money surreptitiously from pocket to pocket. So far as he could make out, it came to twenty pounds short of a thousand.

A thousand! Was there truly so much money in the world? Rustling the notes in his pocket he felt another sharp pang of the appetite and stopped a few cars.

But what was the good of it? He had over a thousand now, and he was dead with fatigue. 'I'll call it a day,' said Bert, and rubbed out the drawings.

Night had fallen by the time he reached his kip. Lying on his pallet that evening he read through the advertisements of shops for sale in the *Daily Telegraph*, put a cross against a dozen, and fell asleep. That night he wasn't taking his clothes off, not even his Sunday best. He knew better than that.

It was not until the afternoon that he came upon the shop he wanted. There it was, the small panes, the sweeties, the cigarettes, the flies, all complete. 'Merry-dew's' said the sign.

He went in and found a small, sharp-looking man behind the counter, an ageing man with bristly white hair and a wisp of goatee beard. There was a sprinkle of white hair on his nose, too, each separate stake leaning sharply forward, as if the nose had long been expecting an attack. It made him look very fierce.

'What do you want for the shop?' Bert asked. 'I saw it advertised in the *Telegraph*.'

The man put his hands flat on the counter and looked him straight in the eye, or he would have looked him straight in the eye if Bert had not been so fascinated by his nose.

'Not a cent less than eight hundred pounds. I paid every penny of that for it, and it is freehold. If my wife had not passed away....'

'Is that lock, stock and barrel?' asked Bert, who knew the expression but not what it meant.

'Eight hundred pounds, lock, stock and barrel, and not a penny less.'

He slapped the counter with his palm and looked extra fierce.

'Well...' Bert began.

'Don't think I can't wait. I can. I don't mind if I have to wait a year, but that is my price.'

Bert raised his right hand into the air.

'Hold it out,' said Bert.

'Hold what out?' Mr Merrydew was completely taken aback by this.

'Your palm, man.'

'My palm?' He turned his hand up and looked at it. Bert slapped it heartily.

'Done,' he said.

'What's all this?' asked Mr Merrydew.

'That's how we settle bargains in Wales,' said Bert. 'You said eight hundred pounds, lock, stock and barrel.'

'And not a penny less.' He was on safe ground again.

'I can pay you now,' said Bert. He threw a bundle of notes on the counter.

'Wait, wait,' said the little man. 'This is all wrong. You haven't seen the accounts...'

'I don't want to see the accounts.'

'Your surveyor, the accountant, the inventory, then the solicitors....'

'Can you be out of this shop by five o'clock this afternoon?' asked Bert.

'This afternoon! But it takes three weeks!'

'Three minutes, that's my way,' said Bert. 'Here, you count them yourself. Mine is not a head for figures.'

He pushed the bundle across. Mr Merrydew, his hair bristling more defensively than ever, wiped his mouth, stared at Bert with round eyes, stared at the notes and wiped his mouth again. Joy, cupidity, mistrust, chased each other in his features. Then his hands fell on the crisp notes and he started counting.

'Hundred and forty-four... Your solicitor,' he mumbled.

'I haven't a solicitor,' said Bert.

'Two hundred and ten. You must get a solicitor.'

'Search me,' said Bert.

'Six hundred... This is not business, Sir.'

'It's good money, isn't it?'

That started a train of ideas in Mr Merrydew's head. He held a note up to the light, turned it round and held it up again.

'Why don't you bite it?' asked Bert.

'Eight hundred. Shall I... shall I count the rest?'

'Don't you bother,' said Bert, stuffing the remainder back into his pocket. 'I'll be back at five o'clock.'

'A receipt! You must have a receipt. I don't know what to say to this.'

'There is no need for you to say anything, man. You get out by five o'clock, see!'

Bert opened the door and shouted down the staircase.

'Anita! You shut that shop now and come along up.'

'All right, Bert.'

'And he was out by five o'clock, too,' said Bert to me. 'But he's round every day. He can't get over it. He keeps thinking there must be a fly in the ointment somewhere.'

'You can't blame him, Bert. You should have offered him five hundred to begin with, then six hundred, and so on.'

'Yes, I suppose so. Would you like to see where Anita sleeps? She has a lovely little room above this one.'

I could hear Anita coming up the stairs.

'Some other time.'

'Not a word about the pills, remember.'

'Not a word,' I said.

'There she is!' said Bert jubilantly as the door opened. 'I ask you, Mr Starling, is there another shop in London has a little woman looks like that!'

'Oh, shut up, Bert. I'm hungry. What is there for supper?'

'I do the cooking,' he explained. 'She is no good at it, but you can't have everything, can you? Now tonight we'll have a royal spread. What about some ham and eggs, fresh laid eggs, Anita? That suit you?'

'If it doesn't take too long. I'm simply famished. We'll lay the table.'

'Expect me in five minutes,' said Bert, and walked downstairs.

'Do you like it, Mr Starling?' she asked.

'I think it's grand. How about you?'

'I've never been happier.'

'Truly?

'Well, look at me.'

She certainly looked it. She was radiant.

'You shouldn't give up your work as a model, though.'

'But Bert doesn't like it! And I don't mind.'

'It's hard on Joubert.'

She tossed her head and made a little grimace.

'And Bill?' she asked. 'What's become of him?'

'He is looking for you everywhere.'

'You won't let on, will you?' she asked swiftly.

'Of course not, but it's rather hard on him, too.'

'I don't want to see him again, ever,' she said.

Bert came stumbling up the stairs. 'I've been out to get the beer,' he panted, rolling half a dozen bottles on to the floor. 'I expect the ham is burnt to a frazzle.'

Anita laughed happily. 'Don't you think Bert is a dear?' she asked.

We had a great night, finishing off with the Collier's Lament for Father and Mother. When eleven o'clock struck from a neighbouring clock he made urgent signs to me to stay where I was and told Anita to go off to bed. 'Up you go,' said Bert.

'I don't want to go, yet.'

'No cheek to the boss. Hop it. Time for little girls to be in bed.'

She did go at last, slowly and unwillingly, I thought.

'Why did you want me to stay?' I asked. 'That's what you meant by those signs, wasn't it?'

'Oh well,' said Bert, 'you know what women are. It's safer when there is another man around.'

'I'll come to the wedding,' I said.

But I could see that it wasn't weddings that Bert was bothered about. It was christenings.

I stayed with friends for three days and left no address at the flat. On the morning of the fourth day I was back in town and within half an hour Roper was talking to me on the telephone.

Had I been away? Yes. Why had I been away? Why did I not leave the address? Why had I not told him that I was going?

I did my best, but it was a poor, unconvincing best.

'Can you come and see me this evening?'

'Sorry, Bill, but I have an engagement.'

'What is it?' he asked quickly.

It takes me time to think out my lies. I fumble and get awkward. He laughed and rang off.

About eleven that evening, when I was thinking of turning in, he came round to the flat.

'You are back early!' he mocked.

'Yes,' I said. I had not been out at all, and he knew it.

'Why the prevarication? What are you hiding?'

'Nothing. I wasn't feeling very well, that was all.'

I felt more and more uncomfortable, and showed it.

'One ought to accept the conventional lies on their face value,' said Roper. 'Nothing more becomes a man. Where's Bert?' he shot out.

'Haven't you found him?'

'No, but you know where he is. You started. You looked guilty. Out with it.'

'I tell you I don't know.' The best I could do was to sound irritable and peevish.

'I'll find her on my own, then,' he said grimly.

He was looking strained and unwell, as if he had not slept.

'You are not still thinking of that girl?' I asked.

'Oh no, not at all.'

'Honestly?'

He jumped to his feet.

'You damned fool, I think of nothing else.' He paced about the room. 'Ever been hungry, really hungry?'

'Once or twice,' I admitted.

'Then you know.'

He sat down again. 'Drink is no good. I have tried it. Work is no good. I can't work. Do you want to see me go crazy?'

'Don't talk nonsense, Bill.'

195

'Where is she? Where the hell is she? Why don't you tell me? You've found them. I know that. I can see it in your face.'

'I've told you...'

'You've told me a pack of lies. Very well, then, I'll go about it my own way, but I'll find her.' He looked so desperately determined that I was alarmed.

'Why, what do you mean to do?'

He stood by the door, the handle in his hand, looking over his shoulder at me.

'Bert is known to the police. You told me so yourself. All I have to do is to whisper a word to Scotland Yard, say that he disappeared with a tenner, and he is in the net. They'll find him for me. I might as well use your telephone,' he went on coolly, and came back into the room.

'Wait, Bill. Let's talk. I'll get you a whisky.'

He sat down again and I poured out the drinks.

'You wouldn't do that. Bert hasn't been in trouble for years, and...'

'I am not thinking of Bert. I am thinking of myself. And he pinched the pills. Don't forget that.'

'I put him on to it,' I said.

'You!'

'I could see what they were doing to you,' I began, but he cut me short.

'Where is she?'

'I shan't tell you that.'

'Very well, then, it leaves me the Yard.'

'This is going to hurt you,' I said, 'but you've asked for it. She is with Bert....'

'Of course she is. I know that.'

'She asked me not to tell you where they are hiding. She never wants to see you again.'

'That's a lie.'

'It's true, Bill. I told you how well the two of them get on together. Better forget and cut it out.'

'I must see her. Where is she?'

'She's in love with him,' I said brutally.

I could see the muscles working in his cheek, but he pulled himself together.

'Where is she?' he asked softly.

'I am not telling you.'

He got up and put on his hat.

'Don't forget that he has the pills,' I warned.

He left without another word.

Early next morning he rang me up again.

'I'll give you one more chance,' he said. 'If you don't tell me where she is I put the police on to Bert.'

I slammed the receiver down and hurried round to the shop in my car. Bert himself was serving behind the counter.

'Quite an early bird, Mr Starling,' he beamed. 'Come right in. Anita is upstairs making the beds. We are not busy this morning. I am not using the pill, see?' he whispered.

I nodded.

'Merrydew comes round every day for fear the customers or the travellers are cheating. He is terribly afraid of anybody getting the best of me. When he thinks how easily he could have done me in he gets into a sweat and runs round to see nobody else is grazing on me. It's funny, people are.'

'Listen, Bert, something serious is happening. Mr Roper is after you.'

'What for? I don't owe him anything?'

'No, but he wants to see you.'

'Anita?' he asked quickly.

'I am afraid so.'

'Well, she does not want to see him, She has told me so.'

'I know, but he wants to see you... her. He's trying to find out where you are.'

'That's all right. He can go on looking for a year of Sundays. He won't find us.'

'He's using the police.'

'What does that matter? The flatties are good friends of mine. Two of them call in regular for their baccy.'

I had to tell him. I did not like doing it, but I had to. He was completely bowled over by Roper's perfidy. 'It isn't as if I had stolen anything,' he wailed. 'I didn't touch a thing except that box of pills, but give a dog a bad name... It is Anita he is after, and he is not going to get her. If she liked him, that would be different. He could have her for keeps, if he wanted to.'

'You will have to skip. I'm afraid you'll have to give this up and go away somewhere. For a while, at least.'

'Oh no, I am not budging an inch.'

'But you must.'

He came round the corner and whispered in my ear.

'What about a pill? I can put the flatties off with that. I can put him off. What do you think?'

I had not thought of the pills.

'It would be better to hide for a bit.'

'No,' said Bert obstinately. 'I have not done anything wrong, and I am staying right here. Wait a minute.'

He went upstairs and after a while came down again.

'It takes twenty minutes, but they won't be all that quick. I have told Anita you are staying to lunch. You will, won't you?'

I agreed to stay and see how things went.

'You walk upstairs and talk to her. I am going to make things buzz here by and by.' He winked at me, and I understood.

I spent the rest of the morning with Anita. 'It's my day off the shop,' she said, 'and I do the cooking. Do you know anything about cooking, Mr Starling?'

We were having a hilarious time in the kitchen when I heard someone talking in the shop. I slipped out and saw a policeman going out through the door.

'That is not so bad,' said Bert, in a low voice. 'What he told them was that I had some papers of his, and he wanted to see me. He works for them, the flattie told me, so they were willing to help him out. He knows where I am now, though. Well, let him come.'

'You won't do anything rash, Bert.'

'I want to have it out with him. He is not going to see Anita again so long as she does not want to. I promise you I will not do anything unless he makes me. If he is reasonable, everything is all right. He told you about charging me to frighten you, but you see, he is not a bad man really.'

I was glad that Roper had discovered another way of finding Anita. But I was far from feeling as optimistic as Bert.

'I shall be going after lunch,' I said, 'but you will let me know if anything happens.'

Bert telephoned two days later to say that nothing had happened. Roper had not been round, and he was wondering if he should go and beard him at the laboratory. I advised against that, but even through Bert's bawling it was plain that this waiting was getting on his nerves. He wanted to have things out at once.

I could only counsel patience, but I was a good deal more mystified than Bert. I remembered Roper asking me if I had ever been hungry. It was not like him to wait for his meals.

Bert was on the telephone again at tea-time the next afternoon. He was shouting so much that I could not hear a word. I begged him to lower his voice.

'Anita's gone,' he said.

'What do you mean: gone?'

'She has left the shop. She has disappeared.'

Bert, it seemed, had left the shop about one o'clock for a walk through the streets with Merrydew. The walk had turned into a tour of inspection of other shop windows, and Merrydew had got so excited and fierce over various displays that they had not come back until after three. The shop was open, but Anita was not there. Bert had asked all the neighbours, but none of them had seen her go. She had just disappeared. It was not like Anita, Bert pointed out, to leave the shop like that.

'Ever been hungry, really hungry?' Roper had asked me.

He wanted Anita, and Anita was gone. How, then, had he managed it?

I gave it up and weakly hoped that everything would turn out right.

Soon after dinner Bert was on the telephone again.

'I am getting worried, Mr Starling. She is not back yet. Are you quite sure he had no pill?'

He was so distressed that I took the car out and ran round to the shop.

As I entered he waved a letter at me.

'I have just got this,' he said. 'Read it and tell me what you think.'

It was from Anita, and very short. 'Dear Bert. Don't worry about me. I have gone away with Bill. Give my love to the shop. Anita.'

'We can't do anything about that,' I said gloomily.

'I would never have believed it,' said Bert. 'No, honestly I wouldn't. But there you are, that is a woman all over. So long as you are sure.'

'I am quite sure.'

'She might have told me,' said Bert, 'but perhaps she didn't like to say she had changed her mind. There is one thing I know about her, though. She is a nice girl and would not do anything wrong, wrong for her, I mean. I hope they are happy.'

Did I, or did I not, detect a certain relief in Bert? It was difficult to say.

'I am not sure that he is Mr Right for her,' he went on, 'but there you are, that is her business. She knows best.'

I admired and envied him his simple faith in the girl, the breadth of his tolerance.

'Didn't she tell you she disliked him?' I asked.

'Yes, I know, but you can't depend on that. You know what women are like. Some of them go to the altar whispering I hate you. Or so I have heard.'

'Do you really think she was in love with him?' I pressed.

He looked somewhat disturbed. He was finding it difficult to reconcile the Anita who had kissed him and the Anita who had run away with Roper.

'Let's close the shop and go and have a drink,' said Bert.

'One thing more. I telephoned the laboratory and there was no reply.'

'So did I, but perhaps they have gone away somewhere. Let's go and drink Good Luck to them.'

Bert, at any rate, was quite satisfied, but there were still fringes of doubt and misgiving in my mind.

Anita left the shop on a Monday. I did not telephone the laboratory again until Wednesday. Roper answered the call.

'You are back?' I said fatuously.

'I have never been away.'

'Oh. I rang you up several times on Monday.'

'I heard the ringing.'

I did not ask him why he had not answered.

'How is Anita?'

'She is very well. Why don't you come up and see us this evening?'

'I hardly like butting...'

I have a gift (if it can be called a gift) for saying the wrong thing. He interrupted me.

'Wait a minute. I'll ask her.'

He was back again pretty soon.

'We are going out to dinner, but you could come round later. Shall we say nine?'

'All right, Bill.'

I put the receiver down with a sigh of relief. I had been suffering from the embarrassment I always feel in contact with the newly wed or the freshly liaisoned. I had been put out, too, by Roper. He had always snapped over the telephone, and he had been unexpectedly easy and simple.

I nearly put off going. I wanted to see them, but there was an element of 'snoop', of illegitimate curiosity which was somehow a little shameful. But the curiosity got the better of me and I was there soon after nine.

Roper was on his own in the laboratory, reading. He was in evening dress. He threw his book away and sprang up to meet me.

I was immediately aware of a change in him. Roper was ugly and I knew his ugliness feature by feature. He was ugly still, feature by feature, but he was wearing his ugliness with a difference. The best way I can put it is by saying that the lighting of his face had changed. It was as unexpected as a transformation on the stage. The sharp, bleak, white lights were gone, and with them that swift cynical aware-ness which was his main characteristic. The diabolism had vanished, but I could only note without understanding what had taken its place. The expression was still clean as a whistle, but warmer, less subtle, more natural. Above every-thing there was an eagerness, an optimistic vivacity dead contrary to his old defensive alertness. It was as if he had suddenly come out of the shadows into broad daylight.

It took me by surprise. Many of my friends have accepted a woman unto themselves and the immediate result has been a visible softening of the brain, a bashed fruit look allied with an insufferable complacence and condescension. I have often wondered how their women can stand it. I had not expected that in Roper, but I could have borne with it. I was nonplussed by this; it was new to me.

'Well, how are things?' I said. Life must go on as if no miracles ever happened.

'Have a drink,' said Roper, and poured out.

'You not having one?' I asked.

'I've cut it out a lot.'

If he had said: 'I get drunk another way now,' and leered a bit, I would have felt more at case. This new Roper baffled me. He was simple and friendly, too, without reserve. He even asked me what I had been doing, whether I had found a job, how the inquiry into the solicitor's affairs was progressing. That, perhaps, was the most staggering of all. He paid no attention, customarily, to other people's affairs. That was their own business, and generally a mess.

'I wish you would take some of the money, Jim.'

'I never liked that affair,' I said.

'I don't feel too well about it myself, now.'

'Send it back, then.'

'I probably will.'

I was through with my drink before I realised it. I felt nervous and constrained. He poured out again.

'What are the plans?' I asked.

'We are getting married. High time to settle down, you know.'

I could only gulp down some more.

'Date fixed and all that?'

'Oh, there's no hurry. I shall want you as best man.'

'Getting married in a church?'

'She wants it.'

'Okay then,' I said weakly. This was too much.

'She's jimming herself up in the bedroom. She'll soon be here.'

'Fine,' I said.

'How is Bert?' he asked.

'Not so bad,' I said cautiously. 'It was a shock when Anita disappeared, but he's all for people doing what they want.'

Roper nodded and I was going to pump him some more when he took the wind out of my sails by saying quietly:

'You gave me to understand they were living together.'

'Did I?' This was hardly the proper kind of talk about the woman he was going to marry, but the honesty and courage had not evaporated.

'Did you think so?' he went on.

'No, of course I knew they were not, but I thought it better to mislead you at the time.'

'Why?'

'Oh, to hell, Bill.'

'That was not very fair to her.'

'Sorry.'

'That's all right. I don't bear you a grudge. I can understand why you did it.'

'It was to save her. Give me another drink, will you.'

'I wouldn't, if I were you.'

'Just one more.'

I heard the bedroom door open, and I jumped to my feet. Anita was coming in, and she was smiling. I have told you already how her beauty affected me, what a fresh and surprising revelation it was each time I saw her. But this time it was different altogether. My heart missed a beat, and I could only stare. She was radiant, as if candles had been lit behind the skin of her face. Her eyes were starry... but I will not go on with it. I don't read much poetry, but I still remember the shock of delight which went through me when I came for the first time upon the line: 'And jocund day stands tip-toe on the misty mountaintops.' It was the same shock I had then, as if a long-scaled fountain had started gushing. I turned to Roper. He was standing by my side and the muscles in his cheek were working as I had seen them work before under some deep emotion.

Someone told me once that we only live to the fullest intensity in rare moments, moments so rare that a lifetime does not hold more than four or five of them. That time when Anita stood in the bedroom door was one of them for me, the greatest of them. I shall not forget it, and if I have a regret, it is that at my death the memory of it will die out of the world. But perhaps it does not die. I have a feeling that such things are imperishable.

But we cannot live at such heights of vision for long, and in our healthy (is it healthy?) English way we were down at the foot of Pisgah in double quick time.

'Hello, Anita!'

'Hello!'

'You're looking grand.'

And so on, and so on, the threadbare inexpressive banalities of the everyday. We talked, about nothing, laughed, over nothing, drank, a little. And I watched her all the time, partly out of curiosity, partly because I could not take my eyes away.

How do women show love? One can barely tell, but it is unmistakable nevertheless. It is an atmosphere, in the main, a context in which some small, hardly distinguishable gesture or look is entirely different from what it seems. The things she did were ordinary enough; the words were commonplace, but word and look were nevertheless charged and transformed by the mysterious energy of love. She adored him, blindly.

When I get caught up in the company of some self-absorbed couple with the dew of this magic fresh upon them I escape as soon as I possibly can. They are not interested in me; I am an impediment and a nuisance. And to tell the truth, I am not usually interested in them, for people in love are as flatly dull to the outsider as they are vividly interesting to themselves. But this evening I stayed long. I stayed too long. I knew I ought to go but I did not want to go. We were such a happy trio that I fooled myself into believing I was in some part at least a contributor to that happiness.

But towards eleven o'clock, when the thought of leaving was well out of my mind, I found myself standing up and saying that I must go. I bent over Anita's hand and kissed it.

Now I had never in my life kissed any woman's hand this side of the Channel or the Atlantic. When I kissed Anita's hand it seemed no more than, for once, a heartfelt recognition of beauty's due. It was not until Roper was showing me to the door that the oddness of the thing struck me. Why, I asked myself, had I kissed her hand? And like a flood the explanation came pouring in upon me.

It was Roper who was making me go. It was Roper who had made me kiss her hand.

Roper had got hold of a pill.

It is difficult to convey the sense of calamity that surged through me. Everything, in the light of that simple fact, became clear, Anita's disappearance, Anita's betrayal of her feelings for Bert, Anita's adoration of Roper, all but the change in Roper himself. That was as dark a mystery as ever.

'I want you to see something I have in the car,' I told Roper, trying hard to keep my voice even.

'Some other time, Jim.'

'No, now. It really is important.'

He was very unwilling, but I insisted.

'I shall not be long, Anita.'

When we had reached the street I asked him to walk along for a short distance.

'Must you?' he asked.

'Yes, I must.'

Half way down the street I stopped under a lamp post.

'Bill, you've got hold of some more.'

'Some more what?'

'Don't pretend.'

He did not say a word for a moment.

'How did you know?'

'You used it on me to get me away.'

'Well, you don't object to that, do you?' He laughed a little in his old manner.

'No, of course not. I was a fool to stay so long. But it's damnable, what you're doing to Anita.'

'What do you mean?'

'She doesn't love you, and you know it. She dislikes you.'

He gripped me by the arm so tightly that I nearly cried out.

'You've seen, haven't you?'

'It's the drug,' I said stoutly. 'I know it's the drug.'

'That's a lie, blast you. What do you know of Anita?'

It was true. I knew very little about Anita. And he had protested so violently that I was shaken.

'I took a pill because I thought Bert would try and stop me taking her away.'

'How did you get a pill, anyway?'

'When I was working on the drug I dissolved one of the pills but did not go on with it. I remembered it a few days ago and crystallised the stuff out. I am going back now.'

'That's your last, then.'

'My very last.'

'Bill, for God's sake, tell me the truth. Are you using it on her now?'

He did not answer for a while, and when he did it was with a kind of defiant intensity.

'I believe that her feelings are absolutely her own.'

'You know best.... I believe you.'

He went back to the house then and I drove home.

It was only later, lying in bed, that I began to doubt. I could not sleep, and smoked one cigarette after another into the small hours. Our talk repeated itself over and over in my head. He had not answered my question, the one vital question: was he using the drug on her now? He had told me something else which was not an answer except by implication. 'I believe that her feelings are absolutely her own.' But why, if he believed that, had he not given me a simple 'No'?

Either he was using the drug on her or he was not. Why the ambiguity? Why the hedging?

As the hours wore on I managed to piece together an explanation which made some sort of sense.

He had used it on her to get her to go with him. Even if she had wanted to go I didn't think Anita would have gone like that, without a word to Bert. It wasn't like her. He had taken her home by force, and once there I had no doubt he had influenced her again. I didn't like dwelling on that. 'Ever been hungry, really hungry?' I remembered his look and the tone of his voice as he said it. He had passed the feeling over to her, made her want him as avidly as he had wanted her. No, it didn't bear thinking about.

And then he had 'fixed' the emotion. I remembered our own experiment in the laboratory. All he had to do was to 'will' that the state of mind should continue, and it would continue even when he himself was working or thinking of other things so long as she stayed within range and the drug lasted. There was no need for him to go on interfering once he had 'fixed' the emotion. We had not carried our experiment far but we had suspected that it would work in this way.

I didn't believe that Roper had wanted to get her that way, but there had been no other. And he was hungry. Was he fooling himself now? Was he trying his damnedest to believe that he was not, in fact, putting any pressure on her and hoping against hope that she was truly feeling the things she did feel of her own accord? It looked very like it. That was the only explanation I could think of for the way he had both evaded and answered my question.

When you want to believe something badly enough you

end up by believing it. Even hard headed people like Roper go under.

If that was the case, what would happen when she woke up to herself?

I knew so little about Anita, Roper himself had rammed that home. Perhaps she was genuinely in love with him, perhaps she adored him. Perhaps I had been completely wrong about her attitude to Bert. It was quite possible.

And yet...

I had no doubt Roper believed what he had told me, but he himself was not sure, not absolutely. If he were, he could make certainty doubly so at any moment. All he had to do was to snap off, to will her release. Then he would know. But I was pretty sure that he had not done that. He had not dared, because he was still uncertain.

And that must be a thorn of hell in the rose for him. He must be going through the devil's own torture, wondering, looking forward to and dreading the time when she would be released. I had seen what had happened to him. This was no longer lust, no seven days' cure for an itch of the flesh, as he had told me it would be. Roper had been caught himself. He was in love with her.

I counted the days. The crisis would come on Saturday afternoon, about three o'clock.

The moment of truth....

I could not sleep, for thinking of it.

Thursday and Friday I could not get it out of my mind. It was none of my business, I kept reminding myself, but it was no good. I went to see friends, tried a cinema and a leg show, but it was not much good. The worst time of all was when I was in bed. If I stayed awake, I thought of Roper and Anita. If I slept, I dreamt about them. And that was worse.

By Saturday morning I felt like a rag. I didn't know what to do with myself. I read the papers through, walked about the streets, had two or three coffees, and then quite suddenly decided to ring up Roper.

I didn't know what I was going to say to him, but the moment he answered I blurted out the question which had been bothering me.

'What time does it wear off?'

'Three o'clock, why?'

He sounded quite calm and sure of himself.

'Oh, I don't know, just interested.'

'You can come round if you like.'

'At three?'

'If you like.'

'I might pop in later.'

'Good. We shall be seeing you there.'

I don't know why, seeing that nothing had been changed, but that made things much better. It must have been the way his voice sounded, so firm and calm and controlled. Well, if he was feeling like that I didn't see what I had to bother about. I had better forget it.

I went to see Bert. There was a new assistant in the shop, and I could not help laughing a little to myself. She was fiftyish, her hair in a straggle; she breathed like a grampus, and was very anxious and uncertain about the change. I asked for Mr Phillips, and she shouted up the stairs for him. She called him Mr Phillips, too.

212

Bert asked me up and we had a long talk. I began by teasing him about the new assistant.

'She is not Anita, of course,' said Bert, 'but there you are, she's got two kids at home and is down on her luck. She's shaping fine.'

'Still using the pills?'

'As a matter of fact I am. Trade is fair booming down this bit of street. Come over to the window. There. Do you see the Stores? He's a nice little man got that, only things went wrong with the rent. He'll pay it in no time at this rate.'

'You've been sending them across, have you?'

'You know how it is. Let's have some fun whilst the going is good. There are not so many pills as all that.'

'They affect you, Bert. I told you about Mr Roper.'

'Oh, they don't seem bad for me. They make me feel grand.'

But all the same I thought the pills were having their way with Bert, too. But they were working oddly. Bert had always been a kindly creature, a decent, well-tempered man. He had always been prepared to help anybody, if he could do so without any great inconvenience to himself. It seemed to me then, listening to his talk about his neighbours, the assistant downstairs, the owner of the Stores across the way, some kid who had developed measles next door, that this quality in him had been intensified. It might be because he was now in easier circumstances, but I doubted it. There was the same quality of excess about his good heartedness that there had been about Roper's evil. Not that Bert had lost his sense of humour, as philanthropists are inclined to do. Far from it. But his largesse to the neighbours seemed to me indiscriminating, largesse thrown at them with both hands, gleefully and uncritically.

'You become an addict,' I warned him. 'You want to go on taking them and can't leave off.'

'The more the merrier,' said Bert lightly.

We had lunch together at a pub and went for a walk afterwards. He asked me if I had seen Anita and Roper, and I told him how things were with them. I kept Roper's pill to myself, though.

I kept glancing at my wrist watch and at three we were back at the shop. I told Bert I had to be going, and took the car round the corner to the nearest telephone booth, but could get no answer from the laboratory.

The fears which had been simmering in me for days bubbled up and boiled over. I ran back to the car and drove round at speed to Roper's place. The tall, gaunt woman let me in and smiled her acidulous smile. She looked guilty, as if she had been caught listening in the hall.

'Have they gone out?' I asked.

'Do you mean Mr and Mrs Roper?'

'Of course.'

'They are in, I believe,' she said primly.

I raced up the stairs and knocked at the door. The flat was silent; ominously silent, I thought, but dismissed that as nonsense. They must have gone out after all. I knocked once more, but this time I heard footsteps coming to the door. They came very slowly, and in my anxiety I rapped again. The door was opened and Roper stood in front of me.

The first thing that struck me was that the light in his face was gone. It had darkened down again to the old expression of sardonic contempt. The second thing I noticed was that his hair was rumpled, his tie askew. I stepped in quickly and shut the door.

'Where is Anita,' I asked.

'She's in there, in the bedroom.'

'What's the matter with you, Bill? What's happened?'

'Go and look.' He walked over to a chair and slumped down in it. I went over to the bedroom door and rapped on it.

'Anita!' I called. 'Why doesn't she answer?' I asked him.

His face contorted, and he flung an arm across his eyes.

'For God's sake, Bill. Nothing has happened?'

'She's dead,' he whispered. I could hardly hear him.

'How...?' But I stopped, appalled.

'I killed her.'

'I'm going, I'm going,' I babbled. I could think of only one thing. I must get away at once. I must get to the car and drive, drive to the world's end.

'Don't go. Don't leave me,' he cried, and then he broke down, sobbing bitterly. I stayed rooted there, looking at him, in a mindless trance. All power of thought or movement had gone out of me.

And then he began talking, talking, talking. It went on and on, like a river in spate. And I listened to him, still rooted to the same spot, hearing what he was saying, but almost without understanding, as if he were speaking in another language. I remember crossing to the bench and pouring myself a whisky, the bottle rattling against the glass.

What did he tell me that afternoon? Three o'clock and he and Anita lying on the bed, he himself with his eye upon the clock, certain, almost certain that all was well, that this tenderness and overflow of love was no illusion. But nevertheless apprehensive. The bedside clock had tinkled the hour and he had watched her like a cat watching a mouse, his heart hammering. The minutes sped by, and still the same rapt, still face, the heavenly undisturbed beauty. But he was sure now, sure, sure. His heart beat wildly. His love for her knew no bounds or measure. Their life together was blossoming out like a flower.

And then, abruptly, her eyes turned upon him in swift realisation; alarm; memory of the five days pouring in through the floodgates and hate, shame, violent distaste. She was pushing him away, spitting at him with rage, wailing out for Bert, Bert, Bert, oh Bert. And the rest was blackness. He had felt what his hands were doing, but his brain was scared. He had acted as a machine acts when it catches up the loose end of a garment and goes on devouring, mindlessly, mechanically. His hands had touched her soft throat, but the rest had not been him at all. The hands had worked of their own accord, with their own vitality and logic, like a machine.

'My hands killed her,' he said.

What else did he say in that long, dreadful monody? He wanted me to understand, beseeched me to understand. The hunchbacks, the maimed, the halt, the blind, the crooked, the squint-eyed, the impotent, the ugly, yes, the ugly, too, – all those roped off from the normal in their own enclosure – did I realise what it meant? The distortion of mind, the never-ceasing fever sealed upon them by some accident of fate for which there was no remedy. Their number was legion, one in ten, one in a hundred, what did it matter? A legion, and all of them living in some lonely circle of hell, a prison from which there was no escape. They did everything they could, they rationalised, they fought in themselves a ghostly battle which lasted each waking moment of a lifetime. They might appear sound and normal to the outside eye, but each was simmering in his own wretchedness. They longed, they ached, they beat upon the walls, but in the heart of each was a fixed and settled despair.

And with him it had been ugliness. Did I know that he thanked God as a boy that his mother was dead, lest she should be ashamed of him? Did I know that he shrank each time he caught his father's eye on him, and he had loved his father. To appear in company... the agony of it, the stress and strain of looking as if he did not care, as if he accepted, rejoiced even. And women. How he had longed for the love of one woman, one woman at least who would prove that it did not matter, that his ugliness was not a barrier! One, simply one, that was all he asked for. And for five days he had known it, known the delights of other men, the superb joy of the normal.

'I fooled myself that she was in love with me, that I was accepted. And then... back to hell, to prison, to the old frustration and distortion. It was too much. My hands...' He stared at them and lowered them slowly. 'Did you see how my mind was washed clean? Five days. But I am not going back to that. I refuse. I want to die.

'And yet I can't. I have tried and can't.'

He got to his feet, walked to the bench, and picked up a tumblerful of liquid.

'A coward, too. I didn't know that.'

I had not been thinking much about what he was saying. I was seeing Anita, dead, in the next room, beyond that door. I wanted to go in, to look my last on her, and yet I had a horror of it, too. But little by little the stunned sensation ebbed, and I began to feel again in the quick of me the alarm which had coursed along my nerves when I first heard of her death. I must do something, and do it at once.

The first thing was to stop Roper talking. That could be no longer borne. I took the tumbler from his hands and poured him out a stiff whisky.

'Drink that,' I said.

He obeyed at once, as if he had been a child.

'What are you going to do now?'

'Do?' he asked.

'Wake up. You've got to do something. Go away. Run. Anything. You can't stay here.'

'Why not?' he asked stupidly.

'Because of the police. Do you hear? Sooner or later...'

'I'll go,' he said.

I picked up his hat and handed it to him. He held it in his hand.

'Put it on,' I said.

'Where are we going?' he asked.

'Out, anywhere.'

And all the time I knew I was forgetting something that was of the utmost importance to us. I had felt it rather than known it when I was thinking of Anita. Now the feeling came upon me stronger than ever.

'What have we forgotten?' I asked at the door.

'I don't know,' said Roper wearily.

And then it flashed startlingly into my mind.

'The money?' I asked. 'Where's the money?'

'It's still under the bed,' he said flatly.

'But we must get it. If the police find it they'll know.'

'I'll wait for you,' said Roper.

'Bill, listen, we've got to get that money.'

'I don't want it,' he said dully. 'It doesn't matter.'

No, it did not matter to him. I realised that. But it mattered to me, enormously. When it came to murder, a robbery mattered little. But I would be hopelessly implicated. The money must be removed.

'Bill, please,' I implored.

'Please what?'

'Fetch that money.'

I saw him shudder as he leant against the door.

'No,' he said.

I tried to make myself go into the room. I had to. I tried to drive myself, and yet I could not do it. I took hold of Roper's lapels and pulled him towards the bedroom door. He resisted and wrenched himself free.

'No,' he said, and I saw how sick and yellow his face was.

I went to the door myself and tried to pluck up the necessary resolution. But I knew it could not be done. I had a vivid flash of myself down on my hands and knees tugging the suitcase from under the bed, Anita staring at me, and I knew it could not be done.

I hustled Roper down the stairs and out to the car. I had to open the door for him and push him in. Then I got into the car myself and drove it away.

I knew even then that it was hopeless, that I had made a mess of it. We had run away and nothing could be done about it now.

'Did your landlady see us go out?' I asked.

'I don't know.'

I caught sight of a clock and saw that it was ten minutes to four. The landlady made tea for them and took it up. I had not even locked the door. At four o'clock she would take the tray up, go into the laboratory, and find no-one there. She would probably knock at the bedroom door, go in, too. And then it would be all up.

I could always deny that I knew anything about it, could tell them that I thought Anita was out, that Roper had suggested we should go for a run. But they would get me over the money, probably suspect complicity in the murder, too. We had ten minutes, perhaps, before the hue and cry.

I remembered the landlady listening in the hall. Perhaps she had heard the cries. That, at any rate, was before I had gone up.

Roper had gone stupid. He was sitting in his seat, not saying a word, staring ahead. There was, I knew, no hope for him. He was not making any effort to save himself, and I could think of nothing that I could do.

I pulled up in front of a tea-place and got out.

'Come along, Bill. I want a cup of tea.'

He got out and followed me into the restaurant. The waitress brought us our tea, and I poured out.

It was hopeless, hopeless. Nothing could be done. At any moment now the general call would go out. It would not take them more than a few minutes to get the number of my car and we would be caught taking tea together. There was nothing to be done.

Roper ought to go. I didn't believe that he realised what was happening. It was all wrong that he should be making no effort to escape, hopeless as that would be. He was away somewhere in a dream of his own, stupefied. I felt that I had to warn him, make him aware of what was about to happen.

'Bill.'

'Yes.'

'The police will get you in a few minutes now.'

He stirred the tea slowly with his spoon.

'They will hang you for this,' I blurted out.

'Hang me?' He was startled. 'It mustn't come to that.'

'What are you going to do then? For God's sake, wake up.'

'Take me down to the river,' he muttered.

'Don't you want to try and escape?'

But his face was blank again.

'I can't think straight,' he said. 'I feel drowsy. If only I had another pill....'

It was as if a magnet had been placed amongst my scattered thoughts and they had all swooped together into a coherent whole. I jumped to my feet and called for the bill. The waitress seemed to take an age, and in a fever of exasperation I threw down a ten shilling note and hustled Roper out to the car.

The pills! Why had I not thought of them before? But we must go hell for leather to Bert. In Bert alone was there any hope of extricating ourselves from this mess.

I expected to be stopped each moment by some police

221

car on the look out. I had never driven like that in London before. Once, stopped by a red light, I waited for an opportunity and dashed through a gap in the traffic amidst furious hootings and blarings.

'Where are we going?' asked Roper.

'To Bert,' I said.

He turned quickly towards me. 'Why to Bert?'

'It's our only chance. The pills.'

He surprised me by laughing sardonically in his old manner.

'Your only chance, you mean.'

It was true. I had been thinking of myself. Bert would give me a pill or two and I could get out of the country, disappear somewhere, anywhere. I was sure Bert would do that for me. But for Roper? When he heard that Anita was dead? I was not so sure, and Roper no doubt felt certain that he would not.

'Get there then, quickly, before they catch us.'

'It is a chance,' I repeated.

'For you. I don't want a chance, but I don't want to hang either.'

He was very much more himself. I stole a glance at him and he seemed almost as eager as I was.

'Don't you think he will help you?'

'He will kill me.'

'But...'

'It is what I want,' he said harshly.

I slowed down at that. I wanted to get to Bert but I did not want to land him in trouble.

'Go on. Go on,' he said feverishly.

222

'No,' I said. 'I am not taking you to him.'

'Don't be a blasted fool. He won't get into any trouble. He's not going to stick a knife in me. Bert will kill me because I shall ask him to do so. I wanted to try that experiment. I always thought you could make a man die if you suggested it strongly enough. And I shall want to die. Push on.'

I did not hesitate after that. It would be for Bert to decide. It had nothing to do with me.

I asked the new assistant if Bert was in and she answered that he was. Roper and I went behind the counter and climbed the narrow staircase. Bert heard our footsteps, came to the door and greeted us boisterously.

'Mr Starling! Mr Roper! Why, this is just like old days at the laboratory. Why didn't you bring little Anita on too, then we'd have been a proper party. How is she, Mr Roper? I hear I am to congratulate you.'

'She's dead,' said Roper.

'Shut up, Bill. Tell me, Bert, is there anyone living in the top room?'

'Not since Anita left. But what is this...?

'Wait a minute. Bill, I want five minutes alone with him. You can go up the stairs to the bedroom.'

Roper turned unwillingly, but went up without a word. I shut the door and turned to Bert.

'It's true, Bert, she's dead. Something dreadful has happened and I want to tell you about it.'

I told him everything this time, about the bank robbery, the money under the bed, the death of Dobbs, of Anita's husband, of Anita herself, the whole sorry business from beginning to end. I told him a little, too, of what Roper had poured out to me not two hours since in the laboratory.

'Poor girl,' said Bert softly. 'Poor little girl. She was a nice girl, was Anita, the nicest girl that ever breathed. She wouldn't hurt a fly, really.'

I was bewildered by the way he took it. I had expected horror and indignation, but not this pity and sorrow without a trace of vindictiveness. He said nothing about Roper for a long time.

'And now, I suppose, they will hang the poor man,' he said at last.

I said nothing, watching him. He was standing by the window, looking out towards the street.

'Mr Roper is not a bad man either. It was this drug that made him do it. He was quite all right but for that.'

He turned towards me.

'Do you know, Mr Starling, what I think about people who murder? I think most of them are sorry for it, and that must be dreadful. It is no good hanging them. The poor fellows can't live long enough to put right what they have done, not if they lived a hundred years. It is terrible to hang them in the way we do.'

'Some of them go on murdering if they escape,' I said.

'But not men like Mr Roper. People like him are not like that.'

The door opened suddenly and Roper came in.

'Bert,' he said roughly, 'I couldn't wait any longer. I want you to do something.'

'I'll be glad to do anything I can. I am terribly sorry for this.'

'Have you got a pill in you?'

'Yes, I have, a fresh one. I took it this morning.'

Roper's eyes were dark with excitement, but he had himself well in control.

'Sit in that chair, facing me, Bert.'

Bert obeyed him without a word, but he looked a little scared. They were within two yards of one another. Roper asked me to give him a cigarette, and took one himself. All three of us smoked for a while, saying nothing.

'I don't know when they will be coming along, but they might be here at any moment now,' said Roper coolly. 'I suppose I ought to go through with it. I don't quarrel with the hangman. I deserve all they propose to do to me. But shall we say simply that I don't care for the idea.'

'Well?' Bert exploded.

'That is not the way I want to die, and I don't see why I shouldn't choose my exit. I want you to use that drug on me, Bert.'

He said it simply and unemotionally, as if he were proposing a walk down the street.

'I think it can be done. All you have to do is to will that I die. I shall help you. I want to go, and shall not offer any resistance.'

'No, before God, no,' cried Bert. 'I have never killed anybody, and I don't want to.'

'As a favour, an act of friendship....'

'No, I am not touching you, Mr Roper. That is too much to ask. I do not wish to touch you and I am not going to be your judge.'

Bert jumped to his feet, but Roper asked him to sit down again.

'Please, Bert.'

'Never, never, never,' said Bert, beating his fists on his knees.

I saw the old wry look come into Roper's face, a hint of cynical mischief and contempt. There was rising passion, too, in his eyes.

'Very well, then.' He threw his cigarette on the floor and ground it under his foot. Then he leant forwards and looked Bert straight in the eyes.

'Do you remember how beautiful she was? Think of her brow, her mouth, her eyes, Bert. She loved you with all her heart. She was going to marry you. You were going to live here, in this little shop, happy ever after. "I think you're a dear, Bert," "You make me laugh, Bert." Do you remember?'

'Don't, Mr Roper.'

'I killed her,' he taunted. 'I murdered her, squeezed the life out of her.'

'Oh God. Poor girl, poor girl,' said Bert.

'She called out your name before she died. Bert, Bert, Bert, oh Bert.'

Bert's brow was beaded with sweat and he was wringing his hands.

'Kill me, man. Kill me.'

'Mr Starling,' said Bert, turning to me, his eyes full of tears. 'Make him stop. This is more than man can bear.'

'Can nothing make you do it?' asked Roper fiercely. 'I'll make you do it.' He jumped to his feet, his fists clenched.

I ran to the window because I had heard the screech of brakes outside. It was a police car which had pulled up behind my own, and men were pouring out of it. I saw a sergeant, two constables and two plain clothes men. Almost at the same moment another car pulled up, and more men scrambled out. The sergeant looked up and saw me at the window. He stared at me for quite a time, and then began waving his arms about and shouting. Some of the constables ran round the corner. To cut us off at the back, I thought. The plain clothes men were examining my car, going through the pockets and looking at the papers.

The sergeant called the two detectives and spoke to them. Then the three of them, along with two of the constables, advanced towards the door. By this time both Bert and Roper were looking over my shoulders.

'That's that,' said Roper.

Bert grabbed hold of Roper's arm and mine. 'Keep quite calm now,' he said. 'This is where I come in. You let me deal with this. It will be all right. Don't you do anything rash.'

I heard the assistant shouting up the stairs. 'Mr Phillips! Mr Phillips!' and Bert opened the door. 'Let them come up,' he said, but even before that permission had been given they were trooping up the narrow stairs and making a great noise. Bert backed slowly from the door.

The Sergeant came in with a bounce. He was a big man and his face was red with excitement. The plain clothes men and the two constables were at his shoulder, all gazing at us, holding their truncheons in their hands.

'You're Bert Phillips, aren't you?' asked the Sergeant.

'Mr Albert Phillips,' said Bert, smiling at him.

They crowded into the room, and before I knew what was happening my arms were pinioned by my side. I saw that the same thing had happened to Roper. He was looking desperate.

'We want you for that murder at your flat,' said the Sergeant to Roper. Then he turned to me. 'You were there, too, soon after. Know anything about that bank robbery?'

'Yes, we did that,' I said. There was no use in lying.

'Thought so,' said the Sergeant. 'Well, we've no time to waste. To the station.'

He turned round and made for the door. The two men at my side drew me along with them.

'Bert, use the pill on them,' said Roper.

The Sergeant swung round and glared at him.

'What was that? What did you say about a pill?'

'Keep your hair on, Sarge,' said Bert. 'Nobody's going to hurt you, man.'

'I'll talk to you later,' said the Sergeant, and stumped down the stairs.

The poor assistant, breathing more heavily than ever, was staring at us with round eyes. 'What am I to do with the shop, Mr Phillips?' she cried.

'You can have it, Lizzie. Yes, you take it. I mean that. It is all paid for.'

When we reached the pavement, Bert called for the Sergeant.

'Look, Sarge,' he said. 'We're very sorry not to fall in with your plans, but we've got to be going along now.'

'Bring the – along,' said the Sergeant.

A crowd had collected in front of the shop. I remember the humming and shuffling noise it made. A press photographer was busy taking picture after picture of us.

The men at my side dropped my arms and I was free.

'Come along, Mr Starling. Come along, Mr Roper,' said Bert, leading us towards my car. 'Make way there.' The crowd fell back. The police stood rooted on the pavement, staring at us but not moving a step.

'Goodbye, Sarge,' said Bert. Roper had got into the back seat and Bert was sitting by my side. 'Are you ready?' he asked me.

I started up the engine and began to move out from the pavement.

'Do you think the flatties ought to salute?' asked Bert. 'Yes, I think they might,' and the next instant they were indeed saluting and the crowd was sending up a lusty cheer, as if we were a wedding party setting off for church. The cameraman had gone wild over his pictures. I saw him snapping the saluting police over our car.

'Where do I go?' I asked Bert.

'Out west. We'll have a holiday in my old village. I haven't seen it for a month of Sundays. What do you say, Mr Roper?'

I heard his hard, bitter laugh from the back seat.

It took us eight hours to come down to this little mountain village in which I am now, and all the way down we were dogged by police cars. They were never very far away. An attempt was made beyond Oxford to close the roads to us. The police had blocked it up with two lorries across the way. We waited there patiently until they had moved the lorries, a police car watching the whole proceedings from the back of us, almost exactly, so far as I could judge, two hundred and fifteen yards away.

We arrived at this village about one in the morning. We crossed a stream and the car lights brushed the white-washed walls of a narrow street. 'Keep your eyes open for the Red Lion,' said Bert.

The Red Lion was on the left, and in complete darkness. We climbed stiffly out of the car and rapped the knocker loudly. By and by a head haloed by candle-light came out of an upstairs window to look at us, and after a time we could see through the fanlight the candle coming down the stairs. A short, round barrelled man appeared at the door in a cotton nightdress, the candle held high. We walked in without a word and the door was shut behind us. 'It's too late to explain things,' Bert whispered to me. 'I am telling him what to do, see?' In a very few minutes we had been allotted rooms, and were in bed. My room looked out on the village street, and through the window, by craning my neck, I could see the lights of the police cars splashing the road beyond the bridge.

Sleep eluded me. The room was stone dark. I remembered how difficult it was to fall asleep in London during a black-out when the familiar haze of light was missing. The images which are the curse of sleeplessness rose in my mind and faded slowly – the Chief of Police at a desk staring fixedly at a photograph of his men saluting a murderer, a bank robber, and a street singer. ('Not so much a case for the police,' I murmured, 'as for the Archbishop of Canterbury.') The image of Bert, the new Bert; of Anita. But it was to Bert that I returned again and again. He stood at the bottom of the bed, looking at me as he had looked when I told him of Anita's murder, no horror, but pity and gentleness in his eyes. What did that mean? Bert was a street singer, a glad and temperate man, but condonation of murder was the last thing to be expected of him. And yet, condoned he had, with love, with pity for the victim as well as for the murderer. He did not seem to realise the deed of blood.... No, that was not right. He did realise it, but not on the surface as a matter of brutal hands and choking breath, but in the depths, as a pitiful tragedy of souls. Oh, but the pills were affecting him, too, turning him, not into an ogre, as they had done Roper, but into something more unfathomable and monstrous still: a lover.

Had he forgotten that Roper *was* a murderer?

After a heavy breakfast of ham and eggs I went for a walk with Bert through the village. He was as excited as a boy, grabbing my arm continually, stopping and pointing to some object or other. That was the school he had gone to. That was the Baptist Chapel, with the Methodists right across the road, 'swearing blue murder at each other'. Not so far away, in a similar building, squat and square and ugly and grimly roofed, were housed the Independents. 'They believe anything,' Bert told me. 'Three chapels, and only one pub, that is what is wrong with this village. Not a bad little birthplace, though, do you think?' It might have been worse, I agreed. It was, at any rate, well set. Through the gaps in the houses I could see the surrounding hills, browned now by the summer suns, but emerald green, I imagined, most of the year. That morning, the sun shining on the whitewashed walls, lace curtains fluttering in the small windows, the noise of the river in our ears, the tang

tang of an anvil echoing through the street, it was all I desired. I had not yet seen the rains close in upon it and beat it to its knees.

We walked up the street, to begin with, past a small General Stores on the left, the school on the right, the Post Office, the three chapels, then cottages, a farmhouse, and that was all save for a biggish Georgian building glimpsed up a drive and over lawns. That, Bert told me, was where the General lived, the Squire who owned all the village and the land around. We even saw the Squire himself, talking to a gardener near a clump of rhododendrons, a tall, bony man holding himself very upright, shaggy in heather green shooting jacket, a peaked cap far forward and shading his eyes. 'A bit of old Satan, but not as bad as the dam,' Bert said, but right as rain if you saluted him. Many a time had a penny been thrown him at that gate for a click of the heels and a smart salute. 'Even then I was at the butcher's, as they say,' said Bert. 'I had started this begging game before I had finished with mother's milk properly.'

We walked down the street again, and everywhere it was 'Hello, Bert, you back? Forgotten your Welsh, speaking only the squeaky language, I suppose.'

'English is the squeaky language,' Bert explained to me. 'I hear you have a grand motor car, Bert,' said another. 'Made a fortune in London, no doubt?' Bert clapped them all on the back. 'You know how it is, money does not stick to me, somehow,' he protested whenever charged with the motor car. 'How is Dafydd? How is old William? How is the Reverend Pritchard?' he would ask. And whenever he did so I noticed that a sly look would come into the interlocuter's eye and he would whisper a good deal in Bert's ears, Bert breaking through with exaggerated interjections: You don't tell me, man! Who would ever believe that, eh?

We called at the cobbler's and found a bald gnome of a man with a leather apron across his chest and his mouth full of nails, the tang of old boots and fresh leather filling the cellar in which he worked. He spat the nails out and he and Bert talked together for half an hour in the rapidest Welsh. Judging by the expressions fleeting across Bert's face – of surprise, content, dismay, and alarm – I suspected that gossip was being pumped into his system at very high pressure. When some extra sensational point was to be made, the gnome picked up a nail and hammered it into a boot with a triumphant bang. There for you! he seemed to say, what do you think of that?

Bert was greatly excited by the time we left. 'The Baptist Chapel is split in pieces,' he told me. 'It's cloven like a cow's foot over the Holy Ghost, and as if that was not enough, what do you think? The Baptist minister goes and pokes an umbrella in the Methodist preacher's belly and there's hell popping. Everybody is taking sides, meetings every night, and a rare fight last Sunday on the Common. It's lucky we are,' he went on enthusiastically, 'to land right in the middle of the biggest scrimmage since the Independent deacon ran away with the funds.'

Bert, to my great relief, seemed himself again.

'You see more life here in five minutes, Mr Starling, than in Piccadilly Circus in a year.'

'They are not talking about us, are they?' I asked.

'The Holy Ghost, in the main.'

233

'I mean about the murder. They must have heard about it over the wireless.'

'But I have stopped all that,' said Bert.

'The wireless?'

'No, I mean the talk. I have made them feel it is all right about that.'

'You mean, you have used the drug on them? The whole village?'

'I had to do something, hadn't I? There's the Baptist minister,' he whispered, nudging me.

I surveyed the Baptist minister and we passed on.

'Looks as if he were a smart one with an umbrella, does he not?' said Bert. 'Did you see how he cut me dead? That is because someone has told him I have been to the cobbler, and the cobbler is on the wrong side about the Holy Ghost.'

Bert, at any rate, was happy. He shook hands and hailed people all down the street, insisted particularly on shaking hands with those who protested that their palms were wet or dirty. I was amused to see a woman who had been scrubbing a doorstep protest, wipe her hands in her sack apron, Bert waiting patiently the while, and then shake for a whole minute. 'A good little woman,' Bert explained. 'I never forgot the toffee she gave me once when I was a kid.'

Down by the river the character of the village changed. The houses gave way to cottages, small, stuffy, bedraggled, with holes in the sodden thatch of their roofs. 'This is where the poor ones live. As bad as some of Camden Town, is it not?' The noise of the river, pleasant enough in the rest of the village, was a deep roar here. 'This is where I was born,' said Bert, 'and here it was I learnt to sing from that river. My people, these are.'

He walked along a flagway by the riverside and entered cottage after cottage. I stood waiting for him by the bridge, my thoughts elsewhere by now, for there, a short way along, were the police, waiting patiently. I saw them look at me through a field glass, one after the other, and then close into a bunch. They are discussing me now, I thought. Nothing has been changed. They are guarding every exit, lining every hedge, waiting for Roper and for me. The pills will last, how long? and then we shall fall into their hands. There is no escape. I might as well walk over to them now and give myself up for all the good it will do me waiting here.

Bert came back, a raggle-taggle of dirty children at his heels. He shook his head dolefully. 'Things are terrible,' he explained. 'The Squire has turned off three of them and sent another one to prison for catching a cock pheasant by the tail. They don't talk about the Holy Ghost down here. No. They are cutting fresh holes in their belts. Pity you did not get that money under the bed. We could use it here.'

'I have been thinking, Bert, that I might as well walk over to those police now. They are bound to get us, if they wait long enough.'

'While there is life there is hope,' said Bert. 'Only that is not the kind of thing I like saying to the poor.'

The queer inward look was in his eyes again.

Roper was still in the dining-room, staring blankly at a book. There was a bottle of whisky and a syphon of soda water on a tray by his side.

'Hello, Mr Roper,' Bert hailed him. 'We have been for a

walk through the village. You must come out into the sun, man. It is not good sitting here like a spider in a web.'

'A fly, Bert, a fly. I have been listening to the special bulletin on the wireless.'

'Oh, what did they say?' I asked.

'They can't, of course, make head or tail of it. You felt that between the words. They don't try to explain. They simply say that we are armed and desperate. They made a special appeal to the villagers not to thwart or resist us in any way. They say they will deal with us in good time. We are surrounded, it seems.'

'That is true enough,' said Bert.

'How many pills are there left?' asked Roper.

'About ten.'

'Fifty days,' I said.

'That is a long time,' said Bert.

Down by the bridge I had felt the first discomfort which always heralded, in my case, an attack of malaria. I knew, by now, each symptom of the paroxysm. The discomfort would last an hour or two, then lassitude, headache and nausea, my skin cold and blue, the temperature racing up to 103 or 104. This cold stage would be followed by one of extreme heat, the headache would be splitting and the thirst unquenchable. That might last for an hour or two, and I would fall into a sweat, the whole of my body relaxing in sweet comfort. Then a sleep. The attack usually lasted ten or twelve hours, and after that I would stay between the sheets for two or three days, recovering.

There was nothing for it but to go to bed and lap up all the quinine and fluid I could lay my hands upon.

Bert was telling Roper about the village, the chapels, the Squire, the labourers down by the bridge, but I was too restless to listen. I went out to ask the landlord for quinine and to arrange for a certain amount of nursing. He sent out at once for the quinine – fortunately they sold it in the General Stores – and I was introduced to a sister-in-law, a sturdy, efficient-looking woman who would see me through the worst. I went back again into the dining-room to tell them that I was going to bed.

'I don't understand them,' Bert was saying. 'It is so easy to be happy. All you want is a little human kindness, and there it is. The Squire has plenty of money, so what does it matter to him if the three men are back to work? Nothing at all. And there is that cock pheasant. It is no use sending a man to gaol for that, and fancy the Holy Ghost setting them by the ears too! It is wicked, that is. It does not make sense. All they want is a little human kindness, and the pheasants and the Holy Ghost don't matter.'

Roper was smiling his old sardonic smile at him.

'You seem to think that it matters,' he said.

'Everything matters, Mr Roper.'

'Nothing matters... much. They all want to be happy, true, but they certainly don't want to be good. They can't see how it is possible to be both. One rules out the other. The only thing to do with them is to give them some simple game to play, like making money, and then leave them to it. Goodness means not breaking the few rules of the game, but even at that most of them foul when then can, when the referee's not looking. Your human kindness would upset them much, much more than my badness. But go your own way. Give them your famous recipe. What's to stop you?'

'You think it would do?' asked Bert eagerly.

'Human kindness?' said Roper. 'Human kindness is all boloney. But try it, Bert. Give it them hot, all the human kindness you can. Make them love one another. Why not? They haven't tried it yet, and everything else has failed.'

He was laughing at Bert. I could see that, but Bert was taking it seriously. I could have stopped the business then, I think, but I was feeling too listless and ill to care. I told them that I was in for an attack of malaria and went upstairs to bed.

'Now look, Mr Roper, they *can* be happy,' I heard Bert saying as I went through the door.

Roper came up to see me later.

'Everything going to order?' he asked, sitting by the side of the bed.

'Yes,' I said. 'I'm in the North Pole stage now.'

'The drug,' he said, 'works in a mysterious way. Have you been watching Bert?

'A little. Why?'

'You know how it got me, but it affects him in a different way. He's... melting with tenderness, a pat of butter in the sun. He's no more himself now than I was a few days ago. The drug seizes upon the main motive in you and bloats you with it until the thing is monstrously out of control. It's making a tinpot god of him as it made a pocket devil of me. He's oozing with the milk of human kindness.'

'Can't you get the pills from him?'

Roper shook his head and went on with his theme.

'Bert is as mad as I was, but it's the obverse side of the coin. He wants to make them happy, to give them joy.

238

We're going to see some odd things in this village, more disastrous things than my killings. You can't stop him now.'

'You're not trying to stop him,' I said. 'You are egging him on. For God's sake don't let's have any more foolery.'

'Why should I stop him?' asked Roper. 'I have a sense of humour.'

I was going to urge and beg him to do what he could when the nurse came in with a heap of blankets and hot water bottles. Roper slipped off the bed.

'I must send a wire to the Press Association. The outside world ought to be in on this. Bert could arrange to get the reporter through. There's a lot to be done.'

He left at that, but late in the evening, when I was in the throes of the hot stage, he brought in a fresh-coloured young man who wore glasses and looked unnaturally sharp. 'The reporter's come, by air,' said Roper, but I could only groan and wave them away.

The morning sun was shining through the window when I woke up. Two days in bed, I thought, at least two days, and Roper no doubt encouraging Bert in his fantasies, egging him on mischievously, no longer caring what happened but squeezing a last few drops of sardonic humour out of the world before he left it for good. My thoughts were so dismaying that I reached out for the bell pull and tugged. I heard a far tinkle in the bowels of the house.

It was Roper who came. 'Did you ring?' he asked innocently. 'Want the nurse?' But I was not to be put off with that.

'What is happening?' I asked.

Roper pulled up a chair and got his pipe going.

'Great events,' he leered. 'The thing started last night. But naturally you don't know. Bert is keeping you and me and the reporter out of it, a special exemption obtained with some difficulty. He wants us to be happy, too, particularly me. But I persuaded him and he gave way.'

'What's up?' I asked.

'The great reign of love and kindness in the world,' grinned Roper. 'First of all he took the reporter round the village, explained to him about the Holy Ghost and the Baptist minister's umbrella in the Methodist minister's navel, got him to talk with the labourers down in those hovels by the bridge, tried even to barge in upon the General and his dam. There are subsidiary rows here too, and Bert was thorough. The schoolmaster – he calls him the Schoolin' – is up against Jones the Post Office, and half the village accuses Evans the postman of reading their precious postcards. The reporter says there is so much news here that it would take him a month to cover it all, tells me it is the most passionate place he's ever come across.

'After the grand tour I had the reporter alone with a bottle of whisky for half an hour and gave him the low down about the drug. Don't look so alarmed. He's a tough young man and didn't believe a word of it until I brought Bert in for a demonstration. I didn't, of course, let him know everything. I told him that I had invented this drug and had lashings of it corked up in bottles and could keep the police at bay for years and years and years. The Home Secretary will collapse when he reads about it this morning. I never thought a man could type as fast as that young fellow. The story of the century, he called it, and said he would be retiring soon if this went on.

'When he had wired it from the Post Office – Bert opened it up for us – we came back here and the landlord brought us another bottle. Bert made his speech then about human kindness, the reporter taking it all down in short hand. It was quite moving.

'I didn't think it seemly that the millennium should be ushered in without a little ceremony...' Roper gurgled at me.

'You don't seem to be enjoying this,' he said.

'Go on.'

'I got the landlord to bring us a red cushion, and Bert sat cross-legged on it, on the floor, like another Buddha. "Now for a spot of medicine," he said. Bert, you know, has no dignity. Then he closed his eyes. Presumably he was giving it to them. We, of course, were out of it, and the reporter looked sceptical again. I told Bert to "fix" the emotion, and then we went to bed, the reporter laughing to himself and not believing a thing.'

'Didn't you go round the village to see?'

'It was too late.'

There was a good deal of noise downstairs and I asked him what it meant.

'The first effect, so far as I can see, is that the licensing laws have been suspended. The pub is open all day and the price of beer has been lowered. The boozers have knocked off drink. What you hear are the teetotallers finding out what it is like. That's a long way towards human redemption, when you think of it.'

'And the singing, up the street?' I asked.

'I don't know, for I haven't been out yet. I'll take a stroll and let you know.'

He was not back for nearly two hours. All that happened in the meantime was that Bert rushed in pell mell, his eyes wild with excitement.

'Look here, Mr Starling, you don't want to be out of this, do you?'

'Yes I do, Bert.'

'Say the word and I will give it you, good and strong.'

'I... when I am better, perhaps.'

'Hear that singing?' asked Bert, and was out through the door again before I could question him.

'I wish you could get up,' said Roper, sitting in his chair again. 'I am almost scared. Bert should have doled them out the dose. He shouldn't have been so wholesale.'

'What do you mean?'

'Well, take the chapel business. I am not very clear about it yet, but I know that the Baptist minister fell on the Methodist minister's neck this morning and that they both wept. Quite shamelessly, in the street. Then they went into a huddle with the Independent minister and within an hour they had amalgamated the chapels. There's only one, now, with three ministers. They chucked away their beloved dogmas in handfuls, pretty nearly did in the Holy Ghost, so far as I can make out. The singing you heard was the first meeting of the United Chapel. Louder and more enthusiastic than the river.

'The postman is forgiven all round – never seen such handshaking and hugging. The Schoolin' is drinking downstairs with Jones the Post Office. But most dramatic of all, the Squire has taken on the three men again, and what Bert calls his 'dam' has been down in the hovels collecting handfuls of children and giving them baths and clothes and meals at the Big House.

'You ought to be up. You're missing the biggest thing of your life. They all love one another. They all love you as you walk along. The beastly thing is in their eyes, naked and unashamed. It's... kolossal, as the Germans would say. "Bigger than Evan Roberts'" revival in nineteen-o-five,' says Bert. There's one thing that's bothering him, though. There's a small reshuffle going on, men leaving their wives to live openly with other women. The blacksmith has two young things. And nobody cares! Bert wanted to stop that, but I persuaded him not to. Human kindness, you know, must be given a trial. Pure and unadulterated kindness.'

Roper went off into a peal of laughter.

'The reporter almost lives at the Post Office. He hasn't had time to shave. Do you realise that all this is going out into the world? Imagine your club this morning.'

I tried, and shuddered.

'I warned you it would be worse than my killings,' said Roper.

Late that afternoon Roper came along with the reporter and sat by the bed for half an hour.

'The police doing anything?' I asked.

'Not a thing,' said the reporter, 'but I am wondering how long it will be before the wires are cut. This story is getting uncomfortable for the Government.'

243

'The Government?' asked Roper. He was pricking up his ears.

'Well, think of it,' said the young fellow cheerfully, 'a murderer, a bank robber, and a loonie, and not a chance of catching them. Makes them look silly. And then this business in the village. Pretty bad, and a lot of people outside thinking it's grand, no doubt, especially now that the Squire's gone batty.'

'What has happened to him?' I asked.

'They've been giving things away, you know. Free stamps. The G.P.O. won't stand for that. Free beer, almost, down below, very demoralising. Then the General Stores, ladling things out to all comers. And along strolls the Squire, saying he's giving them the village on a plate. No more rent. Just sign along the dotted line. I haven't sent that story out yet.'

'Why not?' asked Roper.

'Why, damn it, property rights. That's going too far.'

'Send it out,' said Roper. 'Everything that happens.'

'But property?' objected the reporter. 'That's not funny, you know. It's dangerous.'

'Bert didn't make him do that,' objected Roper. 'All that he's broadcast is the emotion of human kindness. He's given them the medicine, but no directions for use.'

'If human kindness makes them do that kind of thing,' said the reporter, 'all I can say is, look out!'

'Put it on the wires,' said Roper. 'By the way, has Bert talked to you yet about the march on London?'

'What!' we cried together.

'This is obviously too good a thing to keep for one potty village,' said Roper calmly. 'I thought Bert had told you about it. We're going to London later on. Bert is hankering to give the Cockneys human kindness, too. He'd like to give it to the whole world. He's frightfully wholesale.'

'You can't reach more than two hundred and fifteen yards,' said the reporter.

'Double the quantity, double the distance ... probably,' said Roper.

'But this is revolution!' The reporter was aghast, staring at him.

'Why not?'

'Look here, you people have been pretty decent to me. I don't want to send out anything which will make things worse for you. Do you honestly want this story sent out?'

'Why not?' asked Roper again.

'Very well, then,' and he was out like a bolting rabbit.

'Things are beginning to move. Funnier and funnier,' laughed Roper.

'You are not really going to London?'

'I hadn't thought of it, but I'll see what Bert says.'

We had our first communication from the Home Secretary two mornings later. The postman told Roper that he was wanted on the telephone. 'Who is it?' asked Roper. The postman went back to ask and returned to tell him that it was the Home Office. 'Tell them,' said Roper, 'to telegraph.'

'We might as well have it in writing,' said Roper. I had got up and was lying on the couch, for bed had grown unbearable.

The communications between Roper and the Home Secretary (acting for the Cabinet) lie before me as I write.

As I go on decoding I am beginning to realise that this manuscript will have to be smuggled out of the village. Not a whisper of that correspondence has leaked out to the public, and I don't suppose it ever will unless I take my precautions. Roper's father will know what to do with it....

'Use numerical cypher. Not to be released to press,' was the first instruction to Roper.

'I know nothing of cypher,' said Roper, 'but suppose we call Z a hundred and work backwards.' His wire to the Home Secretary, in a jumble of letters, reads simply: Will this do?

The first offer was a guarantee of safety, to any country abroad that we wished, provided that all the drug was left behind or destroyed.

Roper refused.

The next offer added a thousand a year, each, for life.

Roper refused.

The offer was increased to ten thousand apiece.

Roper refused.

You must understand that I saw none of these wires at the time. When I asked Roper what the Home Office wanted, he told me that it was unconditional surrender, and I believed him. This correspondence was given to me later, by Roper himself.

'What do you want?' asked the Home Secretary.

'Nothing,' answered Roper.

'Open to suggestion,' said the Home Secretary.

Roper does not seem to have replied to that.

'Reasonable suggestion will be considered,' urged the Home Secretary. And again Roper did not reply.

The Home Secretary repeated his offer of a safe conduct abroad, and our pensions were increased to twenty thousand pounds a year each.

'Can always make more drug and come back,' answered Roper wickedly.

The Home Office spent some time over that, and before they could think of any way out Roper sent them his last wire.

'Are servants of inevitable historical process. Coming to London Thursday.'

I can imagine the fierce joy with which Roper cyphered it, he who did not believe in people, in a process, or in any inevitability. How carefully he must have worked at it to obtain the right note of wrong headed political fanaticism! How he must have revelled in it! He wanted to die. His life was finished, but he meant to go down with flying colours, mocking to the last. He wanted to frighten them out of their wits, and it must have added sauce to his humour that the thing they so dreaded losing was, in his opinion, itself a fantasy. Property as such had never meant anything to him. Why should it mean anything to anybody else? Let them quake. And to crown his joy, there were only eight pills. They had nothing to fear.

It was typical of him, too, that he should have ignored Bert and myself completely. I don't know about Bert, but I could have lazed very comfortably on twenty thousand a year in exile. Not (I feel sure now) that the Cabinet ever meant us to get away.

The wire was sent at three o'clock, Tuesday, and Roper must have been sending it off whilst the reporter and I were down by the bridge, watching the police.

247

'What the devil are they doing?' asked the reporter.

I couldn't say. Quite a number of blue uniforms and glinting buttons were bunched together about a hundred yards down the road.

'Bert is at the Red Lion,' said the reporter. 'They are just outside the magic circle, and they are up to something.'

The blue uniforms parted, and out of their midst appeared an enormous figure, covered with a bulky material from head to toe. He looked like some woolly White Knight of the tournaments, and there was, in fact, a kind of metal lance in his hand, a lance which trailed a wire along the ground.

'Looks as if he were fishing in the road,' I said.

'Got it,' said the reporter brightly. 'He's insulated. Or thinks he is. They've probably dished you with this. Bert's brainwaves against the engineers. What's the betting?'

'Bert should be here,' I said.

'No time for that. He's coming on, isn't he?'

The giant figure was certainly beginning to shuffle towards us.

'You're jiggered,' said the reporter. 'He must be inside, now.'

'Not yet.' But I wondered.

The figure came on another yard or so and stopped.

'Resting? Or Bert?' The reporter looked at me.

'We'll soon see.'

But the figure advanced no further. After a while some policemen came forward, lifted the thing up bodily and bore it away.

'First round to Bert,' said the reporter. 'I won't deal with this. Some of the boys are across there with the bobbies and will be covering it. If they let them, that is.'

We walked through the village together, and since it was the last time I was fated to do so I would like to give a thumbnail sketch of what the village life was like during the 'reign of Bert the Good,' as the reporter called it. The villagers were happy. There can be no doubt of that. Even in the faded and sultry air of August there was a springtime joyousness in the way they talked, and walked, and worked. I am told the Welsh sing more than we do at most times, but surely they did not trill like this normally. 'Like living in an opera,' said the reporter. A woman beating a mat at the door would break into a lilt. It was caught up elsewhere, from house to house, the singing spreading like a fire. There was a tremendous 'boy scout' atmosphere. Lads, and men too, hurried to help the women carry buckets of water from the river. I saw a stripling take over an old man's barrow and swing it along the road as if... as if he were being paid to do it. I knew their heart's joy by the look in their eyes, by their carriage and mien, by a tenderness I had not seen in any people before. They were all like young people in love, with an inexpressible dew upon them. Indeed they were in a sense, in love, in love with everybody and everything. I caught a glimpse of the Squire walking up to his house with a child dancing and singing and hanging on each hand, an idyllic glimpse which brought Rhenish wines and Provencal suns to my mind. The village had been born anew.

And like Roper, I was a little scared.

After lunch on the following day I took a short stroll in the bright sunshine and then turned back towards the Red

Lion. I was not more than ten yards from its door when something went 'slap' into the wall of a house to my right. This was followed by the sound of a hard bang from across the river. I pulled up, startled, watching the layers of whitewash fall to the pavement in a tiny cascade. The next instant I felt a searing pain in my left wrist, and realised that I was being shot at. Bending double, I leapt for the door, the sharp ping and whine of bullets in my ears. I flung myself through and caught Roper as he was running out to see what was happening.

'Keep inside,' I shouted. 'They're firing.'

'Did they hit you?'

I lifted my left arm and looked at it.

'A graze above the wrist,' said Roper. 'Come into the dining-room and we'll see to it.'

He was busy with an improvised bandage when Bert came in. He had been out in the garden at the back with the landlord.

'Did I hear something?' he asked.

'They are shooting at us, now,' said Roper.

'What for?' he asked. 'Oh, I see. But they don't kill people for robbery.'

'They'll shoot you, too, Bert,' said Roper. 'They'd like to finish all of us.'

'But I haven't done anything!' said Bert.

Roper laughed.

'They do not want to shoot me because I can make them happy, do they?' asked Bert.

'Don't be a fool,' said Roper. 'Yours is the deadly sin. If there's one thing the world won't stand for, it's universal happiness. They've always killed anybody with a recipe for that.'

'Do you mean that if I walk out into the village...'

'You're mutton,' said Roper.

'But nobody is going to kill a man because he makes them happy!' said Bert. 'It is not natural. There is something wrong, a big mistake somewhere.' He was very distressed, and hurt, and his eyes were full of pain. 'Everybody in their senses wants to be happy,' he went on.

'Yes, in their senses,' said Roper.

'If they do not want me to make them happy...' said Bert miserably.

'You mustn't give in,' said Roper. 'You've got to go on. People should be happy. You are right.'

'I know I am,' said Bert, his face lighting up. 'My heart tells me I am.'

'You have to use generalship now and defeat your enemy. There are people who don't want to be happy. Good. Smash them.'

'No, no smashing,' Bert protested. 'Human kindness, that is what they want, too. You see, they don't know yet what it is like.'

'London tonight,' said Roper.

'No, we don't,' I said. 'We stay here. There's been enough nonsense already. I'm damned if I move a step.'

'But you must come, Mr Starling,' said Bert gently. 'Listen to me now....'

'I refuse, point blank. You can do what you like, but I'm staying here.'

Roper took me by the arm and led me to the window.

'You're coming with us,' he said.

'It's mad.'

'Of course it is. But there's no way out for you by staying here. They won't let you go now. Face up to it.'

'But what can you hope to do in London? He has only eight pills left. What can you do?'

'Nothing,' said Roper. 'Absolutely nothing. I know that as well as you do. But we can give them five days of hell before we quit. Five days of Bert's happiness. It comes to the same thing.'

'It's insane,' I protested again.

'Are you coming?'

'No.'

'Very well.' He crossed over to Bert and whispered something in his ear.

I saw what was going to happen and began protesting against it violently. But I was not more than halfway through a sentence when the whole panorama changed and I was asking eagerly what time we were to start. Bert came up to me and laid his hand on my shoulder with a friendly squeeze. 'You must come with us, Mr Starling. You do not want to be out of a thing like that.'

Certainly I did not want to be out of a thing like that. I was all for it, wanted to get going at once. Looking back upon it now I realise that Bert did no more to me than change my mind about the visit to London. Otherwise I was still the same, still outside the magic of his happiness. But I wanted to go to London.

It was Roper who planned the details.

'Please take another pill, Bert.'

Bert took out the box and swallowed one.

'Two o'clock now,' said Roper. 'You will take one at hour intervals. That means that you will have six inside you by seven o'clock. You must tell me if you feel ill. We don't know how many of these pills can be safely taken.'

'How are we to find out about the range?' I asked. 'It may not be increased by taking additional pills.'

'Don't do anything about that until I tell you, Bert. Keep to this village, the two hundred and fifteen yards range. Don't will anything beyond that.'

Soon after Bert had swallowed his third pill the reporter came to see us. Roper told him about what was happening. The reporter whistled.

'You are not really going to London?'

'Tonight, but don't send the story out until we've finished our tests.'

'Okay. Any message to the great public, Bert?'

'Tell them I am bringing them human kindness,' said Bert simply.

I had watched Bert closely that afternoon. He was simple, kindly and affectionate, much less boisterous than usual. The drug, I reflected, was working deeply in him, beginning even to show in his features. I was, in truth, a trifle awed by a quality of stillness in his face, a reflection of the dream which had captured his soul. An absentmindedness, an otherness, made him in a sense profoundly pitiable. I felt my heart bleeding for him as he left the room.

'You can watch the tests if you like,' Roper told the reporter. 'By the way, the moment we leave the village they'll be coming to themselves. That,' he grinned, 'should be the best story of all.'

'You don't think the villagers will go on with this?' he asked.

'Do you?'

'Why not?

'Bert must have been doping you,' said Roper.

The garage was at the rear of the pub and could be reached from the back door without showing myself to the riflemen on the hills. At twenty past seven, when the last of the six pills was becoming effective, I went out and started the car. I left it to warm up and returned to the dining-room.

'Now we must try it out,' said Roper. 'Carry on, Bert.'

'What's happening?' I asked.

'You'll see in a minute. If it succeeds, that is.'

I heard, after a while, the sound of cars coming up from the bridge. Roper walked out of the room and I followed. He passed through the door without any hesitation and we stood in the street, watching the cars coming up the road. There were six, and all of them were full of police. They came to a standstill in front of the Red Lion.

'What a good feeling of security the police give you,' said Roper. 'When did the orders to kill us come through, Sergeant?' he asked the driver of the first car.

'This morning, Sir.'

'Any soldiers out there?'

'A company of Fusiliers arrived at dawn, Sir. They're the only ones, so far.'

'Machine guns?

'Yes, Sir.'

'No field guns?'

'Not that I know of.'

'We'd better be going now. Jim, drive the car out. Three of your cars,' he turned to the Sergeant, 'will go in front of us, and three behind. They are to keep close.'

I went to the garage and drove out the car. The others manoeuvred until they had taken up their positions. Roper got into the back of my car, and Bert sat by my side. A few of the villagers, the landlord and the reporter were watching.

'Historic occasion,' said Roper to the reporter. 'March on Rome and all that.'

'I'll send through a snap that you're coming.'

'You must get an interview with the Squire when we're gone,' grinned Roper. 'Start them off, Bert.'

We moved down the village street and over the bridge. It was an eerie feeling, moving freely on the roads again. Driving through the ring of police and soldiers was particularly queer. I saw a red-cap officer stare at us as we flashed past. Bert, I knew, was merely giving us free passage, forbidding them to shoot or block our way, and the officer must have realised the full enormity of what was happening. No wonder he stared.

'Do you know what the range is now?' I threw over my shoulder to Roper.

'No. All I know is that it has increased. I am pretty certain we are outside machine-gun range, though.'

'Why?'

'They haven't fired on us.'

'That's because they are afraid of hitting these other cars,' I said.

'Oh yes!' laughed Roper. 'What do you think you're up against, the Peace Pledge Union?'

We did not know, then, that the reporter's flash had been sent out at once over the wireless. It was not until we were clear of the mountains and across the border that we became aware of what was happening. We had seen small groups by the roadside, but had paid no particular attention to them. When night fell the powerful police headlights showed us that the hedges were lined with people. Handkerchiefs fluttered as we sped past, and in the villages there were shouts from the crowds, three deep on the pavements. Whether they were shouts of rage or encouragement I could not make out.

'England is not going to bed tonight,' said Roper.

As the hours wore on and we cut our way steadily through the heart of the country the crowds grew more rather than less. In places they were so thick that we had to crawl through them at a snail's pace. The windows of a whole countryside were lit at three in the morning as though it were early evening. Our progress was obviously being telephoned through as we passed along, and possibly broadcast. I heard the blare of a wireless from an open door about two o'clock.

'Mr Starling, I am not feeling very well,' Bert whispered to me.

'I am sorry, Bert. Shall we stop? Do you still want to go on?'

'Oh, yes, I cannot disappoint them,' he said.

I asked him then, as a favour, to take away the compulsion he had placed on me at the Red Lion. He agreed at once, but there was little difference, save that my old sense of the insanity of the venture returned. For this was a mad thing we were doing. The sight of the crowds by the roadside brought it vividly to mind. Insulated in our small village, we had not understood what was happening outside, not realised how stirred the whole country had been. We had set in motion an enormous machine which was now out of control, and I recognised, although it was with dismay, that there was no drawing back. We were committed.

We took much longer over our journey to London than we had taken over the drive out. We were not at Uxbridge until half-past four in the morning, when we turned into a roadside bar for a drink of tea and a snack. The weather had turned colder, a blustering wind was rising, and I felt sore and chilled. Bert, taking pity on the police, asked them to come with us, and some of them preceded us into the bar. The instant the heavily moustached, Italian-looking barman caught sight of Roper his eyes rounded with dismay. 'So you've bagged them, have you?' he asked the Sergeant. I thought he looked very crestfallen.

'The boot's on the other foot,' said Roper. 'Tea and sandwiches, and jump to it.'

The man's face beamed. 'Like a grasshopper,' he said, and went about his job.

There was a newspaper on one of the chairs and I picked it up. It was a Midnight Special, and on the front page were our photographs in large. Roper snatched it from me and turned the pages over quickly. He began laughing softly to himself, and then uproariously.

'What's the joke?' I asked.

'Stock Exchange closed,' he said. 'Enormous traffic blocks

on the roads because anybody who's got anything to give away is fleeing to the country, Fleet Street making arrangements to print in the provinces, all banks and most of the big shops shut, the Cabinet out at Chequers, Broadcasting House out of action, the Bank of England shipping its gold at the Port of London, continuous prayer during the crisis at the Abbey, Mayfair deserted and solicitors hiring bread vans to cart their leases and documents as far away as they possibly can. Six pills,' he whispered. 'Six little pills. Lord, how terrified they are of love!'

'I don't blame them,' I said. 'They don't know we have run out of the drug.'

'But what's the matter with them? The reporter made it quite clear that Bert did not force the Squire to hand over his houses. Bert merely filled him with human kindness, and that is how the Squire interpreted it. Others needn't interpret it in the same way. If there is no unkindness in gold at the vaults, what has the Governor to fear? Can't you love your fellow men and keep your vaults bung full of gold? What the devil is Mayfair running away from? Is it built on unkindness? Can't the newspapers thrive on love? Can't you broadcast it? What is the matter with them? They are praying for our success at the Abbey, at any rate. They must be.'

Roper was hugging himself with the joy he was getting out of it, his eyes blinking with malice.

'One would think,' said Roper, 'that this was not a Christian country.

'Bert!' he shouted. 'My God, the man was snoozing!'

'I am tired,' said Bert.

'See that he keeps awake, Jim. He can sleep all he wants

when we've reached Hyde Park and he has "fixed" his human kindness.'

Roper imitated Bert's voice, sing-songing the 'human kindness'.

It was beginning to rain when we left the bar. It poured pitilessly on the heads of the throngs as we approached central London. I have a jumbled impression of windows crammed with heads, of seas of umbrellas and glistening mackintoshes, of an occasional upturned face, mouth wide open, yelling hoarsely, the water coursing down the skin. Most of the women, I noticed, stared silently at us as we went past, but a large number in the crowd waved their hands and cheered. I was not surprised that they greeted us so warmly. These, I reflected, were the people who had nothing to lose, or those who would be glad enough to barter their possessions for happiness. God knows there are plenty of them in London.

'Sergeant,' said Roper when we had arrived at Lancaster Gate, 'take us to the tea-house in Kensington Gardens. We shall make that our headquarters.'

'I took Anita there once,' he told me with an expression I could not fathom.

Our cavalcade of cars turned into the park. We passed the sentry who paces round that mysterious lodge (I have often wondered what they keep there), crossed the bridge over the Serpentine, its water lashed by the rain, and stopped at a wicket gate leading into the Gardens. A few yards beyond was the pavilion.

We trooped into the tea-house, the police at our heels.

Bert was strangely quiet and weary. I took him by the

arm and asked him how he was. 'I am not feeling too well, Mr Starling,' he said. 'No, indeed,' he added with a sigh, passing his hand over his brow. 'Where are those woodbines, I wonder. I could do with a whiff.' He put his hand into his coat pocket, drew out a piece of string, some letters, a pocket knife, the pill box, his few crumpled cigarettes and a box of matches. 'Could you let me have those two pills, Bert?' I asked. 'Of course,' he said, and gave them to me. He lit his cigarette and crammed the odds and ends into his pocket again.

Roper came in from another room. He was followed by a dozen young men. I had seen one of them before, but could not remember where. It teased and puzzled me, but I said nothing.

'Newspaper men, Bert,' said Roper. 'Could you leave them out when you put the stuff over?' He turned towards the men. 'That is what you want, isn't it?'

'It would be a pity if we grew so happy that we chucked our work,' grinned one of them.

'If they want to stay out,' said Bert quietly.

'Can we see him at it?' asked one of the others.

Bert was smoking happily, leaning against the counter.

'I am doing it now,' said Bert.

'Smoking a fag?' the man asked. I cannot imagine what he had expected.

'They are good cigarettes,' said Bert. 'Have one.' He sent his packet on the rounds, but no-one touched it.

'Do you want to be in this time, Mr Roper?' he asked.

Roper laughed. 'You know the answer, Bert.'

'It is a lovely feeling.'

'Fixed it yet?' asked Roper.

'I am doing that now,' said Bert.

One of the news men said something I did not catch and the others laughed. The man I had seen somewhere had left, I noticed.

'You people had better go and see the fun,' said Roper, and they trooped out.

'I could do with a cup of tea,' said Bert. 'It is a small upset of the stomach, I think.'

I asked one of the waiters to bring him a cup of tea.

When I came back Roper was asking him to keep the crowds back from the pavilion. The police were quite unable to deal with them. Bert nodded.

'Pity I am not well, Mr Starling. I do not feel that I am doing my best for all those people out there. I must not let them down, must I?'

I gave him a chair to sit on and went out into the rain to watch the crowds. They had drawn away from the pavilion now and were milling around in a happy, haphazard way, laughing and shouting. In spite of the rain some of them had started dancing clumsily on the grass, and in the distance I could hear a ragged burst of singing.

I thought it would be pleasant to walk amongst them for a while before I went back to the pavilion for my sleep. I was already mingling with them when, above the shouting and laughter, I heard a long shrill scream in the air and there was a crash on the far side of the pavilion. There was a large and deathly silence which seemed to fill the world, and through it there came the scream of a second shell. Bits of the pavilion hurtled high into the air and the crowd roared into a panic. Shell after shell went into the house. 'Bert, Bert, Bert,' I cried, running and stumbling blindly towards him, but I knew in my heart then that he was dead. Nothing could have lived in that inferno. I felt myself lifted into the air by a blast of wind and flattened out.

I do not suppose that I was on the ground for more than a few seconds, but when I lifted my eyes again the pavilion had disappeared. I found myself weeping with rage, shaking my clenched fist at those distances whence the shells had come. 'Bert!' I shouted into the now still world. 'Bert!' But I knew it was no use, and my heart sickened and sank in me.

I do not know how I got out of the Gardens, but I was walking along a deserted street and remembering now the man whose face had seemed so strangely familiar. He was one of the plain-clothes men who had arrested us, and Bert had exempted him. The field guns in the suburbs had been waiting for his message, beyond reach of the drug. They had not waited long.

The telephone works quickly. Bert's reign of human kindness had lasted five minutes. Then they had blown him sky high. Poor Bert, with six pills in him, and mad as a hatter, I suppose.

It was a long time before I thought of Roper, and longer still before I remembered the pills in my pocket.

Why did I come back to this village? I do not know. There was nowhere to go and like a hunted animal, I suppose, I made for the lair, the known place. I was obsessed by the feeling that I would find sanctuary here and some remnant, at least, of the spilled happiness. I turned automatically to these brown hills from the screaming hate of the shells.

I remember swallowing the first of the pills down a side street and walking guiltily through by-ways until it should take effect. It was not yet working when I stole a motor car, dropped wearily into the seat, started the engine and drove away. In a traffic block on the North Circular road a man leant out of his car and shouted to me. 'The three bastards are dead, and serve them damn well right. Blown to glory,' he said, but then he recognised me and nearly fainted. I had to make him forget it.

I abandoned the car and slept in a barn that night, but next morning, after a feed at the farmhouse, I was given a lift on a lorry out westwards. At Chester I stole another car and was back in the village by evening.

Alas for human nature! It was the little round barrelled landlord who told me what had happened. The children had left the Big House, the Squire was collecting his rents again, the United Chapel had been riven in three and the factions over the Holy Ghost had grown more bitter than ever. The evening we left the village had turned into a snarling dog fight, each man claiming from his fellow whatever he had parted with during the previous five days. The boozers were rolling up to the pub and the teetotallers back in their obdurate and embittered prejudices. The landlord thought that it would take fifty years to put things right, the Welsh being very Welsh, with memories as long as a donkey's ears.

By next morning the police were back again, ringing the village round. I sent them a message, told them exactly how things stood, asked for seven days' grace. It was granted.

And now the seventh day expiring and the last pill working its last effects at eight o'clock tomorrow morning, I have only to decide how I shall make my exit.

I have made arrangements for this manuscript. After dark last night I talked to one of the three men discharged again by the Squire. It will float down the river in a biscuit tin, and when the police are gone the man will search the eddies and the weirs, recover it, and see that it gets to Roper's father. I gave him all the money I had and know that he will do me this last service – for Bert's sake.

How, then, shall it be with me? Tomorrow morning, when the drug is no longer working, I shall walk over the bridge towards them, and this time it will be no graze on the wrist. For I am, as all the world knows, a dangerous and desperate criminal. What the world does not yet know is that, alive, I am also somewhat embarrassing.

That is the end. Nothing remains for me now but to congratulate the devil on all his works.

Foreword by Adrian Dannatt

Adrian Dannatt is a writer, artist, curator and critic based in New York and France.

Cover image: *Love* by Keith Bayliss

Keith Bayliss is an artist and freelance arts educator based in Swansea, whose work has been exhibited throughout Europe. He has developed and co-ordinated numerous exhibitions, as well as writing articles for various publications.

LIBRARY OF WALES

The Library of Wales is a Welsh Assembly Government project designed to ensure that all of the rich and extensive literature of Wales which has been written in English will now be made available to readers in and beyond Wales. Sustaining this wider literary heritage is understood by the Welsh Assembly Government to be a key component in creating and disseminating an ongoing sense of modern Welsh culture and history for the future Wales which is now emerging from contemporary society. Through these texts, until now unavailable or out-of-print or merely forgotten, the Library of Wales will bring back into play the voices and actions of the human experience that has made us, in all our complexity, a Welsh people.

The Library of Wales will include prose as well as poetry, essays as well as fiction, anthologies as well as memoirs, drama as well as journalism. It will complement the names and texts that are already in the public domain and seek to include the best of Welsh writing in English, as well as to showcase what has been unjustly neglected. No boundaries will limit the ambition of the Library of Wales to open up the borders that have denied some of our best writers a presence in a future Wales. The Library of Wales has been created with that Wales in mind: a young country not afraid to remember what it might yet become.

Dai Smith
Raymond Williams Chair in the Cultural History of Wales,
Swansea University

LIBRARY OF WALES
FUNDED BY

Llywodraeth Cynulliad Cymru
Welsh Assembly Government

CYNGOR LLYFRAU CYMRU
WELSH BOOKS COUNCIL

SPORT

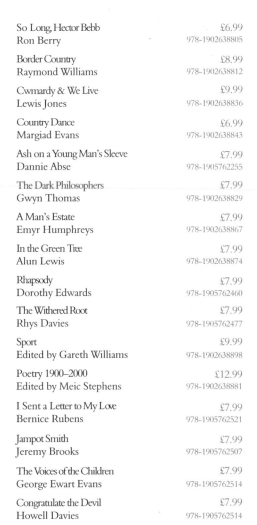

LIBRARY OF WALES

So Long, Hector Bebb	£6.99
Ron Berry	978-1902638805
Border Country	£8.99
Raymond Williams	978-1902638812
Cwmardy & We Live	£9.99
Lewis Jones	978-1902638836
Country Dance	£6.99
Margiad Evans	978-1902638843
Ash on a Young Man's Sleeve	£7.99
Dannie Abse	978-1905762255
The Dark Philosophers	£7.99
Gwyn Thomas	978-1902638829
A Man's Estate	£7.99
Emyr Humphreys	978-1902638867
In the Green Tree	£7.99
Alun Lewis	978-1902638874
Rhapsody	£7.99
Dorothy Edwards	978-1905762460
The Withered Root	£7.99
Rhys Davies	978-1905762477
Sport	£9.99
Edited by Gareth Williams	978-1902638898
Poetry 1900–2000	£12.99
Edited by Meic Stephens	978-1902638881
I Sent a Letter to My Love	£7.99
Bernice Rubens	978-1905762521
Jampot Smith	£7.99
Jeremy Brooks	978-1905762507
The Voices of the Children	£7.99
George Ewart Evans	978-1905762514
Congratulate the Devil	£7.99
Howell Davies	978-1905762514